REAPER

REAPER

QUINCY HARKER, DEMON HUNTER
BOOK TEN

JOHN G. HARTNESS

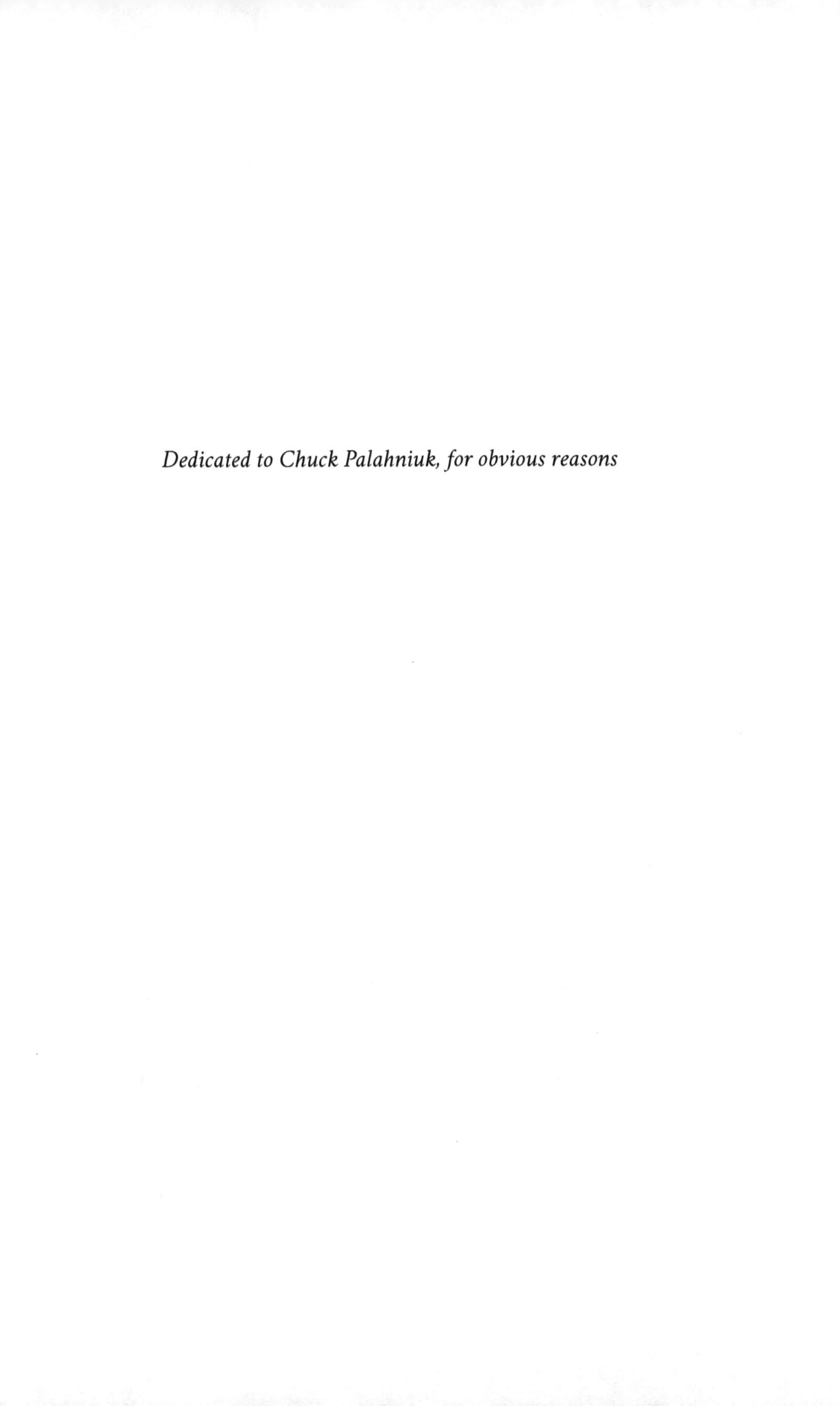

Dedicated to Chuck Palahniuk, for obvious reasons

1

You take me to the nicest places, sweetheart," I said as I pulled the hood of my raincoat over my head. One of the benefits to growing up in the earlier parts of the twentieth century, I actually own a raincoat designed to keep water off me, not just a hoodie that gets soaked in the lightest drizzle. This one was a weatherbeaten old London Fog trench with a hood that I'd picked up in a thrift shop because it reminded me of one I had back in World War II, before my life imploded and I went batshit crazy. Admittedly, what I was looking at on the streets of Charlotte wasn't any less nuts than some of the things I saw in mid-century Europe.

I was standing on the edge of a sand trap next to a pond on an exclusive golf club in south Charlotte, looking at a naked dead guy curled up in the fetal position. A blue folding tent kept the rain from washing away any evidence that might have remained, but it felt an awful lot like a losing proposition. It was closer to sunup than sundown, and the body had been discovered by a pair of amorous teenagers several hours before. The ground was soaked, and the sand trap was more mud trap than anything, thanks to the rain rolling in mid-afternoon. According to the weather app on my phone, it wasn't letting up for another day at least. Any physical evidence would have to be under the body to be of any use. "Who is it, and why are we here? This looks a lot more like a CMPD thing than ours."

"It would be, if this was the first body to be discovered like this. And if there was any obvious cause of death. Look at him, Harker, he's in perfect condition. Too perfect." The lean Black woman crouching by the body was Department of Homeland Security Deputy Director Rebecca Gail Flynn, who also happened to be my fiancée. Or girlfriend, depending on how annoyed she was with me about not setting a date for our wedding on any given day.

"So he's healthy. Except for the being dead part," I said. "What makes this ours?"

Becks looked at me like I was being intentionally obtuse, which I certainly wasn't. I can be obtuse without even trying, like tonight. "This is the fourth mysterious corpse to appear in the last six weeks. Every one of the victims has been in peak physical condition. In the other cases, no cause of death could be determined, even with an autopsy. That doesn't seem weird to you? Four men in perfect health found naked and dead scattered around one city?"

Okay, that *was* pretty odd. I opened my Sight to get a look at things in the supernatural spectrum, and everything became perfectly clear. And completely opaque at the same time. I knew why this guy looked like there was nothing wrong with him, and it wouldn't be much of a stretch to assume the other victims were similar. But that spawned a larger question. Who was murdering lycanthropes and leaving their bodies out in the open for anyone to find?

An hour and a half later, we were in dry clothes sitting in the living room of our apartment, my Uncle Luke relaxing in an armchair with my cat purring in his lap. "Quincy, are you certain this man was a werewolf?"

"He was a were-something," I replied, pouring a healthy slug of bourbon into a glass. It wouldn't get me drunk, my metabolism is too supercharged for that, but the burn helped dash away the last of the night's chill. "I can't promise what type, but he was definitely a lycanthrope."

"You can see if someone's a shifter with your Sight?" Becks asked, coming out of the bedroom with a sleep kerchief tied around her hair. She looked adorable in flannel pajamas, but her expression was definitely one that brooked no nonsense. She petted Nameless, the cat, and perched on the arm of one of my sofas.

"Yeah, and if the other victims were lycanthropes, it explains why there were no visible injuries. Weres heal when they shift, even if they're dead. So if he was killed as a wolf, or whatever he could turn into, and he shifted back, he'd look perfectly healthy. Assuming he wasn't shot in the head or dismembered," I said. "Some shit even magic can't fix."

"If we can get the other bodies, would you be able to tell if they were shifters, too?" Becks asked, holding out her hand for my glass. I handed it over and made myself another.

"Probably," I said. "How long have they been dead? I've never looked at a were's corpse with my Sight that's been dead any significant amount of time, so I don't know how long they retain their magic after death."

"My source inside CMPD says this has been going on for about six weeks, but she didn't feel comfortable calling me until this one."

"You still have connections inside the police department?" Luke asked. I swear to God seeing him stroke the cat's gray fur put me in the mind of Dr. Evil, and I kept waiting for him to hold a pinky up to his mouth and ask for a million dollars. Of course, he already had a million dollars, and way more, but that's what happens when you live for centuries.

Oh yeah. Luke, or Lucas Card as he went by lately, was more famously known as Count Vlad Tepes, or just Dracula. My family tree is weird. I turned to see Becks' response, since I'd been wondering the same thing. She left the Charlotte-Mecklenburg Police Department on less-than-favorable terms after actions the cops took during the protests in the summer of 2020, and I was as surprised as Luke that she had an inside source.

"There are some women within the department, younger officers of color that I mentored when I was there. A few keep their ears to the ground for me and give me a heads up when something spooky comes across their radar."

I raised an eyebrow. We worked for the Department of Homeland Security's Paranormal Division, but that Division didn't exist, as far as the public knew.

"Look, Harker, everybody in the department knew I was dealing with some weird shit before I left. So now if one of my ladies hears something that would have probably landed on my desk when I was there, they make sure I know about it." She downed her purloined bourbon and rattled the ice cubes at me.

I took the glass and freshened up both our drinks, like the good bartender/boyfriend/magician I am. "Six weeks? Are the bodies still on ice?" I asked, handing Becks her glass and sitting at the far end of the sofa so I could face both Luke and her.

"One is. One was claimed by relatives, and the other was disposed of after it was unclaimed for thirty days," she replied.

"Do we know where exactly it was buried?" Luke asked.

"We are not robbing graves," I said, my voice hard. "I still get twitchy around shovels after that night outside Constantinople."

"Istanbul," Becks corrected.

"Not Constantinople?" I asked, the corner of my mouth twitching up.

"Don't start," she said.

"Quincy, you do not get 'twitchy' as you say, around shovels because of that unfortunate incident in Turkey. You get twitchy because you are afraid someone will ask you to perform manual labor," Luke said.

He wasn't wrong, exactly. But the whole Istanbul thing *sucked*. Luke had been hiding in a coffin in a small family cemetery on account of us being out too close to sunrise and not having time to get to a light-tight room. I was digging him up when a farmer thought I was there to do unspeakable things to his dead granny's corpse. It took me the better part of four hours to pick all the birdshot out of my ass. Admittedly, I got off easier than the farmer. I think it took him six weeks for his arms to heal enough so he could wipe his own ass again.

"No matter the reason for Harker's twitchiness, there's no body to dig up. The remains were cremated and put into storage. Nothing to see there," Becks said.

"Then I guess we look at the other dead guy," I said, downing my drink and standing up. "Tomorrow."

"Tomorrow?" Luke asked.

I peeled off my shirt in response and started walking toward the bedroom. "Unless you think he's going to be any less dead after sunrise, I'm going to grab a couple hours sleep and go see a dead man about a fur coat in the morning."

"I'll get you in to examine the body, then I'll work on finding out who claimed the other victim. If we can talk to his pack, we might get some insight into who killed him," Becks said, following me into the bedroom and closing the door. She wrapped her arms around my neck and kissed me, her soft flannel pajamas rubbing against my bare chest in delightful ways. "Tomorrow," she whispered, then nipped at my earlobe.

"I shall return to my apartment. With the cat," Luke called from the den. Becks and I fell laughing into the bed, where we didn't get nearly enough sleep.

2

This wasn't my first trip to a morgue, not by a long shot. But one of the biggest changes in my life since getting together with Becks and starting to work for official government agencies was that I no longer had to break into morgues to investigate weird shit. We just walked in the front door in broad daylight, showed our badges to the balding middle-aged drone at the front desk, and told him what we were there for.

We'd barely gotten uncomfortable in the molded plastic-and-steel chairs in the waiting room when a cheerful round Asian man in scrubs came through the double swinging doors and walked over to us. "Director Flynn?" he asked, walking over to me. I jerked my thumb at Becks, who stood and extended a hand to him.

"I'm Deputy Director Flynn," she said, shaking his hand.

"I am so s-sorry," the man said, a slight flush coloring his cheeks. "I'm Doctor Yang."

Becks shook his hand and looked at me.

"It's okay," I said, standing up. "Happens all the time. On account of me being so much older. Quincy Harker," I said, holding out my own hand.

Dr. Yang looked back and forth between us, confusion all over his round face. I am a *lot* older than Flynn, but I don't look my age. When my powers kicked in as a young man, my aging slowed to a crawl. I'm over a century and a quarter old, but I look like I'm barely forty. Becks is in her late thirties, young for her position, but we look pretty much the same age. I try not to mention this too often, because my couch is uncomfortable and I really like sleeping with my fiancée.

"Um…okay," Dr. Yang said, obviously wanting to get the conversation back onto more familiar footing. "Come on back. Alex said you were here about one of our John Does?" He turned and headed back through the double doors, probably as much to get out of the uncomfortable conversation I'd put us in as anything else.

"Yes," Becks replied. *Don't annoy the coroner until we get the information we need*, she said over our mental link. Ever since I used some of my blood to heal a mortal injury Flynn sustained on a case, we'd been tied together. We could communicate without speaking and sense each other's presence and emotions over a huge distance, unless one of us took pains to close down the connection. Or unless someone severed it somehow, which generally ended very badly for whoever had that stupid idea. "We understand that he was brought in nude and with no apparent injuries."

Yang held up one finger as we walked. "Sorry, I don't like discussing specific cases in the public areas of the building. Some of our clerical staff are…not accustomed to some of the things I see in my work."

"Got bitched at for making somebody's executive assistant lose their lunch?" I asked with a smirk.

"More or less," Yang said, pushing through another pair of swinging doors. I wondered for a moment why there were so few normal doors in the place, then remembered that most of their customers arrive on stretchers.

We followed the short man into the heart of the morgue, passing through one empty autopsy room and into a large room with tables in the center and dozens of drawers lining the walls. There must have been room for three dozen bodies in the place, and judging by the name placards on each drawer, most of the spots were occupied.

"That's…a lot of dead people," I said, looking around. And given the number of bodies I've dropped in my day, it takes a lot to impress me.

"You should have seen it during COVID," Dr. Yang replied. Then he sighed. "No, you shouldn't have. It was nothing I ever want to live through again."

I could relate. The COVID-19 pandemic wasn't my first experience with overcrowded morgues and funeral homes, but I sincerely hoped it was my last. I've seen enough mass graves from all over the world to last me a lifetime. There's a lot of good to be said for living a very long time, but having lived through the flu epidemic of 1918, the Holocaust, and Pol Pot's killing fields, I knew the horrors that nature and mankind could inflict upon the species long before the first victim of the novel coronavirus got the sniffles. It doesn't get any easier for having survived a pandemic before.

"Hopefully this spate of mysterious deaths won't turn out to be contagious," Flynn said, putting a hand on the man's shoulder. It was a pretty clumsy attempt at condolence, but Yang seemed to appreciate it nonetheless.

"I don't see how it could," the doc replied, his cheeks reddening slightly as he looked at Flynn's hand on his shoulder. "Since I couldn't determine a cause of death at all." He opened a drawer at chest height and slid a body out of a long metal roller tray. "There is nothing wrong with this man. No injuries I can see, either by visible exam or on x-ray. No illness of any kind, no organ damage discovered during autopsy. No poisons or drugs in his toxicology report, no alcohol in his system, not even anything out of the ordinary in his stomach contents. I can find no reason that this man shouldn't be walking around in perfect health."

"Except for the part where he's dead," I said. I stepped closer to the body and looked it over. He looked like a lot of the werewolves I've met—tall, muscular, a little hairier than most people, without a scar to be seen anywhere. He didn't even have the little callous most people have on their index finger from holding a pen for years. He looked too young for a smallpox vaccine scar, which might have been the only thing he kept. A lot of weres still have scars from before they were turned, but if they were born shifters, the normal childhood bumps and scrapes didn't even leave a mark.

I dropped into my Sight and examined him again. Yep, definitely a lycanthrope. There's something in their aura that lingers long after death, a kind of greenish brown "woodsy" aura that marks them as creatures that wear multiple shapes. His was faint, but that was to be expected after nearly a month on the slab. With my Sight active, my other senses were more acute as well, and I could smell a faint hint of thick musky scent. This wasn't just any shifter: this was a were-bear.

That put everything into a different light immediately. What the hell could do enough damage to a were-bear that it would die before being able to shift? Normal bears are big, strong, and way faster than they have any right to be, and the whole thing about them not being able to climb trees is abject bullshit, which I learned to my horror one afternoon in the Black Forest. But were-bears were stronger, faster, and even more massive, as they tended to shift into the Grizzly or Kodiak varieties. So, whatever had killed this guy, it had almost certainly killed a nearly half-ton beast with claws that could rip through sheet metal and enough power to rip a human in half.

This was…not good.

We spent another half hour pretending to examine the body before confiscating his personal effects, which consisted entirely of a necklace with an odd pendant that looked familiar but I couldn't place right away. We bid Dr. Yang farewell, and after he pressed his card into Flynn's hand and implored her to call him if she needed *any* more help, we stepped back out into the Carolina spring sunshine. I took off the hoodie I'd needed first thing in the morning and in the conscientiously cold morgue and followed Becks to her government-issued Suburban.

"Have you ever thought about driving around in something a little less 'I'm a federal agent'?" I asked. "Besides, this thing has to get absolutely shit gas mileage."

"The car came with the badge, and I don't have to pay for maintenance, so I'm pretty good to look like a fed. Also, I *am* a federal agent, and with the engines we've got in our fleet, I get sixty miles to the gallon, so gas isn't really an issue."

"Wait, what?" I asked, sliding into the passenger seat. "Are you telling me you've got a magic motor in your Suburban?"

"I'm not telling you anything other than it gets better gas mileage than your Honda. You don't have clearance to know the details," Becks said, cranking the SUV. I noticed it did run a lot quieter than most enormous parking spot hogs.

We rode over to Southend for lunch at Phat Burrito, a locally owned joint that made burritos the size of my head. I got a Dos Equis to go with it, and Becks gave me a dirty look. "We're on the clock."

"I'm a wizard," I replied. "It's literally impossible for me to get drunk off one beer, and I really like Dos Equis."

"And as an independent contractor, I guess I don't get to tell you how to do your job, just what job I want done and when I need results by," she said. "But as your fiancée, please stop making me look bad by drinking on the job."

"Okay," I said, walking up to the counter and getting a soda. I finished my beer first, but I did switch to Coke. I figured that had to count for something, especially since I picked up our burritos while I was there. "So now what?" I asked, unwrapping the hunk of tortilla, beans, cheese, rice, chicken, guacamole, and salsa bigger than my forearm.

"Now I watch you try to eat that without wearing it," Becks said. She'd opted for a more fashion-safe, yet cowardly, burrito bowl. "Then I go to the office and look for similar cases in the surrounding towns while you go home and do some kind of divination spell to see what the hell that necklace is."

"And by 'divination spell,' you mean look it up on Google," I said, a little bit of cheese dribbling onto my chin.

"Magic takes many forms, Harker. You recognized that thing, even though you have no idea from where."

"Maybe Luke will know when he wakes up."

"Don't try to rouse him early, you know his attack cat is very protective." She wasn't joking. Nameless was supposed to be my cat, but more and more he seemed like my uncle's familiar. It wasn't fair. I'm the guy who actually casts spells. If anyone should have a familiar, it's me. But cat's gonna cat, and I know better than to try to force affection on a creature with tiny daggers strapped to the end of every finger. If you ever want to know if someone understands the concept of consent, ask if they have cats. They'll teach you about not touching anything that doesn't want to be touched, and *fast*.

"There might be something in one of Luke's books that will jog my memory," I said. "Maybe I'll put in a call to a local Alpha I used to drink with back before you made me all respectable. If there's something going after the local shifter populace, I bet he knows about it."

"Respectable?" Becks scoffed. "I don't think that word means what you think it means."

I chuckled and shoved more burrito in my mouth, trying to come up with a good way to approach a werewolf who threatened to rip my arm off and beat me with it the last time we met.

Didn't I tell you I was gonna rip your head off and shit down your neck if I ever saw you again, Harker?"

"I'm pretty sure you said you were going to rip my arm off and beat me to death with it, Saint," I replied, hoping I looked a lot more relaxed than I felt.

I wasn't relaxed, not at all. I didn't think Saint could kill me, but I definitely didn't put it past him to make a hell of an effort. If you asked somebody to draw their prototypical werewolf in human form, Jason St. Laurent would probably be how most people saw it. He was taller than me, and I'm a few inches over six foot. He was broad across the shoulders and thickly muscled, with wavy dark hair and a grizzled beard. If it sounds a lot like I'm describing Joe Manganella from *True Blood*, it wouldn't be the first time someone has drawn that parallel. Not me, though. Not more than once. Saint backhanded me right off my barstool the first and last time I made the comparison.

Saint was ostensibly the leader of a motorcycle club called the Caswell Howlers, a social club with a headquarters staggering distance from Presbyterian Hospital. I guess he really was the leader of the Howlers, but the Howlers were also his pack. Shifters, all of them, and I don't mean transmissions. Most of his pack were wolves, but there were a few bears, jackals, panthers, and at least one red-tailed hawk named Cindy.

Cindy was the reason Saint threatened my life. Not because I slept with her, although I did. But because I wasn't a lycanthrope and I slept with her. Why that all fell on me, I didn't know, but I've learned that it's better not to ask too many questions when somebody wants to murder me over a sexual encounter. And yes, it's happened often enough that I have rules for that sort of thing. Cindy and I had a fling a little more than a decade ago, and Saint informed me that I was under no circumstances to see her, speak with her, and certainly not screw her again.

Being a sober individual known for my good judgement and skills at conflict avoidance, I did all three. Did I mention Cindy is also Saint's niece? So I knew when I walked into the clubhouse that I was taking my life, and my arm, into my hands. But the full moon was a couple weeks away, so at least Saint wasn't going to be moon-crazy when he tried to murder me.

"You making jokes now, Harker?" Saint demanded, stepping out from behind the bar with a baseball bat in his right hand. I guess he had thought better of beating me to death with my own arm.

"I remember you used to think I was pretty amusing," I said with my best "let's not ruin your floor with a lot of blood and brain matter" smile.

"That was before you banged my niece then disappeared on her." It's really hard for humans to actually speak in a growl. The best most people can manage is a Clint Eastwood rasp. But Saint, he had the growl down pat. It was a rumble that sounded like it originated somewhere around his kneecaps and rattled around his entire intestinal tract before bubbling out of his mouth, coated in a thick layer of threat.

"For the record, you were responsible for the disappearance," I said. "You told me to get lost and stay lost. So I did."

"Except now I'm looking at you in the middle of my clubhouse." Two steps forward and he was officially looming over me.

I don't like being loomed at. It makes me feel short, and I don't like feeling short. I also don't intimidate easily. Something about staring Lucifer in the eye and basically telling him to go fuck himself makes it a lot harder for mere mortals to scare me. I decided it was time to stop playing at being Quincy Harker, nice guy who doesn't want to get in a fight, and time to be someone a little more true to myself.

Time to remind Saint that when demons and monsters whisper stories about me they don't call me Q, or Harker, or even Quincy. No, the monster under the monsters' beds is only called by one name.

Reaper.

I looked into Saint's eyes, something I try to avoid doing because they really are the windows to the soul, and my soul is not something most people can handle looking at for very long. I channeled a little bit of magic into my orbs and let them glow with a purple fire flickering just behind my pupils. "Back the fuck up, Saint," I whispered. "Or everyone in here is going to see their Alpha turn into my beta in a hot second."

I didn't try for a growl, just kept my voice very low and steady. "You know who I really am, who I am when I'm not having fun drinking and chasing skirts. You got to see a little bit of what I can do when those Hell's Angels rolled up on us in Richmond that night, and you saw a little bit more when that trio of wolves came into your clubhouse looking to step to the Alpha. But you've never seen all my tricks, or even a quarter of my power, and I've had ten years to get better and stronger."

"And I've had ten years to become a better shot," came a female voice from behind me, followed by the sound of a cocking pistol.

Okay. I guess it was gonna be the hard way. I drew in more energy, siphoning magical energy from everything around me to augment what I kept stored. I wrapped my entire body in a hazy shield of purple energy, then spun around, bringing my left hand up to snatch the barrel of a Colt 1911 out of the hands of a very startled young woman with long auburn hair and a smattering of freckles that I knew full well traveled down far past the neck of her Harley-Davidson t-shirt. I put my right hand in the center of Cindy's chest and gave her a gentle push, which of course sent her flying back a good ten feet because of the magic coursing through my muscles.

I turned back to Saint, dropping to one knee as I did. His massive fist swished through the air over my head, and I stood up, landing a magically enhanced uppercut on the point of his jaw. His eyes crossed and he staggered back a couple steps, but he didn't go down. He always was a strong mother. He shook his head to clear the stars from his vision and grabbed the baseball bat with both hands, ready to take my head off with one swing. I wasn't having it.

I called power and shaped it into a purple sphere, then flung it right into the center of his chest with a shouted *"Forzare!"* The ball of kinetic energy caught him square, flinging him back to crash into, then backward over, the bar, taking out the bottom shelf of liquor. I felt a little bad about that. Kicking Saint's ass was one thing, but there was really no need to destroy perfectly good booze.

"You wanna cut this shit out now, Saint?" I called. "Or am I going to have to break a sweat?"

"I think I'll break your spine instead," said a massive Black man with a shaved head and a goatee. I mean, really? Where did this guy get his fashion advice, *Luke Cage*? All he was missing was the tinfoil tiara. He was close to seven feet tall and four hundred pounds if he was an ounce, and as I watched, his skin thickened, he grew even taller, and a pair of ivory tusks sprouted from his jaw.

Great, I thought, *a fucking were-elephant.* And me without my silver anything. This was probably gonna sting. He took one step forward and lashed out with an enormous fist, easily the size of my head. My only saving grace was that he was too big to be fast, so it was more like fighting Andre the Giant post-*Princess Bride* than back when he was doing cartwheels all over Europe. I ducked and slammed a fist into his left kneecap, sending it sideways and putting the big shifter through two tables on his way to the ground.

Another, much smaller, man leapt at me, wrapping long skinny arms around my face and neck while screeching like some kind of deranged monkey. He bit my ear, and I reached up over my left shoulder, grabbed a ponytail, and flipped him across the room. "That's not the kind of howler you're supposed be, Monkey-boy." A pale white arm came up from the collapsed chair he landed under, middle finger extended.

I turned back to the bar where Saint had regained his feet and found myself staring down the barrels of a very large shotgun. "You know that won't get through my wards, right?" I asked, the smirk still on my face.

"I know this is a mix of cold iron and blessed salt, so I'm willing to give it a shot," Saint replied. "Are you?"

I wasn't. I didn't think cold iron or salt could screw with my shields on their own, but together they might be disruptive enough to put me down. Besides, I really wasn't there to fight. And I certainly wasn't there to slaughter a group of relatively harmless biker lycan-thropes. I raised both my hands and said, "You win. You beat the Reaper. Now can we talk, or do you want to see if I'm really immortal?"

A wave of whispers and muttering rippled through the bar like a fart in an elevator. "Reaper?" "*That's* the Reaper?" "I thought he'd be bigger." That kind of stuff. I'm used to it, mostly.

Saint put the shotgun down and grabbed an unbroken bottle of Wild Turkey, then stepped out from behind the bar and stalked past me to a door marked "OFFICE—FUCK OFF." He turned back when he noticed I wasn't following. "You comin'?"

I followed. After I grabbed a pair of glasses. I don't really get sick, but I really prefer to drink like a civilized Reaper when I can.

4

So what the fuck do you want, Harker? And why did you have to wreck half my bar?" Saint asked, leaning back in his desk chair and putting his motorcycle boots up on a scarred corner.

"For the record, I only started wrecking shit when you got all up in my face. And most of that was when your pet elephant fell down and went boom. When the fuck did you add a were-*elephant* to your pack? Isn't that a little far afield for wolves?"

"We don't discriminate," Saint said, taking a long pull off the bottle and passing it to me. "Jermone came to us about five years ago after he got trafficked here for his ivory. Some asshole realized that his tusks grew back every time he shifted, so he wrapped the big guy in silver and forced the change on him over and over again. Poor bastard was down to a hundred-thirty pounds when we got him out."

I poured myself a healthy slug of Kentucky's only notable export and passed the bottle back across the desk. "You could have called for help, you know. I was in town."

"Didn't need your help," Saint replied. "And sure as fuck didn't need the drama that seems to pop up every time you're around."

17

He had me there. I'm kind of a shit magnet, even when I'm not trying to stir any up. I guess it's my winning personality. Or maybe my complete lack of impulse control. Or the zero fucks I have to give about how people perceive me. "Fair enough," I said. "Any of your people go missing last night?" I asked, ready to quit dancing around and get to the real reason I was there.

"It ain't a fucking dorm, Harker. I don't know where all my folks are every minute of every day. But nobody's missing that I expected to be here, if that answers your question."

"It kinda does, but let's get more specific. Is this guy one of your wolves?" I held up my phone, marveling that once again it had survived a Quincy Harker fistfight. The new cases Homeland had built for me and Bubba were worth however many thousands of dollars they cost the taxpayers.

Saint sucked in a breath and his eyes widened at the photo of the most recent victim. "Willy. He's not pack, but I know the kid. What happened to him?"

"That's what I'm trying to find out," I said. "I figure the best way to find out what happened to him is to find out who he was first. So who was he?"

"He's a stupid kid from somewhere in flyover country. Nebraska, maybe. Went on some church trip to build houses for poor people in Canada or some shit, got himself bitten, and when he turned fuzzy a few weeks later, he ran away from home and landed here."

"He went through his first shift alone? Did he kill anybody?" Weres could eventually control themselves when in their animal form and, except for the three nights of the full moon, were in control of their changes. They *had* to shift for the full moon, no matter what, but the rest of the time they had a handle on it. Unless they got badly injured or really pissed off.

"No," Saint replied. "He got lucky. He told me he'd been off alone fishing when he changed and woke up butt naked with half a deer carcass strewn all around him."

"That must have been fucking terrifying," I said.

"It's an Alpha's worst nightmare, a newly turned lycanthrope going through that alone. Okay, I guess it's my second worst nightmare. My worst is that the baby were kills somebody. Anyway, he hooked up with a few other para kids around town and got into a little trouble, but nothing major. Vandalism, petty theft, a few burglaries down in Ballantyne, that kind of shit. Then they fucked up and tried to rob Jermone in a park one night."

"Oh, there's no way *that* ended badly," I said, remembering how much of my mojo it took to lay the big were-elephant out.

"Yeah, you called it." Saint nodded and took another swig from the bottle. I couldn't tell if he was playing at being a hardass not using a tumbler, or if he thought drinking from the bottle would keep me out of his liquor. Either way, I reached across the desk and poured myself another slug. "Jermone's a peaceable guy until it's time not to be, so when four idiot kids jumped him, he tried to keep it chill until one of them landed a good punch on him. Then he went all gray and stompy on their asses. He brought the whole lot of them back here, we patched them up, and I had a conversation with the crew about how to behave in a city with multiple groups of paras."

"You mean, you told them if they fucked around with any of your people again, you'd string their intestines from streetlamps," I said. I'd gotten the same "conversation" from Saint about twenty years ago. In my case, it didn't stick. I thought it probably went better with a bunch of scared kids that he actually could disembowel without too much effort.

Saint ducked his head and gave me a grin. "Yeah, that was about the gist of it. But then Willy started coming around the clubhouse. He never made like he wanted to join the pack, and he certainly didn't want to ride with us. The kid never even looked hard at a bike." The incredulity on Saint's face was funny. It was like he couldn't fathom someone *not* wanting to ride a motorcycle. "But we're not gonna shove some kid out in the cold just because he's not a member, so I let him come and go as he pleased. He's been bouncing around town for about the last two years."

"When was the last time he bounced through here?" I asked.

"Been a couple months. He actually looked good, you know. Better than usual. He was clean and well-fed for a change. Usually these street rats are scrawny, haven't showered in about a week, and are broke. But Willy paid for his drinks, was cleaned up, and had on clothes that looked like they'd seen the inside of a washing machine recently. I figured something had turned around for him. I was happy, you know? Even though he wasn't one of mine, I had a soft spot for the little idiot. Now he's dead. Fuck."

"Yeah." I took another sip of Saint's bourbon. "Did you talk to him? Maybe poke around a little about what changed for him?"

"I didn't, but I think Cindy did. He always followed her around like a puppy dog, offering to bus tables for her, do dishes for her, that kinda shit. Reminded me a little of some other guy who used to hang around my niece. Only difference was, I liked Willy."

Okay, that one stung. But Cindy was a beautiful woman, and given that lycanthropes age slowly, she looked a lot closer to twenty-one than to the fifty she was really pushing. "You think she might know more?" I asked.

"Maybe. But she ain't gonna tell you. She was *pissed* when you stopped coming around, Harker. Pissed."

"You told me never to darken your door again, remember? That's what the whole fight we just had was about."

"Yeah, I might not have mentioned that to her at the time. Better to have her hate your guts than mine. I gotta live with her." He tipped the bottle in my direction, and I begrudgingly toasted him with my glass. I couldn't argue his logic. Since Saint never mated, Cindy was his Alpha female, basically the second in command of the pack. A real argument between Alphas could tear a pack apart, and he didn't think a fling with me was worth that. Hell, *I* didn't think a fling with me was worth that.

We are going to have a chat about this 'fling' when you get home, Becks said in my mind. Sometimes, like when walking into a bar run by the uncle of your ex-girlfriend, it gets real inconvenient having your significant other riding shotgun inside your noggin.

"You want to call her in here and ask about Willy, or you want me to leave through the back door and ask her after I'm gone?" No point trying to pressure Cindy into saying anything if she didn't want to talk with me around. She was one of the most stubborn women I'd ever known. *I guess I have a type,* I sent to Becks, getting a mental image of a raised middle finger in response.

"She's mostly over being pissed at you. Let's get this over with, so you can go back to never setting foot in my bar again." He tapped on his cell phone, then set it back down on his desk. "She'll be back in a minute. She's stocking the beer coolers right now."

Sure enough, less than two minutes of uncomfortable toxically masculine drinking and glaring at each other later, me and Saint were rescued by Cindy sweeping through the door. "What do you want, Harker?" she said, standing in front of Saint's desk. "I've got a bar to run, and a bunch of broken furniture to replace, thanks to you."

"Willy's dead," Saint said, cutting off the argument before we got started.

Cindy looked like she'd taken a punch to the gut, sitting in the other visitor chair with a soft "oh."

I gave her a second to collect herself before opening my mouth to start asking my questions. She held up one finger, and I sat back, silent.

"When?" she asked.

"Last night."

"Where?"

"We're not sure. The…his body was found on a private golf course, but the scene indicates he wasn't killed there."

"How?"

"We don't know. Without a crime scene, and since all but the most grievous injuries heal as soon as one of you shifts, we can't tell what happened, or where, or why." The last was to save her from asking yet another question I didn't have an answer to. "I was hoping you could tell me where to find his friends, so I could ask them about it."

"You gonna ask them questions, or slaughter them?" Cindy asked.

I took a second before I answered, giving the question the weight it deserved. I'm not known for my restraint. "I'm going to question them first. Then, if it turns out they killed him, and that they killed the other shifters that have shown up mysteriously dead around town over the past six months…well, then I'll probably slaughter them."

"How many others?" Saint asked.

"How do you know they were all shifters?" Cindy jumped in.

I held up a hand to forestall any more questions. "Willy is the fourth victim. I can only confirm two of them as weres. The other two bodies were disposed of before I could get a look at them. But I spoke to the coroner this morning, and he said the other two John Does were found the same way—naked, in relatively populated areas, and with no apparent cause of death, even after an autopsy. They were in perfect health, except they were dead."

Saint sat back in his chair. "None of our people are missing, so they aren't pack, but that doesn't make me feel much better."

"How many unaffiliated shifters are there in Charlotte?" I asked.

Saint looked at me like I was an idiot. "How the fuck am I supposed to know, Harker? That's what unaffiliated means. Shit, I don't even know how many members are in the other packs, much less who might be walking around fuzzy three nights a month that don't run with a crew."

"Crap," I said. Then an idea hit me. A possibly terrible idea, but it was the only one I had. "How friendly are you with the other Alphas?"

"We're pretty territorial, but as long as nobody pisses on the wrong fire hydrant, we kinda have a live and let live arrangement."

"Would they take your call? Maybe come to a meeting?" I asked.

Saint was shaking his head before I finished my sentence. "There's no fucking way they'd meet here. They'll talk to me, but if I asked them to a meet here, they'd come expecting an ambush."

"What about on neutral territory?" Cindy asked.

I looked at her, and as I realized where she meant, my heart fell, bouncing off all my ribs and stomach on the way down. There was only one really neutral place for cryptids, fae, and other supernatural beings in Charlotte, and it was a place that I *really* didn't want to go back to. But it was probably the only place I could get all the Alphas together to try and figure out who was killing shifters in my city, and how.

Get the team together, I said over my mental link to Becks. *We're gonna have to go to Mort's.*

5

O h, *hell* no!" the brown-skinned woman behind the bar said when I walked in. "Turn your narrow Anglican ass right back around and walk out that door, Quincy Harker! You weren't welcome in here before the last time you trashed my place, and you sure as hell aren't welcome in here now! Do you know how much it costs me every single time you show up at my bar?"

I didn't have time for this bullshit. "Nothing, Mort. I know full well it doesn't cost you a goddamned cent, because Luke pays for the damages. Every time. Now, I've played this game with you for years, because I think it's kinda funny, and because I feel bad for getting Christy involved with my crap, but I don't have time for it today. I've got half a dozen different packs of weres descending on this place for a meet, and I need at least a couple minutes to move tables around and get prepared. So let's put the games on hold for a couple hours, and you can go back to hating me when the meeting is over."

"Moot," Saint said, walking in and immediately starting to rearrange chairs.

I turned to the big wolf. "What?"

"It's not a meet, or a meeting, it's a moot."

"What are you, a fucking were-Ent now?" I asked.

"It's an ancient term for a debate, which is what we're going to be doing. We're going to debate whether or not there's someone hunting lycanthropes in Charlotte, and then we're going to debate whether or not you're to blame. And if we decide that you are, we're going to debate who gets to rip your head off, and who can be the first to shit down your neck."

"You're welcome to try, big boy," I said. "Bigger shifters than you have tried, and none of them ever howled at the moon again. Remember, I didn't give *myself* the nickname of Reaper."

Saint dragged a four-top table across the floor with a spine-wrenching *screeeeeech*, then looked at me with a grin. "No, you didn't. But I'm the Alpha of the baddest pack of shifters in North Carolina. You ever stared down anybody worse than that, *Reaper?*"

I usually can manage not to take the bait. I really have been working on my self-control, and it's been almost a full year since I felt the need to participate in a dick-measuring contest, but I needed to make sure that in a room full of Alphas, they all understood that if they fucked with me, I'd be their goddamned Omega, and not in the smutty ebook way. So I walked over to where Saint had lifted another table, and I slapped it to the floor with one hand.

"Listen, furball," I said, my jaw tight and my voice low, "I've gotten into a fistfight with an Archangel, told Oberon the King of Faerie to go fuck himself, and stared Lucifer himself right in the eye in the Ninth Circle of Hell. You think I give a single flying fuck at a rolling doughnut about you? Motherfucker, I've intimidated scarier things than you before breakfast, then went on to kick the shit out of a Reaver demon before lunch. So if you want to step to me, let's get it the fuck over with so I can have this fucking moot with all your fine furry and feathered friends, and figure out who's slaughtering shifters in my city."

Saint shoved the table aside and took one step toward me, fists clenched at his side, before we registered the slow clapping coming from the door. Yeah, the old slow clap to take all the testosterone out of a room. I turned to see a gorgeous blonde with brilliant white wings and a David Bowie t-shirt standing in the doorway. Beside her, the one doing all the clapping, was a tall man with a sandy ponytail hanging over one shoulder. He wore a white suit with the sleeves rolled up twice, somehow *not* looking like the worst Don Johnson cosplayer in history. Glory and Faustus, who was now really named Fautinir, although he threatened to smite me if I ever called him that. The angels had arrived.

"I thought you two were off on some Heavenly mission," I said, not turning quite enough to leave Saint out of my sightline.

"Oh, we are," Glory said. "But I'm still your Guardian Angel, and as amusing as it would be to watch you two idiots turn this place to a war zone, Luke asked me to pop in and see if I could save him a repair bill. So put the wieners away, zip up your shit, and let's get this place ready for a good old-fashioned moot."

"Okay, first—please don't ever mention my wiener again. It's bad enough having an angel watching over literally everything I do, but I really don't want to know that you've ever thought about my junk. And second—*language*."

"Fuck off, Harker," Glory said as she walked past me to Saint. "I've seen your junk more times than anyone but you, and I'm still not interested." She held out a hand to the Alpha. "I'm Glory. This is Faustus. We're angels. Please don't break Harker; he's got important shit to do."

Saint looked completely stunned by this turn of events. I couldn't blame him. It's one thing to meet an angel; it's another thing entirely to meet one that could grace the cover of the *Sports Illustrated* swimsuit edition. He shook her hand without saying a word, then went back to moving tables. Glory looked over at the bar. "Hello, Mort. Nice body."

Mort gave her a little wave and a nod. "Thanks. Investment banker from Nashville. She wanted perfect pitch, I wanted to be a chick for a week, especially one with the tastebuds for really spicy curry."

"That's a pretty fair deal, especially for you, pal," Faustus said, stepping over to the bar. "Beer me?"

Mort seemed to have some trouble looking at the former demon, just handed him a Heineken and stared at the bar top. "I heard you'd gone home, Faustus. I…" Mort's voice trailed off, and the silence that fell over the bar was heavy for a second.

"Yeah," Faustus replied. "I…Returned."

"Is it…" Mort didn't finish his question, but Faustus answered anyway. Like he knew what the demon was going to ask. He probably did, since he'd been asking himself the same question since The Fall.

"Yeah," Faustus said, his voice gentle. "It's as good as I remembered."

I turned away, suddenly feeling like I was intruding on a very private moment between two beings that had seen the literal dawn of time. Saint was still staring at me, so I stuck out a hand. "Truce?"

He looked at Glory, then Faustus, then shook my hand. "Truce. But one of these days, Harker, we're gonna see who really is the baddest motherfucker in town."

I jerked my chin at Glory. "Pretty sure it ain't either of us, pal."

"I can confirm that, Quincy," Luke said, having done that creepy-ass thing he does where he's nowhere around one minute and the next instant he's standing by your elbow. "But now I believe your guests are beginning to arrive, so if there is more redecorating to be done, we should proceed with it post haste."

"That's our cue," Glory said. "We've got work to do on another plane, but all of you remember…" She pointed to Mort, Saint, and for a particularly long moment, at me, then said, "I'm watching." Then she and Faustus vanished. I noticed Faustus took his beer. Old habits, I guess.

"She's kinda scary, dude. Hot, but scary," Saint said.

"You should see her in armor," I replied. "Even hotter. And way scarier."

<hr>

We got all the tables and chairs moved, but it still took over an hour to get everybody inside, get the "how you beens" and "good to see yas" out of the way so we could actually talk about what was going on. Finally, I stood at the end of a massive conglomeration of bar tables we'd thrown together in a weird conference table shape, and addressed the Alphas, Betas, and Sergeants-at-Arms of eight shifter packs from all over Charlotte.

"I know a lot of you by sight, and more by name, and I'm pretty sure you all know me. I'm Quincy Harker, and I work with the Department of Homeland Security's Paranormal Division—"

"You're the fucking Reaper, asshole," one particularly belligerent Asian were from East Charlotte called out. Apparently he wasn't a fan.

"Okay, sure," I said, holding up both hands to show that I wasn't currently holding a weapon. Not that I didn't have a gun in my belt, another strapped to my right ankle, one duct-taped to the underside of the table, and enough magical energy stored to turn Mort's bar into a smoking crater. But I didn't have a gun in my hand *then*. "Some people call me the Reaper, and I've had a few unpleasant encounters with some of you over the years."

"You killed my brother, you fucking prick!" shouted a heavily muscled Black man with long braids.

"Yeah, sorry about that, Dex," I said. "But we both know Calvin was a dumbass, and a mean one, and that your pack is in better hands with you as Alpha." Dex's brother Calvin had decided about six years ago that he should control all the drug trade on Charlotte's west side, despite his pack having never trafficked drugs before. He killed his way up the ladder of the groups that did move drugs on that side of town, and when a couple of high school kids got caught in the cross-fire, I stepped in. And stepped on Calvin. Hard. Seemed like Dex might have held a grudge.

"Look," I started again. "If we go down the list of everything one of you wants to kick my ass for, we'll be here all night. And if we're here all night, we won't find out why there are at least four dead shifters in Charlotte over the last six weeks."

A low rumble went across the room, and Becks stepped forward. "I'm Deputy Director Rebecca Gail Flynn from Homeland. I'm techni-cally Harker's boss, but some of you probably understand that he's crap at taking orders. But he's right. There are lycanthropes turning up dead all over Charlotte, and we need to find out what's happening to them, and who's responsible."

"Why, so you speciesist fascists can give them a medal?" Ah, the University weres. Another, painfully and demonstrably progressive, party heard from. The young woman standing in front of her chair had close-cropped pink hair, a nose ring, and the patented anti-government snarl of the poli-sci undergraduate. I did have to admire her dedication to her body jewelry, since every time she shifted, she'd have to re-pierce her septum.

"No, so I can teach those motherfuckers why they call me Reaper," I said. I still had my hands raised, but now I wreathed them in purple flame, letting some of that same energy bleed out from my eyes. "I might not know all of you, and I know I don't like most of you, but if anybody's going to slaughter you in my city, it's gonna be me."

"That's my nephew," Luke said with the level of droll you only acquire after your third century on the planet. "Always the diplomat."

6

———————

My display of exceptional restraint (exceptional because it came from me at all, restraint because I neither blew anyone up or set anyone on fire) reduced the tension in the room from a boil to a simmer, and Becks pointed to a big monitor on the bar with four crime scene photos displayed on it. I don't know where it came from, but it seems like any time a government agency is part of a meeting, there has to be a big-ass monitor. I was just hoping she hadn't had time to make a PowerPoint. You don't know suffering until you've sat through eight hours of mandatory federal sexual harassment training, led by the person you are actually having sex with on a regular basis.

"These four men were found naked and dead at different locations across Charlotte over the past six weeks. All the bodies were found on a Sunday morning, and they all seemed to be in perfect health. From the two bodies we were able to examine, we know that they were lycanthropes. We are working under the assumption that the other victims were shifters as well. The autopsy reports showed enlarged hearts typical of high-performance athletes, no trace of injury, and completely clean toxicology reports. Their stomach contents

30

consisted of large quantities of meat and other high-protein foods, and very few vegetables."

"Yeah, we ain't known for our love of spinach," Saint said from across the room, getting a chuckle from the assembled shifters.

"Speak for yourself, fang-boy," a slight lycan with buck teeth shot back. A were-rabbit, if I had to hazard a guess. This got an even bigger laugh.

Becks continued. "All four bodies were found naked, and no clothes or belongings were anywhere in the vicinity. Saint has already identified the most recent victim as a hanger-on named Willy, but we would like your help in identifying the others."

She clicked a remote, and the screen switched to close-ups of the three unidentified victims. A low rumble passed through the crowd as they got their first good look at the dead men, all young, all seemingly in the prime of health, and all very obviously dead on a morgue table.

"The one on the far left is José Marquand," the college were woman said. "He vanished from campus almost two months ago. I didn't even know he was a para, much less a were. I guess he was still closeted."

A lot of nods around the table at that. Many young shifters don't know how to find a local pack when they move to a new area, so it wasn't a big surprise that José hadn't reached out to anyone. It's not like Miss Nose Ring was plastering flyers around campus telling people to meet on the quad naked every full moon to romp through the woods. At least, I assumed she didn't. College in the new millennium might be more open-minded than I thought.

"I think the one in the middle might be Jerry Cans." This was the buck-toothed shifter, pulling out a pair of glasses and slipping them on over his short nose. I swear, everything the guy did made him look more rabbit-like. If he was a were-aardvark, it was proof God had a fucked-up sense of humor.

"Yeah, that's Jerry," said a thick-necked bald white guy sitting with Dex. "I wondered why he ain't been out back of the bar lately."

"Who's Jerry?" I asked.

The big guy glared at me until Dex elbowed him, then said, "Jerry's a bum. I mean, unhoused dude, that squats in a few places around town. One of them is the yard across from our club." "Our club" was Tempt, a strip club on the north side of town where Dex's pack spent a lot of time. It sat across a narrow street from a junkyard, an unfortunate location for a topless bar, but a pretty good one for a front for a coke and meth outfit, which is where most of the club's revenue came from.

"When was the last time you saw Jerry?" Flynn asked.

"What, like I keep track of the guy picking up half-smoked butts off the ground? Come on, lady."

"Behave, Orville," Dex said, his voice low. "She's a fed."

"That's right, *Orville*," Becks said, stepping forward and putting her hands on a table. "And a former CMPD detective. I know all about you guys running drugs out of Tempt, and if you fuck with me on this, I'll make sure there's a cop car parked across the street from your front door every night for the next year. How's that going to affect your business?"

Orville held up both hands in surrender. "Fine, fine. I ain't seen Jerry in at least a month. Maybe two. He don't keep a regular schedule, ya know?"

"Yes, he does," Rabbit Guy disagreed. "He has a route he works, like a delivery guy, or the pallet man. He spends a couple weeks at the junkyard, then a couple weeks in Marshall Park if it's warm, then a couple weeks under the bridge over by J.C. Smith, then a couple weeks down by the John Belk overpass on 77. Then he goes back to the junkyard and starts his lap all over again."

"How would you know, Bunny?" Orville asked, his lip curled up in a snarl. Most lycanthropes are predators, so the ones who shift into typical prey animals are considered second- or even third-class citizens.

"I know because I talked to him, you muscle-bound asshat," Bunny said, pushing his glasses up his nose. "You just threw rocks at him, but he was a good guy. He was smart, and a talented artist. He painted the mural on the side of our shop when we moved onto Central."

"Your shop?" I asked.

"I'm part owner of The White Rabbit," Bunny said, a hint of pride in his voice. The White Rabbit is Charlotte's oldest LGBTQ+ bookstore, and a gathering point for the community for decades. It's entirely possible that Bunny was the store's namesake. I never knew there was a paranormal component to its ownership, though. "We all save our aluminum cans for Jerry, and he'd pick them up about once a month when he was heading from his spot under John Belk back to the industrial park where the junkyard is. He…he was a good person. He didn't deserve to be thrown away like garbage."

"Nobody does," I said, getting nods from everyone around the table. If there's one thing shifters understand, it's rejection and solitude. That's why the bonds of a pack are so strong. For a lot of them, it's the only family they can ever have after being rejected by the humans in their lives. I get that. It's why the bonds I've formed with my people are so important to me.

I turned back to the screen. "Anybody know the last unidentified victim?" My only response was silence. "Are there any other packs, or loosely affiliated groups of weres, that aren't here?" Maybe the last victim would be a member there.

"There's that bunch down by the Arboretum," a woman who had been silent until now said. She was a normal-looking woman, white, in her forties, with a little gray at her temples. Which meant she might have been forty or eighty. She looked to be in good shape and had a slightly feline air about her movements. Maybe a were-cat of some sort. "There's not really an Alpha, or even a membership. I think it's more like a social club. They meet up most Wednesday nights at the Barnes & Noble down there."

"Would you be willing to make an introduction?" Becks asked.

The woman looked at Flynn like she'd grown another head. "You want me to introduce a fed and the Reaper to a bunch of shifters? Hell, no. I barely know them, and I like the ones I know, so if you show up and start doing fed stuff, I don't want to be associated with that. And I definitely don't want anybody thinking I sicced the Reaper on them."

You have got *to do something about that nickname,* Becks said.

If only I hadn't spent so many decades earning it, I replied. I held up my hands. "Okay, that makes sense. But look…" I let my words trail off and gave the woman a "this is where you tell me your name" look.

"Theresa," she said, her voice curt, like even giving me her first name was a struggle.

"Look, Theresa, I really don't want to hurt anyone—" I had to pause to let the snickering die down. "I don't want to hurt anyone who doesn't deserve it. I just want to find out who these dead men are, and what's happening to them, before it happens to more people."

"How do you know these are the only victims?" Luke asked.

I whirled around to stare at him, partly for interrupting me when I was at my most diplomatic, but mostly because he'd raised a point we hadn't even considered. I made an effort to keep my shock under wraps and asked, "What do you mean, Luke?"

He rose and walked over to the monitor, gesturing at the four faces there. "You have the photographs of four lycanthropes who have apparently been murdered in Charlotte recently, but what of other paranormal or supernatural beings that don't leave bodies in mysteriously perfect health? How do we know that this is only a problem of the lycanthrope population? What if someone is once again hunting cryptids and supernatural beings of all stripes?"

Fuck me, I said to Becks through our link. We hadn't even considered that, but it was definitely possible. It wasn't too long ago that DEMON, the government agency that used to be responsible for protecting humanity against paranormal and supernatural threats decided that the best defense was a good offense and went full genocide on every non-human being they could find. We blew DEMON up, in some cases literally, but there was nothing to say that this wasn't another broad-spectrum assault.

"We…don't know that," I said, sitting down on a barstool and holding out a hand. Mort, a great bartender no matter what body he's borrowing, slapped a bottle of Jameson's into my palm.

"How *would* we even know that?" Saint asked. "If somebody left a dead vamp on a golf course, you'd burn to ash in the sunlight before anybody came along to find you. A dead demon would melt into disgusting demon goop, and I don't even know what dead fairies turn into. Glitter?"

"The bodies of most deceased fae return to their home dimension upon their expiration," Luke replied. "And yes, most supernatural beings leave very little in the way of evidence behind. It is one of our natural protections against humanity's prying eyes."

"So how do we find out if there are other types of dead paras in town?" Becks asked.

"We ask," I said. "We identified three of our four known victims by asking the weres. Now we talk to the witches, the demons, the faeries, the vampires, and any other supernatural types we can get to meet with us. If Luke's theory is right and this isn't limited to just shifters, we might have a much bigger problem on our hands."

I looked across the bar at Mort. "Sorry, pal. I think we're gonna need to have a few more moots at Mort's."

"Long as your uncle is picking up the bar tab, you can have as many moots as you need."

7

"What do we know now?" Becks asked, standing in the middle of our living room. It was three days later, and between her, Luke, and I, we'd shaken almost every tree in the Charlotte bureaucratic forest, both legitimate and criminal. Glory and Faustus were still off doing their angel stuff, having just popped in long enough to make sure I didn't slaughter two dozen shifters in Mort's bar.

"Fuck and all," I said. "None of my usual contacts know shit about missing paras. I went over to see Saint today, and he had nothing new from his people, either."

You went to see Saint, or you went to see Saint's niece? Becks asked across our mental link.

Jealousy isn't a good look on you, babe. You can feel everything I feel, so you know I don't have any feelings for Cindy.

I know, but it's fun to watch you squirm.

My fiancée can be truly evil when she wants to be. "None of the fae will speak to me after that dustup with Oberon down in Atlanta, so if there are faeries involved or being victimized, I've got no way of knowing."

"The local vampire covens are aware of seven of their number missing in the past quarter, but some of those seem to be due to the vampire in question wanting a change in scenery. And one was put down for misbehaving."

"Put down?" Becks asked. "I don't remember us going after any vampires in the past few months."

"You didn't," Luke said. I gave Becks a little shake of my head, hoping she'd drop it. Luke has mostly accepted his role working within the framework of the DHSPD, but he's not what anyone in their right mind would call a tame vampire. If a bloodsucker stepped out of line, he wouldn't hesitate to take them out, and he apparently wouldn't even ask forgiveness, much less permission.

"I...see," she said. "So how many of their missing do we think are connected to this case?"

"No more than four. Likely three at most," Luke replied.

"That takes us to seven semi-confirmed victims."

"Ten," I said. Every head in the room swiveled to stare at me, even Nameless, who was perched on Luke's lap as per usual. I swear, the cat spends any more time snuggling with my uncle, I'm going to make him clean the litterbox. Or at least buy one of those robotic ones.

"You said you didn't get any information, Harker," Becks said.

"I didn't. Madame Wanda, however, made some calls on my behalf. Her and that cohort of crazy-haired witches she runs with have some good contacts down here."

"Contacts that won't speak to you?" Becks asked.

"Contacts that kinda tried to kill me a couple times," I said. "But they told Wanda that three witches from different covens have been found dead recently, all naked as the day they were born. Except they called it sky-clad, because they're witches and have to make everything twice as complicated as it needs to be."

"And you wonder why these women tried to kill you," Luke mused.

"They're not all women," I said. "Get with the times, Uncle. Men and nonbinary people can be witches, too. And in this case, that's who was attacked. Two guys and one nonbinary person who looked pretty masculine at first glance."

"So our killer is targeting men, or at least male-presenting people," Becks said. "That's something, at least."

"It might be pretty important, given that men make up less than a third of most covens, and less than a quarter of the ones in Charlotte," I said. "Unfortunately, all the bodies were claimed by relatives or their covens, and they were all cremated, so there are no bodies to examine."

"But we can examine the autopsy reports and photographs," Luke said. "Assuming the coroner will share them with us."

"I think Doctor Yang will give Becks about anything she asks him for," I said with a grin and a tip of my glass in her direction.

"What?" she asked. By the look on her face, she really had no idea what I was talking about.

"Oh, babe, did you really not notice that he was into you? He was completely professional whenever I asked him a question, but whenever you so much as looked at him, he turned into a nervous high school freshman talking to the head cheerleader. It was pretty adorable, actually."

Becks blushed, which made her dark skin seem to glow from the inside, and she took a long swig of her Coke to hide her cheeks. "I'll put in a call tomorrow morning. But tonight, we've got a book club to crash."

"A what?" I asked, looking from Becks to Luke in confusion.

Luke just shrugged his ignorance, but Becks gave me a vicious grin. "The Arboretum pack meets at Barnes & Noble every Wednesday night, remember? Come on, honey, I hear they're talking about *Fourth Wing* tonight, and I can't wait to talk about all the spicy scenes."

Someday I will learn that I embarrass Deputy Director Flynn at my peril.

The bookstore was big, with a coffee shop built into it, a half dozen tables scattered around a cute tiled area in front of the big windows so all the passersby could see what a lovely intellectual time all the book lovers and coffee snobs were having. I was instantly uncomfortable, flashing back to a childhood where my father couldn't walk past the front window of a bookshop without some overzealous clerk following him down the sidewalk with copies of *Dracula* in hand for him to autograph. No matter that he hadn't written the thing, just being one of the famous characters was plenty. After his adventures with my uncle, Father wanted to be a private man, but celebrity pursued him all across London. He finally got his peace in 1914, when he passed away in his sleep. The doctors called it consumption, but I knew that he was never sick a day in his life after his "encounter" with Luke's "wives." No, he died of a broken heart, following my mother in death less than two years after she passed. I was young then, but I've never liked bookstores.

I don't often like weres, either. They're fast, strong, and heal with completely unfair speed. They're tough to put down without silver, and that tends to be a more permanent solution than I wanted tonight. But I had silver-tipped hollow points in the Glock under my hoodie, just in case things went exceptionally sideways.

I sat in an overstuffed chair and picked up a book called *I Was a Teenage Slasher* from a side table. I missed the slasher movie craze of the 1980s, but the book had a unique narrative voice, and I found myself drawn in despite being unfamiliar with many of the references. I sat there engrossed for the better part of an hour before I noticed the tables were filling up. Everyone had the look of a shifter of some type—all healthy, with lithe movements and the loose-limbed grace of people who are somehow always ready to move at an instant's notice.

I see them, Becks said.

Can you tell who's the leader?

Not yet. There are two or three people circulating between tables, but I can't pick up on any body language that tells me anyone in particular is in charge. Wait, scratch that. I think I found her.

And just like that, I'd found her, too. Because standing in front of me, looking down with a warm smile, was a gorgeous redhead who looked to be in her early thirties. She was tall, extremely fit, and had a broad smile stretched across her face. "Are you here for the meetup?" she asked, her voice bright.

I straightened in my seat and leaned forward. "Yeah," I said. "I'm James. James Card. Is there like a sign in sheet or anything I'm supposed to do? I don't have to wear one of those 'Hello My Name Is' stickers or anything, do I?"

She laughed, and a couple at the nearest table looked over, smiling. Apparently my hostess's exuberance was well-known. She stuck out a hand. "I'm Rachelle. And no, there aren't any nametags, or even any real agenda. We just like to get together, meet new people, and chat. Coffee?"

I nodded and followed her over to the coffee bar where she ordered some kind of confection that looked more like a dessert than a coffee. I ordered a large caramel coffee with whipped cream and followed her to a table. We sat down and she leaned forward, making way more eye contact than I was comfortable with. I tamped down my soul gaze because sharing that much of myself tended to either leave someone a gibbering puddle of goo on the floor, or send them running away screaming. But I've learned that I can examine someone's eyebrows very carefully and keep them safe from the horrors that are Quincy Harker's soul. "So what brings you out to our little kaffeeklatsch?" she asked, that smile never leaving her face.

I was starting to trust Rachelle less and less the longer she smiled at me. I suppose there are people in the world who are just naturally cheerful and happy, but I don't run into them often. And their happiness doesn't usually last much past five minutes into meeting me. "I'm looking for someone, actually," I said, leaning forward and lowering my voice.

"Oh?" Her eyebrows went up and she leaned back a little. "I'm in a relationship, sorry. But some of the other girls are single—"

I waved a hand at her, chuckling. "No, not like that. My cousin moved to Pineville about three years ago and told me about this group he met at a bookshop that he really liked. Said they were a lot like our family back home, almost like he'd found his tribe, or his pack." I put a little weight on the word "pack" to see how it landed.

And land it did. Her eyes went wide, and she looked around quickly, then leaned forward, waving me closer. I leaned in, and she whispered, "We don't use that word here, and unless you tell me who the fuck you are and what you really want, I'm going to go full tigress and rip your goddamned face off in the middle of this coffee shop."

"Pretty protective of something that isn't your pack," I said, not moving an inch. At least, not above the table. My right hand drifted toward the pistol under my left arm, and my left called power in case I needed to shield.

"Who are you and what do you want?" she repeated. "I won't ask you again."

"Technically you just did," Becks said, pulling out a chair with a loud scrape that put all eyes on us. She reached into her jacket pocket and dropped her credentials on the table. "Rebecca Flynn, Department of Homeland Security."

"Paranormal Division," I added, sitting back a little and making sure I could be heard by all the surrounding shifters. It didn't take much, since all of them had the same heightened senses I did. I could whisper and everyone with a silver allergy would catch every word, while the baristas, clerks, and human shoppers would be none the wiser. "We're investigating a string of paranormal murders all across Charlotte in the past few months."

"You're investigating murders? That's fucking rich coming from you," a deep voice said behind me. I glanced over and saw a lean Black man with a neatly trimmed beard sitting in the chair I just vacated. I couldn't peg what type of were he was, but he had a Northern English accent and the coiled tension of a predator. Maybe some other type of big cat?

"Why's that?" I asked, keeping my tone and expression neutral. "I'm a DHS contractor here on a case."

"No, you're not," the man said, standing up and slipping his sport coat off. "You're the bloody Reaper, and wherever you show up, bodies start dropping. Well, not tonight, mate. Tonight you're walking out of here without whatever you came for, or you're not walking out at all."

Goddammit. I was really going to have to do something about that nickname.

8

I stood up, holding both hands out to my sides, trying to project an air of peace and calm. The problem is, I don't even know what an air of peace and calm looks like, so I probably just looked like a ruthless asshole about to fill his hands with weapons and go all John Wick on my surroundings. Which was a whole lot closer to the truth, but between Luke and Becks, I was getting kinda tired of people bitching about the cost of my fights. "Look, pal, believe it or not, I didn't come here for a fight. I came here to see if any of your people were missing, so I can try to find out what's happening in my city."

The shifter scoffed. "Your city? *Your* bleedin' city? What the bloody hell lets you call it your city when someone us been livin' here since you were pissing your nappies?"

"Son, I haven't worn nappies since the turn of the fucking century. The *twentieth* century. You furballs aren't the only ones who age slow, and while I didn't come here to start a fight, I'll fucking well end one if I need to. So why don't you put on your dandy little frock coat, sit your lanky arse down, and let's talk this out like the civilized folk do?" I let a little of the London gutter slip into my own accent, a tone I hadn't used in nearly a century, but it came back as natural as breathing.

I knew guys like this growing up. I never had too much trouble with them, because I was a scrapper from an early age, but some of the neighborhood boys had it in for my little brothers because our parents were famous and we were pretty well-off. So I ran with more than one pack of little ragamuffin shitheads all over London and wasn't shy about throwing hands even before I developed the ability to throw fireballs at people who annoyed me. And this idiot was definitely annoying me.

I saw the store security heading in our direction and held up my badge. "Grab a doughnut, Barney Fife. Nothing to fucking see here." The rent-a-cop turned on his heel and headed for a door marked EMPLOYEES ONLY without even a little bit of ado.

"Don't talk to him, Reaper, pay attention to me," my erstwhile opponent-to-be said, the whine of the perpetually ignored creeping into his voice.

"Why?" I asked, stepping forward until I was less than two feet away from him. "Does nobody pay enough attention to you on the regular?" I slapped him across the face, hard enough to sting and embarrass, but not hard enough to dislocate his jaw. Which took restraint on my part.

"You mother—"

I slapped him again. "The next word out of your mouth better be fucking respectful. You say anything bad about my mum and I might get annoyed. You don't want me to be annoyed."

He took half a step forward, all the room he had because I wasn't moving, and bumped chests with me. I've never understood this behavior. It doesn't hurt the other person, and it puts you in way closer than you usually want to be. Like this time. Here was a guy accustomed to being the biggest, strongest, and baddest ass in the room, only he was stepping to someone who was completely unfazed by his intimidation attempts. I was not only older and more powerful, but I was also taller, although he probably had ten pounds of muscle on me. I'm more lean, ropy muscle that doesn't look impressive, but I get the job done. Often by using my head more than my biceps.

So that's what I did. I used my head very directly. I used my head to slam into his nose, breaking it and sending a torrent of blood down his face, making his eyes water, and causing him to stagger back into a pair of shifters who had been enjoying pastries and coffee until they got nearly two hundred pounds of asshole sprawled through their table. I was really wreaking havoc on bar furniture this week.

"You son of a—" he sputtered, scrambling to his feet in the wreckage of the table.

I cut him off with another slap, this one higher up and farther back, rupturing his eardrum and dropping him back to one knee. I watched as his fingers shortened and black fur sprouted along the back of his hand and up his forearm. He was pissed, hurting, and losing control of his change. This had the potential to get real ugly, real fast if I didn't put an end to it.

So I wrapped my fist in a shield and slammed it into his temple, counting on his were durability to keep him from dying. I hit him with a right hand that would have killed a human, and probably put most beings in traction, but he just continued shifting until his whole body was covered in sleek black fur and his features took on a distinctly feline cast. When his lips peeled back in a snarl and I saw the elongated fangs, I barely managed to stifle a laugh.

"Seriously?" I asked. "You're a panther? A real life Black Panther?"

His mouth couldn't really form words anymore, but the roar he let out told me exactly how unamused he was at my comment. He stood up to his full height, any wounds I'd inflicted on his human form completely gone, and roared. The sound drove any remaining customers streaking for the doors, and I took a couple steps back to give myself some room to maneuver.

"If any of you don't want to be banned from the store forever, not to mention see your buddy here splattered all across the ceiling, this would be a good time to talk him down," I said to the assembled weres.

Several of them looked at one another, then bolted for the doors themselves. Rachelle, however, obviously considered herself at least something of a leader in the group, so she stepped between me and Temu T-Challa. "Cut it out, Randy," she said. "He's a fed, even if he is a murderer."

I didn't say anything. Because it was true. I was working for the government, and I have killed more people than cholera, as they say in the movies.

Randy growled but stood his ground. Rachelle looked back and forth between us. "Harker, can I count on you not to attack if Randy shifts back?"

"I didn't start this shit," I reminded her.

"Randy, take off the fur and act like a fucking adult, please," Rachelle said.

"Yeah, Randy, be a good kitty and you'll get scritches," I said. I promised not to attack him. I never promised not to talk my fair share of shit.

Of course, Randy wasn't in any mood for my good-natured banter, or my snarky assholery, so he leapt right over Rachelle's head and straight at me.

Oh well, so much for a peaceful cup of coffee.

I ducked under his leap and rolled across a table, letting it topple over and lower me to the ground a little bit slower than just a straightforward dive, but I still got covered in powdered sugar, sprinkles, and coffee. If I didn't kill Randy, I was definitely going to take my dry cleaning bill out of his ass. Ah, who was I kidding? I don't wear shit that needs to be dry cleaned.

I rolled to my feet just in time to get a chest full of angry Randy. Werepanthers are almost as fast as the real thing. His jaws snapped closed on the air an inch in front of my throat, and I got a hand up between us, palm flat to his chest.

"*Forzare!*" I shouted, blasting him straight back across the coffee shop with a bolt of pure kinetic energy. "Stay down, Puss in Boots," I said as he flipped perfectly to land on both feet with one hand down to steady himself.

Randy just growled and sprang forward, shifting completely into feline form as he charged. I braced myself for impact, but he pounced a couple feet before he would have barreled into me, springing over my head and raking lines of fire down my back as he vaulted me.

"Mother*fucker!*" I yelled, whirling around and calling more power. I spun a shield around my body, giving me a little protection from his claws, but also limiting my mobility, which I could ill afford when I was facing an opponent who was already faster and more agile than me.

Language, Becks said through our link. *There are children around.*

If there are still kids in here, their parents should be arrested. And I've got a little more to worry about than an errant f-bomb. But her mention of kids did get me to let some of my summoned magic flow back into the floor. I couldn't go bringing the whole building down on Randy if there might still be civilians in the store.

Randy charged me again, this time rearing back on his hind legs to hug me with his forelegs and try to bite my face off. My shield protected me, but it stopped neither his rancid breath nor the face full of cat slobber I got, both of which just pissed me off more. But since he wanted to dance, I was now close enough to tango. I channeled fire into my palms and slapped them against his sides, filling the store with the stench of burnt fur and the howls of a werecat who had suddenly gone from predator to prey.

Randy thrashed in my grip and pulled away, sprinting to a far corner of the coffee shop by the front windows. He crouched there, glaring and spitting at me, then sprang at me once more, determined to have Harker entrails for dinner. I didn't try to duck this time, just used my magic to anchor myself and reinforce my shield, then let him slam into me again. It was like running face first into a brick wall, only glowy and purple.

Randy let out a yelp and fell back onto his ass. I laid a punch across his head, ringing his bell once again, and he shifted back to his half-human form, the better to stand and beat the shit out of me with. I noticed that the burns on his sides hadn't healed, so maybe he had to perform a full shift to heal. I filed that away, then kicked him right in his dangly cat balls. His mouth flew open and he made a gagging sound, like he was trying to cough up a hairball. Or maybe two hairy balls.

Either way, I took advantage and punched him right in the throat. Not hard enough to crush his larynx and kill him, but definitely hard enough to make it really hard to breathe for a few minutes. His hands flew to his neck, and my right hand jabbed for whatever passes for a solar plexus on a half-cat, half-human hybrid. He dropped to his knees, and I introduced the side of his skull to my knee, which was finally enough to send his eyes rolling back into his head and his body crashing to the tile floor. As he passed out, he shifted back to human form, leaving me standing over the unconscious body of a naked Black man in the middle of a Barnes & Noble.

This was not how I'd envisioned my night going.

We found Randy's pants and managed to achieve something resembling decency, then got him a sweatshirt from the bookstore and Becks handcuffed him to a chair. The rest of the pack except for Rachelle had bolted, along with most of the store employees and all the customers but one weird guy sitting in the back reading a book called *Dungeon Crawler Carl* and muttering "Goddammit, Donut" every few minutes. The manager stuck around to watch the weirdness, and one cashier with purple hair and a pierced lip hung out flirting with the barista, who said as long as there was anyone in the coffee shop, he had to stay, no matter what. I thought he probably would stick around as long as Lip Ring was giving him the time of day, but let it slide.

"So, Randy, you want to tell me why you went all Wakanda Forever on my ass?" I asked, dragging a chair over and sitting in front of the bound were-panther.

"You gonna make Black Panther jokes all night, or you want to find out who's killing shifters?" Rachelle asked.

I looked up at her with my most innocent expression, which hovers somewhere between Charles Manson and Jason Voorhees on a good day, and gave her my most Hannibal Lecter smile. "Porque no los dos?" I asked. I turned back to Randy. "Talk, asshole."

"I don't know nothing about anybody killing shifters, man. I just got scared when I saw the fucking Reaper at our meeting. Everywhere you go, folks come down with a bad case of dead. These are my peeps, man. I don't want nothing to happen to them."

I leaned forward, letting red magic trail from my eyes. "You ever think that maybe people end up dead when I'm around because dumbasses think fur and fangs are worth a fuck against a guy who literally throws fireballs? You started this shitshow, Randy, not me."

He leaned back, giving him a little distance from my glowing eyes. "Yeah, okay, I shouldn't have started anything. But I heard you threw down with Saint's crew a couple days ago, and those guys are tough, man. Anybody who'll step to them wouldn't have any trouble putting a hurt on some of our people. I was just trying to look out for them."

"He's telling the truth," Rachelle said. "We had lunch with one of the North End Whiskers yesterday, and he told us what happened with Saint's people. And something about blowing up Mort's bar again, too."

I threw up my hands. "For fuck's sake! I left Mort's place in better shape than I found it. We had a goddamned meeting there, that's *all*. I didn't even punch anybody. Not even Mort, and everybody knows how much I like kicking his ass."

"Wait a minute," Becks said, holding up a hand before I really got rolling. "Who are the North End Whiskers?"

This was a crew we hadn't heard of. Not that I try to keep track of all the packs in and around Charlotte. It's a decent-sized city, and most packs are just four or five people who hang out together, like an extended family. I was only really familiar with the larger groups, like Saint's or Dex's, or the ones that got into some really ugly shit. I usually didn't let them live long enough to know their names, though.

"The Whiskers are a bunch of street rats that live up around Camp North End. There's still a bunch of old industrial buildings around there, so they hang out in abandoned warehouses and dumpster dive behind the bars after closing," Randy said. "You didn't know about the Whiskers? Where you been, man?"

"Not going to trendy crowded bars with shitty chairs, loud music that sucked in the 90s, and overpriced domestic garbage beer. If I want to pay four bucks for a PBR, I'll...never mind. I never want to pay four bucks for a fucking PBR," I shot back.

"Well, the Whiskers been around for close to ten years now, and nothing goes on in the north side of town they don't know about. You wanna find out what's up in the cheap parts of town, you gotta be sure to bring some cheddar with you. And I don't mean the kind you get at the grocery store."

I glared at Randy, then looked over at Rachelle for confirmation. She nodded, and I turned to go, not before tossing a small fireball at his face. Not enough to do any damage, just a little puff of flame to remind him who the Alpha was. "Thanks for all your help, pal. I really appreciate it."

"You gonna let me out of these cuffs?" he asked.

"Not my cuffs," I said. "I'm not into that. Much." I walked off with Becks right behind me. *You're not going to unlock him?* I asked her as we got to the parking lot.

He did start a fight in the middle of a crowded store where children were present. That's the kind of thing the local authorities frown upon, isn't it?

You called the cops?

No, and I left the key with Rachelle, but I told her to let him sweat for a bit before she lets him out. He could use a few minutes to sit there and think about his bad decisions.

Damn, girl. Sometimes I wonder which one of us is the meanest.

Oh, it's definitely me, Becks sent with a mental grin. *You make the biggest messes, but I'm way more dangerous.*

I could not disagree with her, not even a little bit.

Camp North End is a bunch of old warehouses and basically abandoned real estate reclaimed and converted into artsy spaces, trendy restaurants, clubs, overpriced apartments made to look old and weatherbeaten but actually newly built with state of the art everything, all nestled in what used to be a decent place to score drugs twenty years ago. I mean, I'm pretty sure you could still find almost any drug you wanted, but you'd have to look a lot harder, you'd pay a lot more, and you were more likely to be scoring off some hedge fund douche named Chad than a biker named Little Jimmy. In short, I liked it better when it was more dangerous. But if that's where I needed to go to find a bunch of rats, I was willing to make a few sacrifices.

At least there was decent beer. Some faux-German beer garden (of course, spelled biergarten because it would have to be to justify their prices) had good dunkelweizen, so I grabbed a pint and a pretzel as Becks and I wandered the area looking for shifters. I kept my Sight overlaid on top of my normal vision, which meant I was more prone than normal to bumping into shit. Looking at the mundane world through the magical spectrum is like staring at the sun through a tie-dyed shirt. Everything is bright colors and shifting blobs of energy, and the occasional supernatural being pops out like a beacon in the night.

Only problem with that was that Camp North End attracted a lot of freaks and weirdos, and that means it also attracted a lot of faeries, witches, and other paranormal beings. So by the time I got my belly full of dark beery goodness, I needed what little refuge alcohol could provide from the sensory overload I was experiencing.

See anything? Becks asked.

No. Well, more like I see too much, but I can't pick out any shifters that might be rats. I saw a couple walking back there near the gelato stand, but they were too muscular. Most lycanthropes share physical characteristics with the animals they turn into. Most aren't as blatant as the buck-toothed were-rabbit back at Mort's, but it would be very unlikely if the pair of buff guys I spotted as weres were anything other than predators. They had the thickly muscled frames of lions or wolves, not the narrow faces and twitchy postures typical of rodents.

You okay? Becks asked.

Yeah, I'm fine. Just a lot of mojo floating around this place. I think we might be better off trying to find them without my Sight. I'm gonna get a lot of interference with all these paras around.

"Okay," Flynn said, pulling out a chair and taking a seat at a round cafe table. "Then what's the plan?"

"Well, rats are natural scavengers, and the Arboretum kids said they liked to go dumpster diving after the clubs close, so why don't we just hang out for a while and see what we see when the crowd thins out?"

I could tell from the wrinkled-up nose that she didn't like this idea. Becks might be the only person I know who hates sitting around doing nothing more than me. "Why don't we see if we can spot them a little earlier?"

"You got a plan?" I asked. I knew the answer was yes because the corner of her mouth twitched up like it does when she gets a good idea.

"Rats are scavengers, but scavengers are often also thieves, aren't they? Why don't we make ourselves appealing targets for pickpockets and see who takes the bait?"

nd that's how I ended up with beer spilled all down the front of my favorite Waylon Jennings shirt, staggering around the edges of the dance floor in a club playing music I'd never heard of, hoping a rat would try to pick my pocket. I love my fiancée, but sometimes I hate her "brilliant" ideas.

The lights were loud, the music was bright, and I know exactly how that sounds. But the sensory overload was so intense that I experienced a kind of synesthesia, where I could almost taste the colors. It transported me back to the 70s, Studio 54, and incredible amounts of hallucinogens. But I tried to keep my head on a swivel and my eyes peeled for scruffy shifters trying to lift my wallet. The small binding spell I cast on my pants would help with that because no matter if I somehow managed to get blackout drunk, my cash would stay put. Unless the thief was also a wizard, but lycanthropes don't usually have the ability to call magic, or the patience to learn how.

I stuck to the edges of the dance floor, shuffling along like the sad old man at the club, bumping up on the odd attractive man or woman. I didn't discriminate, and there were a lot of pretty people around, so I managed to annoy at least a dozen in the first hour I was there. I'd apparently gotten irritating enough that a bouncer came over, tapped me on the shoulder, and invited me to step into the office for a conversation about my behavior. I demurred, but he insisted, and rather than blow the roof off the club (in a far more literal sense than the sound system was capable of), I let him guide me by the elbow into a dark hallway.

"What the fuck are you doing?" the massive bald man hissed at me once we were off the floor. "The boss doesn't like surprises, and you seriously surprised him."

His tone made me think he was way more familiar with me than I was with him, so I dropped my drunk act and looked up at him. He was nearly seven feet tall and built like the proverbial brick shithouse, but he didn't seem particularly angry, just annoyed. "Sorry, pal. I have no fucking clue who you are or who your boss is. So why don't you just take me to your leader or whatever you were going to do anyway?"

He gave me a look like I was the stupidest thing he'd seen all night, which was a high bar in a nightclub, and let go of my arm. "Last door on the right. I'm going back to work." Then he just turned and left me standing there gawking after him.

Not wanting to violate the exceptional amount of trust bestowed upon me, I proceeded down the hall. Okay, yeah, I was really fucking curious now, so I went to the door he indicated and knocked.

"Enter," came a familiar voice, and I pushed into an office that looked like it was decorated entirely off the set of a Universal monster movie.

And standing in the center of the room was the primo monster himself, my uncle, Count Fucking Dracula. He turned, because of course he was facing away when I came into the room for greater effect, and I saw that not only was Luke apparently the owner of the bar, but he'd brought my goddamned cat to the bar as well. Nameless was curled up in the crook of his elbow, glaring at me with his yellow eyes.

"Quincy, what in all the gods' names are you doing here?" Luke asked.

I looked around the office, all mahogany and red velvet, and spotted the thing I needed most in the world at that moment—the wet bar. I poured myself a healthy slug of Macallan 18, knocked it back, poured myself another, then decided "fuck it," and took the bottle with me to sit on the long leather sofa under a painting of the London Bridge. "Why don't you sit down and answer the same fucking question for me, Uncle? And why is my cat here? All the noise can't be good for him."

"Cats go where cats want to go, and after I realized that I was incapable of leaving him behind if he did not want to remain in my apartment, I had custom earplugs made for him." He turned Nameless so that I could see the little pieces of red molded plastic with strings hanging from the cat's ears.

"Okay, just as long as I'm not going to come home to a deaf cat next week," I said, sipping Scotch right from the bottle now. I set the glass down on an end table. Kind of a "drink Scotch in case of emergency" backup. "Now what the fuck are *you* doing here? You *own* this place? Why didn't you tell me about it?"

"Because if I told you I owned a nightclub, you would be here every night drinking up my profits. Remember Dublin?"

"Okay, I might have contributed to the downfall of that pub, but don't you think naming it The Blarney Stone didn't do you any favors? You were actually *in* Ireland. You didn't have to play up the faux-Irish bullshit."

"My poor branding does not change the fact that you consumed ten thousand dollars in alcohol in one month."

"It was a rough month."

"You did that five months in a row!"

"It was a rough five months," I said, my defense crumbling in the face of Luke's accurate recollection of events. I can be excused for not remembering how much I cost him. After all, I was very drunk for about half a year. "But that doesn't answer the question of how you came to own this bar."

"I don't," he replied, walking over behind the massive desk and sitting in the big bossman chair. He deposited Nameless onto a perch beside the desk, where the cat immediately curled up and started purring. Eventually I was going to have to admit that it was his cat now. But I didn't want to. I was getting kinda used to being a cat person. Hell, Becks says I'm half-feral anyway.

I turned my attention back to Luke, who was waiting patiently for me to dial back into the conversation. "As I was saying, I don't own *just* this bar. I own Camp North End. Through a series of shell corporations, of course, and this nightclub is the only business here that I take a direct operational interest in, other than the gelato stand, but I own the entire complex. I bought the property when it was worthless, and when a developer came to me with an idea to purchase the land from me and turn it into a destination, I agreed. Then I bought the developer."

My mind whirled. How rich *was* Luke? I knew he'd been royalty back in the olden days, and I knew he'd invested well, but these were some big-time money moves. "Okay, that all seems pretty smart. But why not tell me?"

"You have been rather occupied the last ten years. Saving the world and all that."

"You were right there beside me most of that time! How did you even have time to pull something like this off?"

"I have very skilled and trusted employees. But Quincy." He leaned forward and nailed me with that piercing gaze that made so many people think he was hypnotic. "Why. Are. You. Here?"

Let's be perfectly clear. Luke cannot mesmerize anyone with his stare. He does not have hypno-eyes, or any other sort of mind control. But he had a massive weight of personality and incredible charisma. He can pressure you into doing whatever he wants, most of the time.

As long as you didn't grow up around him and build up a century's worth of resistance to his skills. Which I have. So I didn't spill my guts because I fell under the powerful spell of Dracula's mind control. I spilled my guts because he's my uncle, one of the very few people in the world I trust completely, and because if he owned this place, there was a zero percent chance it wasn't wired to the gills with top-flight security cameras. "I'm hunting were-rats," I said.

He leaned back, one perfectly sculpted eyebrow climbing toward the sky. "Would you care to elaborate?"

I told him about the meetup at the bookstore, the fight in the bookstore's coffee shop, and the lead I'd gotten on the North End Whiskers, who supposedly operated out of this part of town. When I was done, Luke picked up his desk phone and punched in a number. "Thomas? I need to see you," he said, with no introduction. That's my uncle, all perfect phone manners. "*Now*, Thomas. Thank you. Yes, you may bring one second, but I do not intend to harm you, or allow harm to come to you, while you are on my property." He gave me what I considered a wholly unnecessarily direct glare when he mentioned not allowing harm to come to whoever was on the end of the line.

"Who was that?" I asked when he hung up the phone.

"That was Thomas. He is the de facto leader of the Whiskers, in as much as a loosely affiliated group of rodent lycanthropes can be said to have one."

"You have the Whiskers' Alpha on speed dial?" I asked.

"Of course not," Luke scoffed. "It would be highly irresponsible for me to commit important numbers to anything as vulnerable as a speed dial. Have I taught you nothing about being a criminal? I memorized it. He will be here momentarily."

There was nothing to say, so I just sent Becks a mental message to join us in the office and drained the rest of the bottle. And Luke wonders why I drink so much.

11

Twenty minutes later, a disheveled, slightly built Asian man in his twenties followed the bouncer into Luke's office. He looked around, starting a bit when he saw Nameless, and almost jumping out of his skin when he got a good look at me. His head whipped around, looking for an exit that wasn't blocked by a wall of muscle, and, finding none, turned to Luke. "What's going on, Mr. Card? We ain't done nothing outside our agreement."

I raised an eyebrow at Luke. "Agreement?"

"Thomas and his…family are allowed to commit certain petty crimes on the premises in exchange for serving as an unofficial defense against more serious infractions," Luke said, his airy tone underlaid with a steel that was definitely noticed by our new rodent arrival.

"And we done that!" Thomas protested. "We pick a few pockets, roll a drunk or two, and maybe boost a car if the owner's too loaded to drive home. But we always give the car back when we're done. It might be missing a stereo, or it might not have the fancy rims they left on it, but we give the car back. And we keep the bad stuff from happening."

"What constitutes 'bad stuff,' Tom," I asked, my voice pleasant.

It didn't help. The little rat looked like he was going to pass out just being in the same room as me and Luke together. Made sense. There aren't very many predators more apex than me, and Dracula is one of them. No rat in his right mind would be comfortable staring down both of us. "You know, rapes, stabbings, shootings—the kind of shit happens around every club in the city. But not here. Me and my Whiskers keep the real bad shit out of the Camp, and on account of that, Mr. Card lets us have a little fun."

"And the drugs?" I asked. Nobody had mentioned drugs, but let's be real. Where there's a nightclub, there are drugs.

"Yeah, we sling a little, but nothing too bad. A little Molly, a little weed, even some shrooms and some acid. But no meth, no smack, and no roofies. Never any roofies. We find somebody dosing a drink, we turn them right over to security."

"What about coke?" I asked. Because I'm old, and I remember when cocaine wasn't just an expensive drug, it was a requirement for a night out.

"Sure, we do a little coke, but no serious weight. Most folks around here ain't into that. They just want party drugs. And Adderall. Fuck-loads of Adderall. Probably all the college kids. We see a spike in sales around exam time."

"I'm not here about drugs, Tom," I said.

"Thomas," he corrected me.

Seemed like my rat was getting more comfortable now that he'd decided I wasn't going to explode him on sight. Time to disabuse him of that notion. I leaned forward, letting magic leak out of my eyes and send crimson flecks of light through the room. "I'm not here about drugs, *Thomas.*"

I could hear the nervous little were gulp. Now that he was properly cowed, I went on. "There have been a lot of paras turning up dead all over town the last few months, and nobody seems to know what's going on. Someone suggested you might know something."

"Who said?" Tom asked, puffing up a little at the thought that someone might respect him enough to think he had information. He hadn't quite processed the part where that same someone set him on a collision course with me. "Was it Saint? He's been pissed at me ever since I had a couple of his pups bounced for picking on my friend Luis last month."

"It was Rachelle, down at the Arboretum," I said. I'm not a reporter. I don't give a shit about protecting my sources.

"Oh, yeah. Rachelle. She's cool. Okay, if she sent you, then it's probably okay. You got names? Or pictures?"

I held out my phone with the photo of the four shifter victims on it. Thomas scrolled through the pictures. "Yeah, I know those guys. Rough, how they lost like that." He passed the phone back to me. "You know about the rest?"

"I know there were some vampires killed as well, and a couple of witches. But the faeries and I aren't exactly on speaking terms," I replied.

"Yeah, there ain't been but a couple faeries to play. They usually ain't interested in mundane stuff like money. Been a buttload of demons, though. They don't leave much for cleanup, though, so I ain't surprised you didn't know about them," the shifter explained.

"What exactly are we talking about here, Thomas? Who is killing these people, and who is covering it up?" Luke asked.

Thomas's head whipped around, and he straightened up, like he was surprised. "Oh, you guys didn't know? I figured as plugged in as you were, you'd know all about it. I guess that explains why I ain't never seen you there."

"Seen us *where*, Tom?" I asked. "Quit dancing around this shit before I find a were-cat named Jerry to flip the script and rip your head off."

Tom looked baffled, like he really couldn't comprehend my ignorance. "The fights, man. The Monster Mash."

I opened my mouth to ask what the fuck a Monster Mash was when everything clicked into place. It was a goddamned fight club for paras. Somebody was running an underground fight ring in my city, and supernatural creatures were dying in it.

Tom could apparently see me figuring it out, and could see me getting pissed, because he held up both hands and almost climbed over the back of his chair sliding away from me. "I ain't got nothing to do with it, man. I don't run 'em, I don't bet on 'em, and I sure as hell don't fight in 'em. I'm a lover, not a fighter."

I held up my right hand, wrapping it in purple fire and pointing my index finger at his crotch. "Well, Tom, unless you don't ever want to be anyone's lover ever again, you're going to tell me how to get find this fight club."

"And who is in charge," Luke added.

"And how to get hired to fight," I finished, letting a wicked grin creep across my face. Seemed like it was time to really get my Reaper on.

This fucking sucks, I thought to Becks two nights later as I fake-puked behind a dumpster. *If I'm going to pretend to be drunk, I should at least be able to get a buzz first. Now I smell like cheap beer and cigarettes, and I haven't even had a drink.*

The federal government is not paying for you to get drunk, Harker, Becks replied. *You'd triple the deficit in one night, with your tolerance.*

Well, I'm getting kinda tired of staggering from bar to bar pretending to be a stupid drunken werewolf. These guys need to make a move soon or I'm gonna start drinking for real.

We know that they need a new fighter, since their last guy died, and Thomas said the money fights are every Saturday night, so tonight is their last chance to grab a new victim. Be patient.

Of the very few virtues I possess, patience is not one of them, I replied, unzipping my pants. I might not have been drinking alcohol, but I'd sucked down enough tonic water at the three bars we'd visited that I needed to piss like a racehorse. And since I was already in an alley behind a nightclub, I figured I might as well do what comes naturally. A few seconds later, I let out a sigh of relief.

Are you peeing? Flynn asked.

When in Rome, etc. I replied.

You're disgusting.

And you're jealous. If there's one thing men can do that women can't do equally well, peeing outside is it. I got the mental equivalent of a poop emoji, then a middle finger emoji. Sometimes communicating with Becks was like texting a millennial. Then I realized Flynn *was* a millennial, and I felt even older than normal.

Contemplating my age and making sure I kept my Doc Martens clean were the only excuses I had for not hearing the guy come up behind me, and I guess I'd pretended to be drunk for so long that my senses were a little dulled, so I didn't know anyone was there until pain exploded over my right ear. I staggered forward, tap-dancing over the puddle of piss, and whirled around, right hand raised in a fist and left hand clutching my Johnson.

And spun right into a massive fist that caught me square on the tip of my nose, blurring my vision and making it hard to breathe for a few seconds. And a few seconds was all my giant attacker needed. He was on me like a blanket, pressing a thick forearm across my throat and hammering my ribs with short, sharp punches. I managed to shove him back a step and raised a knee to his groin, but he turned sideways and all I caught was a thigh.

I didn't call magic because the whole point of the exercise was to get captured, but I didn't want to make it too easy on them. I needed to look like a victim, not a willing participant. But I also was pretty pissed off. I mean, who jumps a guy while he's taking a leak? Is there no fucking honor among criminals anymore? I tucked everything away and blocked an incoming punch, then let the next one through, which was a bit of a mistake.

This guy was big, strong, and definitely not human. I couldn't afford to use my Sight to see exactly what he was, but he hit like a Mack truck. His punch rattled my brain, and I dropped my guard unintentionally. That left me open to a quick left, then a massive right, and as my vision shrank down to a small black dot, all I could think was "I really hope I don't fall in the puddle I just made."

12

W*ell, I didn't wake up soaked in my own piss, so I guess that's a win.* More coherent than a lot of my first thoughts upon waking after being knocked out, which usually consist of some variation on "where the fuck am I and what the fuck hit me?" I still didn't have any idea the answer to those questions, but since the last thought before falling unconscious had been worry about falling into my own urine, it made sense that I woke up thinking about pee.

And having to pee. Lots of piss on the brain, apparently. I opened my eyes to take stock of my surroundings and found myself in a small cell. Not the first time, and not the worst cell I'd ever been locked up in. That distinction goes to a bamboo cage in the jungles of Cambodia. Long story, and not a pretty one. But we can sum up a lot of it with the maxim "don't lock the guy with superhuman strength up in a cell made of wood."

I wasn't locked in a wooden cell this time. No, it was more like a typical room in a stereotypical dungeon, which would make this a first for me. I've been locked in a lot of jails, and more than one have been underground, but I've never been trapped in an actual dungeon before, with stone walls, steel doors, and maybe a torture chamber somewhere nearby. I didn't hear screaming, so torture chamber seemed unlikely. But we definitely checked the "stone walls" and "steel door" boxes. There was a hole in the floor from which a truly rancid stench floated up, coating the whole room with a miasma that would have made Vincent Price and his funk of a thousand years run screaming for the hills. I straddled the hole and received myself, sighing with the relief of a man who was interrupted while taking a piss, then knocked unconscious.

Yes, I know how that feels from more than one unfortunate experience. I've angered a lot of people in my life, and a fair number of them have taken it upon themselves to seek their retribution whilst I was taking a leak. Once I zipped up, I took a quick inventory. I still had my clothes, but my phone, knife, and both guns were gone. My wallet was likewise missing, but since I didn't carry any real identification, I figured there was a slight chance I hadn't been recognized by my captors.

Scratch that. I was fairly certain I hadn't been recognized, because if anyone realized the captured one of the most violent wizards on the Eastern seaboard and they had me unconscious in their dungeon, they probably would have killed me in my sleep. So the fact that I woke up and wasn't running around like a whiny-assed ghost trying to figure out who killed me was a strong indicator that I was still alive. That and the whole pissing thing. Pretty sure ghosts don't need to pee. I still had my boots, but the small knife I kept hidden in the sole of my right one was gone, as was the lock pick set I had built into my belt buckle. Whoever searched me did a bang-up job at it.

Next, I reached out to Becks through our mental link, but got nothing. I could sense her, but I couldn't contact her. We'd been through this before when we were separated by great distances, or when there was something blocking our connection but not strong enough to actually sever it. I reached out to call power from the earth around me and found myself cut off from magic, too. I only had the power I usually stored within me and the juice stored in my magical tattoos. I thanked Past Quincy for getting them redone the last time I was in Atlanta.

My tattoo artist, James, was a faerie mage who poured magic into the ultraviolet inks when he tattooed me, turning them into mystical batteries and rendering them mostly invisible under normal circumstances. It took about twice as long as regular tattooing, and hurt about three times as much, so I had gotten pretty lax about having them redone when I drained them. But after needing every ounce of magic I could lay my hands on for a big fight in D.C. last year, and then going to Hell again when I was supposed to be on vacation in the Outer Banks, Becks had insisted I keep the tank topped off. I was glad I listened to her for once. I had a sneaking suspicion that I'd need every fireball I could summon up to get out of this place.

With no phone, no books, and no furniture other than a thin pallet with an even thinner blanket, I sat on the "bed" with my back to the wall and waited for someone to come monologue at me, threaten me, or try to murder me. I'd wanted to infiltrate this fight club, and it seemed like the fight club approved my infiltration. Now I had to figure out how to exfiltrate myself without any backup. Best laid plans and all that.

I might have drifted off because when I heard a key scrape in the lock, I jerked my attention to the door. The drool on my chin was another hint that I might have been snoozing. The door opened and a guy in his late teens or early twenties came in carrying a styrofoam takeout container and a bottle of water.

He put the food on the floor by the door and looked over at me. "Are you okay?" he asked. "Any blurry vision, headaches, or ill effects from the drugs or the knock on the head?"

"Are you my doctor, or my waiter? And I specifically ordered the escargot," I quipped.

He chuckled. "I'm Pete. The guards told me to ask you that stuff. And you got sesame chicken. Everybody got sesame chicken. With fried rice and an egg roll."

"I don't like egg rolls," I said.

"I'm pretty sure the Boss doesn't care," Pete replied, but he chuckled again. "There's a plastic fork in there. If you try to hurt me with it, they won't give you utensils anymore. If you try to do anything with the food or water other than eat and drink it, they'll just starve you. So please behave. I don't like scrubbing brains off the floor." The matter of fact way he said it was pretty chilling. Like he'd had to scrub brains off the floor enough times to have an opinion about it.

"I'll behave," I said. "Where am I?"

"The Colosseum," Pete replied. "You're a gladiator now. After you eat, you'll have your first fight. You win, you get to keep fighting. You win enough fights, you get to go free."

"And if I lose?"

Pete just looked at me, and his eyes were sad. "Try not to lose." Then he turned and left, locking the door behind him.

Well, mission accomplished. I was in the shit now.

I don't know if it was an hour later or a day later, but I hadn't needed to pee in a hole in the floor again, so probably closer to an hour. The door opened and Pete came back in and held out his hand. "I'll take your trash now. If you need to relieve yourself, please go ahead and take care of business. I'll be back in a few minutes to take you out for the show tonight. If you need weapons, we can stop by the armory."

"I suppose a fifty-cal is off the table?" I asked, getting to my feet and handing him the empty takeout container. I downed the rest of the water and gave him the bottle. I'd kept a couple tines off the fork, thinking I might be able to fashion some kind of lockpick out of them, but I'm neither a MacGyver nor a Houdini, so I didn't hold out much hope for that.

"Yeah, we're going melee for this fight, so knives, swords, or blunt weapons only. If you progress, you might get to use a pistol, but I've never seen the Boss actually *give* anybody a gun. He tells all of you that it's possible, and I wouldn't call him a liar, but I wouldn't hold my breath."

"You wouldn't call him a liar because you believe him, or because you know he'd cut you from your nipples to your nuts if you did?" I asked, stepping over to the hole and unzipping. I didn't have to pee much, but if I was going to fight, I might as well empty my bladder first. There are very few things worse than getting hit really hard in the gut and pissing yourself. And I bet you can think of what at least one of those things is.

"A little of both, actually."

"You seem like a decent kid, Pete," I said. "How'd you end up as a prison guard? And where the hell am I, anyway? I haven't been charged, or gotten to call my lawyer, or anything."

"Don't be obtuse," came a deep voice with an Irish lilt from the doorway. "You know why you're here. What I don't yet know is who you are or why you tried so hard to join our little club. If you wanted to get in the ring, you could have simply asked."

I turned around to see who was speaking, but he stood with his head shrouded in shadow, just outside the door. I could tell he was humanoid, and of medium build, and I could see the pale pink skin of his forearms. But that's about it. "You're the Boss, I presume?"

"I speak for him in all things; so as far as you are concerned, yes," he replied.

That was interesting. Somebody was running things remotely, and this guy was just the onsite supervisor. That added a layer of assholes for me to pummel, not counting everyone I'd need to thrash to get out of here with my skin intact. "Okay, so I knew there was a fight club. And I wanted to get in on the action. But I didn't want to be kidnapped. I want to get paid, man. So where do I sign the contract? And how much do I get paid to fight?"

The man laughed, a short, harsh expulsion that was devoid of real amusement. "Paid? Not for the opening bouts, pal. You get room and board, and you're lucky we fed your ass. You make it through tonight, and we can talk about some more perks. We don't make money off you undercard assholes. You're just here to get the crowd revved up for the real fights after intermission."

Okay, so this was set up like a real fighting promotion, with undercard, midcard, and headline fights. "What do I gotta do?" I asked.

"You fight. You're the first fight of the night, and it's a three-way with you and two other humans. Or at least, mostly human. What are you, anyway? You ain't a were, and you ain't vamp or faerie, so what does that leave? Possessed human? Ninth Circle demon in a borrowed meat suit? Some kind of Euro-trash cryptid I don't recognize?"

This was when I realized that I probably should have put a little thought into a cover story. Becks or Luke are both way better at this shit than me, and I'd gotten way too comfortable having Flynn in my head to talk me through a false identity. I couldn't exactly explain that I was Quincy Harker—that was sure to get me promoted to the top of the bill, if it didn't get me decapitated right off the bat. And almost everything else I could lay claim to was either too recognizable or too scary.

So I went with the truth. Or a version of it, anyway. "Cambion," I said, claiming the heritage of a half-demon, half-human hybrid. I did have a sliver of demon in me, inherited from Luke's demon pal Skyffrax, so that should be enough to fool most people who could see my aura. It would also explain my strength, speed, and ability to wield magic.

"Cambion, huh?" Pete said with a whistle. "We ain't had one of those before, Boss. Have we?"

"Not here, no," the Boss replied. "Mighta been one back in Denver, but that was before you were with us. Okay, a Cambion. I can work with that. You types are strong and fast, right? And can cast a little?"

"Yeah," I said.

"Okay, there's no magic in the opening bouts, so we'll have to collar you."

"The fuck you say," I said, reaching for magic. I was still blocked, but I could tell from his shoulders shaking that Bossman was amused.

"These cells are all lined with sheets of cold iron and silver. You can't touch magic here any more than you can touch the moon. But you'll wear the collar, or we'll take your head. We got guys who've killed things a lot tougher than some candy-ass half demon, so if you want to keep your neck intact, you'll let Pete wrap this around it." He held a hand out past my line of sight into the hallway, and when he brought it back into view, there was a silver collar in it. He tossed it to Pete, who motioned for me to kneel.

"I can't really get it fastened good if you're standing, sorry."

I knelt and suppressed the urge to rip Pete's arm off and shove it up his ass as he fastened the collar around my throat. I still felt Becks in the back of my mind, but it was even more muted than before. But I could still sense her, so I knew she was out there. And if she was out there, I wasn't alone. So I let Pete collar me, and then I let him lead me out into the hallway and toward my first fight.

I almost felt bad for the poor bastards who were about to be in the ring with me. Almost.

13

I followed Pete down a long concrete corridor with crappy fluorescent lighting every ten feet or so, leaving large chunks swathed in shadow. I suppose it was cheaper when the place was built, and once the bad guys moved in, it probably made them feel good to have more places to lurk, but the tactical part of me was loving all the places I could hide to get an advantage on the guards when I inevitably broke out. Assuming I didn't just pull the whole building down around me.

I skipped the Armory visit, figuring if all they were going to let me use were sticks or knives, I could do better barehanded against low-level crytpids or paras. After I told them that, Pete and the pair of no-neck goons assigned as my guards led me to a heavy steel door with "Arena" scrawled on it in red spray paint. Going all out on the decor, these guys. The Boss had bailed as soon as the guards had me cuffed, turning right and heading down the corridor in the opposite direction from where they took me. Judging by the slight curve in the corridor, we were walking in a huge circle underneath a massive building. I stood still while the goons uncuffed my hands, and looked over at Pete, who had a shock of red curls atop his head and a smattering of freckles across his nose.

"Hey, Opie, you wanna take this collar off so I can give the crowd a real show?" I asked, giving him my best "we're buds, right?" grin.

He just looked confused. "Who's Opie?" and I felt a serious need for some Metamucil and a pair of Depends. "Besides, the Boss doesn't want the first matches to have any magic. He says you gotta build a fight card so everything is better than the thing that came before it. That's why you three don't get to use magic or shift. You just gotta go out there and beat the hell out of each other."

Not the first time I've been in a situation where I needed to kick a little ass, but the first time in a long time I didn't have either the crutch of my magic, or backup. Oh well, time to kick it old school, as I'm sure nobody but me says anymore. "Okay, then. I'll see you after the bell rings, Pete."

"I hope so, pal. I kinda like you. You're funny."

I reached for the door, but Pete stopped me with his next question. "Hey, what's your name, anyway?"

Oh, balls. In addition to not coming up with a backstory for my species, I also hadn't come up with one for my name. Or anything, really. I thought for a second, then said, "Murray. Murray James." I figured my mother's maiden name and my older brother's name would be obscure enough that nobody would pick up on it.

"Huh. That's like, two first names. Or two last names. Kinda cool." Pete unclipped a radio from his belt and pushed the mic. "Contestant number three is Murray James." He turned back to me. "Go on through, Murray. And good luck."

I pulled the door open and was hit with a wall of sound that Phil Spector would be proud of. I stepped out onto a friggin' basketball court, or at least an open area the right size for one, with at least a thousand seats arranged on risers around the sides. The first row was on a platform at least ten feet high, I guess to keep the spectators from getting too splattered, and there were several rows between that and a set of luxury boxes nestled atop the bleachers. With thick Plexiglass between the floor and the crowd, it looked like a weird mix between a hockey rink and a grass tennis court, only without the grass. The floor was covered in several inches of sand, but I could feel the wood underneath, and if I scraped my foot across, some of the painted lines became visible.

Where the fuck am I? Some kind of basketball bunker? I didn't have long to wonder because as soon as I stopped blinking away the brilliance of the stadium lights overhead, a voice boomed out over the public address system in a kind of hillbilly Michael Buffer impersonation.

"And our final competitor in our opening bout, the Mysterious Mangler, Murrrrrrrrrray JAMES!!!!"

He did his best, but we were the popcorn and hot dog match, so the applause was tepid to be generous. I looked across the sand at my competition, but without my Sight, I had no idea what kind of paras they were. They both wore collars identical to mine, but they were both also much bigger than me. Like, a *lot* bigger. Not taller, but bigger. One guy was maybe six feet tall, but he had to go three hundred fifty pounds, and he looked like a reject from a biker movie casting call. He had a big gut, sleeves of tattoos running down both arms, and a nasty grin on his face. A long scar ran from the side of his jaw all the way up to his eyebrow, and I could tell from the way he eyed me and the other fighter that he was used to fighting, and used to winning.

The other guy was packed with muscle, but it looked more like gym muscle than ass-kicking muscle. He had the face of a man who hasn't been punched nearly as much as he deserved, and the smirk of one who deserved a lot of punching. I made a quick calculation that he was very much not the threat and hoped Biker Bob made the same assessment. If the dangerous guy went after the easy target first, I might be able to take him down while he was preoccupied.

The ring announcer spoke again. "The rules for the opening bout are simple—there is to be no magic, no shifting, and no weapons other than those provided to our combatants. Everything else is fair game. The contestants will fight until both opponents are incapacitated or unconscious. May the best man win!"

A bell rang, and Biker Trash walked in my direction like he had all the time in the world. Great, he'd also decided that Gym Muscles wasn't a threat, which meant he wanted to get the heavy lifting out of the way first, meaning me. I didn't like that idea, so I charged Gym Rat, leaving Biker Boy to whip his head from side to side in confusion. No magic didn't mean I wasn't still stronger than a human, and my speed also was unaffected. I reached Gymkata in two seconds flat, but when I threw a punch that should have sent him straight to Dreamland, my first connected with nothing but air.

A grenade exploded in my left ear, and I fell to the sand. I rolled over and scrambled to my feet to see Gymbo looking at me. "You don't get to attack a prince of the Summer Court that easily," he said with a shit-eating grin.

"You're Oberon's kid?" I asked. "Lemme guess. Your mother's a human and you don't get to go visit Daddy in the Summer Palace because Titania said she'd feed you your own dick if she ever laid eyes on you?" The Summer Queen is not known for her patience with Oberon's philandering. She doesn't actually give a shit if he screws around—one less thing she has to put up with—but she doesn't want to be reminded of it.

Gymbo stopped smiling and sprang at me. And I don't mean he charged me, or even pounced or leapt at me, all things you can do in a fight if you know what you're doing. No, he literally sprang at me. Like a front handspring. He jumped up, bounced on his hands, and flung himself at me. It confused me enough for half a second that he almost nailed me, but I instinctively stepped to the left and snapped a side kick into his ribs with my right boot. He folded over like a cheap suit and dropped to the sand, gasping and puking a little. I took one step closer, slammed my elbow into the base of his skull, and dropped him.

One down. Unfortunately, he was the easy one, and Biker Billy was still heading my way, doing the slow slasher walk like he was a maskless villain in an 80s horror movie. I just sat down on Gymbo's back, folded my arms over my chest, and waited. That did the trick, annoying Biker Benji enough that he put his head down and charged.

Pro tip: never take your eyes off your opponent in a fight if you can help it. If you drop your head and go at somebody like you're a pissed off rhinoceros, one of two things is going to happen. Either you're going to impale your opponent with your skull, which is way less effective than pro wrestling would lead you to believe, or the guy you're fighting is going to do something very unpleasant to you.

Now I've been a lover of American football ever since I moved to Charlotte, and part of me wishes I'd had the chance to play the game in school. After all, officially sanctioned extreme violence is kinda my whole job description. So I stepped to the side and kicked Biker Brent right in the forehead.

In the movie in my mind, that would have snapped his body upright and reversed all his momentum into a massive flip that landed him on his back, out cold. Then I'd get to go backstage with Pete and maybe get some more sesame chicken, which was pretty good for what was effectively prison food. Way better than Cambodia, let me tell you.

Unfortunately, reality didn't green light the movie in my mind, and while Biker Brian did stand straight up, he stopped in an upright position, turned to me, and grinned. Let me repeat: I kicked this motherfucker right in the noggin with a size eleven Doc Marten, and he stood there smiling at me.

"Fuck." That was the most eloquent thing I could come up with, and apparently the crowd agreed with me, as they all let out a collective "OOOOOOHHHH" before transitioning into a resounding chant of "You fucked up!" I couldn't disagree.

Biker Bastard stepped toward me and snapped out a jab with his left. I got my guard up, but blocking a punch with your forearm bones *sucks*. It sucks less than blocking it with your face, but it still sucks. I leaned my head back so the follow-up right whizzed an inch in front of my face, and I barreled into him, hoping to knock him off-balance and try to trap him into an armbar, a leg hold, or something that I might have learned by osmosis watching MMA clips on YouTube.

Gimme a break. When you're super-strong, heal from practically anything, and can throw fireballs, you tend to slack off on your hand-to-hand training.

And when you slam your body into a guy who outweighs you by

well over a hundred pounds, a guy who knows how to brawl and may be even stronger than you are, well, things don't end well for you. And they didn't. Biker Bro wrapped his arms around me in a massive bear hug and started to squeeze. I'd always thought this was a bullshit move, just something wrestlers on TV did to take a break, but when my vision started to sparkle, I realized that I couldn't draw a decent breath. If I didn't do something, and soon, I was going to pass the fuck out. I didn't know if they executed the losers of these preliminary bouts, but I figured probably not. Otherwise we'd have found a lot more bodies.

But I knew that if I lost, I wouldn't be moving up the card, and if they tossed me out now, I had no idea where I was, or if I could get back in. So I couldn't afford to lose. I slammed my forehead into Biker Bro's, but he just smiled up at me, the trickle of blood running down his face seeming to make his grip even tighter. So I did what I do best when the feces has well and truly impacted the oscillator.

I cheated.

Yeah, I know. No rules other than no magic, no weapons, and no shifting, but biting a guy's nose off still felt like cheating. I still did it, and I'd do it again if I had to, but I did feel a little bit bad about it. I leaned down as far as I could, opened my mouth wide, and bit that biker's nose clean off. Well, not really "clean" off because getting through the ridge of cartilage at the top of the nose was really tough, and the side bits were really kinda chewy. But after a little pulling, twisting, and tearing, I got his nose.

That didn't officially end the fight, but it sure took all the fight out of Biker Beastie. He dropped me like a hot potato and staggered back, his hands flying to his face and high-pitched screams coming from his mouth. There was an odd, wet whistling sound with every breath he drew in, and he fell to the sand, gushing blood, snot, and tears in nearly equal amounts.

I spit the nose out onto the sand, looked up into the stands and shouted out, "Is that incapacitated enough for you, bitches? Do I fucking win yet?"

14

Pete led me down the hall, but this time instead of turning left to go back to my cell, he led me to the right for about fifty yards then stopped before a slightly cleaner, but still reinforced metal door. "Winners get upgrades, so you get a better room now."

"What do the losers get?" I asked, wondering if the answer was a slit throat and dumped on a golf course. I had no idea if either of the men I'd beaten were shifters, and in the heat of battle, I hadn't cared. But I knew I left them alive, and there hadn't been nearly enough bodies showing up for these assholes to be killing everyone who'd lost a fight, so I really didn't know what they did with the losers.

"Every fighter has a bad day, or a bad fight. If you're in a higher tier and you lose, you get dropped down a level," Pete said.

"So the guy who used to be in this room…"

"This room used to belong to one of the fighters in the next round. Whoever wins, moves up; whoever loses, moves down. So this room is empty no matter what, and the one next door will go to whoever wins the second prelim fight, but I kinda feel bad for that guy, whoever it is."

"Why?"

"Because you put on a hell of a show, and now he's gotta follow that. Otherwise the crowd is gonna hate him. It won't make a difference in the fight, really, but the fans will be in your corner next week unless he does something amazing, and the crowd support really seems to make you guys fight harder."

"You don't fight, Pete?"

He ducked his head and blushed a little. "Nah, man. I'm totally human, so even with your collars on, you guys would rip my head off and crap down my neck. Which has happened. Literally, in one of the main events a month or so ago. This one huge Torment Demon just grabbed a vampire ninja dude by his shoulders and his head, and pulled his melon clean off! Then he, I swear to God, held the vampire under him and took a steaming crap right down the guy's neck. It was the nastiest thing I've ever seen."

"Sounds like it," I agreed. "So what happens to the guys I just beat?"

"Oh, one of them, I think his name was Terrell, he'll get one more fight. The other guy, the guy with the tattoos? He's done. He'll wake up on a park bench with the mother of all hangovers and no idea where he's been for the last month. Our docs will put his nose back on first, though. That was pretty mean, dude." Now the prison guard at the cryptid fight club was judging me. Great.

"So you get more than one chance to win at the bottom tier?" I was trying to figure out how this all worked, but it wasn't clear yet. There were rankings, and tiers of fighters, but how did they keep all this hidden? And how did they keep everybody prisoner for that long? Paras aren't known for being patient, or docile.

"Yeah, you get three strikes. If you lose three fights in a row, you're done. Unless the first fight you lose is a main event. Then you're really done."

I stepped through the door Pete opened and into my new quarters. This was a slightly larger cell, almost big enough to be considered a room. Maybe eight-by-ten instead of the barely six-by-eight room I'd been in. There was a small partition hiding an actual toilet, and a TV mounted high up on the wall. A twin bed faced the television, and a nightstand held the remote. "Do I get cable now?"

"Dude, you get all the streaming services. The only ones we keep in the real nasty cells are level one conscripts. Everybody else is a volunteer. This is the worst of the volunteer rooms. You win next week and you get some nice shit."

"And if I lose next week? Back to the cell?"

"You got it."

"So everybody but me figured out how to sign up for this shit? How did they make contact?"

Pete shook his head. "No idea. And I probably wouldn't tell you if I did. The Boss handles recruitment, and he doesn't like anybody talking about the bouts to outsiders. He quotes some old movie all the time."

"It was a book first," I said, assuming he meant *Fight Club*. Great book, great movie, killer author. Less useful in this scenario than you would expect, since that fight club only existed in the narrator's completely fucked brain. This one was real, and it looked like I had just volunteered to spend at least a week undercover. I needed to find some way to get a message out to Becks, or she and Luke were going to start tearing parts of Charlotte down to the foundations looking for me. "Do I get to lose the collar now?" I asked Pete as he turned to leave.

"No, sorry. Collar stays on. The Boss says it's easier to leave it on you the whole time you're here than to try and put it back on you later."

Even with the collar still on, I felt a stronger connection to my magic than before, and Flynn's presence in my mind was better, although still not clear. "This feels different," I said.

"Yeah, these rooms aren't shielded as much. The Boss figures you might need magic to heal. It's warded against offensive magic, teleportation, and a bunch of other stuff that might make you a pain in the ass, but you should be able to heal. And shift, if that's your thing."

"It's not," I said, conjuring a ball of purple light and sending it to float in the corner of the room. "This is more my thing."

"Oh, cool!" Pete said. "Wizards always make a good show when y'all fight. Real flashy. But don't try to get out. The walls and doors are all lined with silver. Just not solid like the last level. So you can cast, but you can't blast, get it?"

He looked so goofy standing there grinning at his dad joke that I had to give him a chuckle. "I get it, Pete. Thanks."

"No problem, Murray. I'll be back in the morning with breakfast. You get a little bit of choice in the menu now. Win next week and you'll get even more. Your exercise time is at eight. Sorry, new guy gets the first time slot, as long as he isn't a vamp."

I walked over to the bed and sat down, slipping off my Docs and leaning back, remote in hand. "See you in the morning, Pete."

As soon as the door closed, I reached out to Becks. *You there, babe?* I asked, feeling resistance from the crap lining the room.

Her mental voice came back thin and thready. *Harker, are you okay? What the fuck happened? Where have you been? Luke and I have been worried sick!*

I got into the fight. Not exactly the way I wanted, but I'm in. I got kidnapped and held in a warded room until I fought tonight. I won, so now I'm in a room with less security. But I won't be allowed to leave, so you're going to have to investigate outside while I try to find out who's in charge from the inside.

How long are you going to be stuck there? Can you blast your way out?

Not from here, I replied. *The walls are lined with silver and cold iron, so they'd just absorb anything I threw at them. Makes it hard to talk to you, too.*

Yeah, this is giving me a headache.

Same. But I'm okay, relatively speaking. At least I don't have to piss in a hole in the floor anymore. To the victors really do go the spoils, at least in here. I'm gonna try to talk to some of the other fighters in the morning, and I'll ping you if I find out anything.

You better fucking ping me regardless, Harker. I've gotten used to having you in my head all the time, don't go vanishing on me again.

I won't, babe. I promise. I let the direct connection lapse, and stretched out, closing my eyes and not thinking about how much I really don't like being locked up.

I woke up a few hours later, about three in the morning according to the clock on the TV, which I trusted about as much as the average campaign promise. I heard someone moving around on the other side of the wall from my bed, but it was too indistinct to make out anything. I tried tapping on the wall in some kind of half-assed Morse Code, but all I know is SOS, and that kinda goes without saying if you're locked in a cell in some kind of secret underground sports complex, or whatever the hell this building was.

I got up and moved around a little, stretching to try and loosen up the sore muscles from my fight. I felt pretty good overall—the bonk on the head to get me here had done more damage than the match, but it still felt good to go through a few katas and limber up. I examined my cell closely, but there wasn't much to look at. A twin bed on a basic metal frame, with clean sheets and a thick blanket. Flat screen TV hanging from the ceiling, high enough that it would be a pain in the ass to pull down for a weapon, but low enough that it was possible. All the cables were hardwired, so there was no electrical outlet to try and MacGyver a bomb out of, not that I had any idea how to do that without getting myself fried in the process.

The "bathroom" was as basic as it could be: a toilet, a small shower with a drain in the floor and a fabric curtain on a piece of curved conduit suspended from the ceiling, and a cubby in the wall holding a bar of soap and a hotel-sized bottle of shampoo. I guess conditioner and a nice lavender body wash would have to wait until I won another fight or two. There was a set of shelves built into the wall across from my bed holding a towel, a washcloth, and a pair of loose pajama pants in roughly my size. There was a set of scrubs and a pair of boxers as well. A sink beside the shelf with a toothbrush, toothpaste, and a cup for water completed the furnishings, which were barebones but far from the worst I'd endured. Hell, given the fact that I'd been pissing into a hole in the floor twelve hours earlier, it was downright palatial by comparison.

Still, I would have liked a window, or something to let me keep track of time on my own. I didn't trust my captors any farther than I could throw a Buick, and screwing with your prisoners' sense of time is a tried and true interrogation tactic. Not that anyone had asked me any questions beyond my name. Well, at least being left alone would give me time to work on my cover story, in case someone decided to care. I felt Becks across our mental connection and could tell she was sleeping. She was probably exhausted from searching for me, so I let her sleep.

I could touch magic, at least on a limited basis, so I sat cross-legged in the middle of the floor and worked on some new defensive tricks I'd been wanting to try out. If the next fight was going to be against tougher opponents who had access to more of their abilities, it would be good if I had a new trick or two up my sleeve.

Spellcraft always relaxes me, as long as I'm practicing when no one is trying to kill me, so it didn't take long for me to decide that my magic wouldn't be harmed even a little bit if I leaned back against my bunk to think things through, and I was asleep in minutes.

15

Pete knocked on my door just as I was finishing up my morning ablutions. He knocked, waited about five seconds, then opened the door, walking in with a tray of eggs, bacon, and grits. He tossed me a bottle of orange juice-esque substance, fished a bottle of water out of his back pocket, and set the whole lot on the nightstand.

"Okay, you've got three days before your next bout, so most of that time you can spend however you like. This'll be the last time you get room service, so enjoy it while you can."

I put down the towel I'd been rubbing my hair dry with and looked at him, confused. "Three days? I thought you only did fights on Saturday."

"Nah, we do Wednesday night fights, too. No main events, but it's a good way for you undercard guys to maybe move up."

"So I'll be scrapping with somebody else who won their first-round bout this Wednesday?" I opened my connection to Becks wide so she could hear everything going on. This was good. I'd been worried that I'd be stuck here trying to figure out how be Murray James for a whole week between matches.

"Yep, or maybe somebody who lost a Tier Three fight on Saturday.

You should probably hope for the other Tier One winner, though. Usually the guys who got busted down a tier are really pissy."

That made sense. I could imagine how grumpy I'd be if I was used to sleeping in a bed and had to spend a few days in the Tier One cells. "How many tiers are there?" I asked.

"You really don't know anything, do you? How did you even find us?"

This was dangerous ground, but fortunately it wasn't much of a stretch to feign ignorance. "I don't know anything, really. I heard there was an underground fight league for people like me, but nobody would talk about it. I guess most paras adhere to your boss's philosophy on PR."

Pete chuckled. "Kinda. We've got a hell of a YouTube following, but most people think it's all fake, like indie horror films or something. There's five tiers. Tier One is where you were. Not all the Tier One guys live here; some just volunteer to fight now and then to blow off steam. Tier One is fight until first blood, knockout, or submission, so there usually aren't any serious injuries."

Until some asshole bites a guy's nose off, I thought. "Usually," I said, letting a little color into my cheeks. I wasn't really bothered by chewing Biker Bro's nose off. It was far from the worst thing I'd done in a fight. At least he lived.

"Well, sometimes a fighter gets carried away. And sometimes his opponent has to be carried away, if you get what I mean. But we've got healers on staff for anybody who's going to be sent home. We don't want word to get out that our fighters are maimed for life. That would cut down on recruitment."

"Tier Two is where the fights start to get interesting. That's where you are now. Magic-users get to throw some spells, but your access to power is still limited. Shifters can assume their animal form, but they can't do that half-man, half-beast thing. If they pause midway through a shift, they get tranked and forfeit the bout."

"What about vampires?" I asked.

"Vamps go straight to Tier Three. Vampires and certain types of demons are just too powerful for Tiers One and Two. There wouldn't be a challenge for them at the lowest tiers. We do get faeries sometimes, depending on the type, and a bunch of cryptids. Not Sasquatch, though. They're too badass. They jump right to Tier Three."

"So Tier Three the gloves are off, then?" I asked. "No restrictions on power, no limits to what magic we can access?"

"Mostly. The collars help us regulate your magic, so you're not at full power yet. That's Tier Four. *That's* when the gloves come off. The only thing you can't do in Tier Three is intentionally murder somebody. So if you like threw a fireball at a vampire's face right out of the gate, you'd get disqualified."

"And what happens if I get DQ'd?" I asked.

"You don't want to know. But let's just say that spending a week in the Tier One cells would be a vacation by comparison."

"So what's Tier Five?" I was pretty sure I knew the answer, but wanted to hear it.

"Tier Five is the Main Event. We only do one Main Event fight per week because those are always to the death. You don't have to move up to Tier Five if you don't want to, though. But there's no real paycheck at any of the other tiers. You get some cash into your accounts in the early rounds, but you can't access it until Tier Four or Five. And even then, you can only use it to bet on the fights. You can bet on yourself, or on other fighters. Just tell me where you want to put your money. If you get that far.

"Up until Tier Four, you're mostly fighting for fun and bloodlust. But Tier Five? You win four fights at that level, go undefeated for a whole month, and you get fifty grand and retire as a Grand Champion."

Pete's face practically glowed when he talked about this, but I didn't expect it to be nearly as rosy as he seemed to think. "Anybody ever do that? Take the money and retire?"

"Not since I've been here," he admitted after a pause. "A couple guys have won three in a row, but then they always meet up with somebody stronger."

"No matter how much of a badass you are, there's always somebody badder," I said. *Especially when the Boss can bring in a ringer at any point.* "Do you ever get fighters that come in at the Main Event? Or does everybody climb the ladder?"

"Sometimes there'll be a special attraction come in. We had a dragon one time. An honest to God, no bullshit *dragon.* Boss set it up so *four* Tier Four fighters went up against it. Didn't matter, though. One blast of fire, one swipe of that long, spiky tail, and one big chomp, and it was all over. It was kinda disappointing, actually."

"Well, it can't all be WWE now, can it?"

"I guess not. Anyway, eat up. You've got exercise time in half an hour."

"Exercise time?"

"Yeah, you go to the arena and spar with other fighters in your tier. It lets you get an idea who you'll be facing Wednesday."

Great, I thought. *Now I just have to get through a sparring session without murdering anyone or getting recognized.*

There were three other guys in the Colosseum when I stepped out onto the sand again. I looked around, but apparently they scooped up all the bloody sand like cat litter at the end of every fight night because there was no sign of me biting a guy's nose off to be found. I immediately pegged one guy for a faerie of some sort as he practiced martial arts, his feet barely touching the ground as he moved from pose to pose. He was pretty, kinda like a dark-haired Legolas with lethal intentions.

Another guy had "werewolf" written all over him. He wasn't lean and tall like Saint, but built like a fireplug, with excessively hairy arms, bushy eyebrows, and a permanent snarl etched on his face. He was definitely a ronin wolf, packless. He stared at me as I walked in, challenge written all over his face.

The last guy was more of a mystery, but a dapper one. He looked human and wore a crisp black suit with pinstripes and expensive Oxfords that looked like ostrich. Ostrich Oxfords. That gave me a chuckle. Until I looked at his eyes and saw red. Not like I got pissed off but like his eyes were red. He was a demon, and whether he was wearing a human suit or he was a body-hopper like Mort, that meant that he was the craftiest, most dangerous motherfucker in the arena.

Until I got there.

I walked in and looked around, then called out, "Hi guys! Murray James. I'm new here, and Pete over there says we're supposed to spar. So, uh, who wants to get some practice in?" I pasted on the stupidest grin I could imagine and looked from fighter to fighter.

Nobody spoke, but they all exchanged glances then rushed me. Good, I wanted to get it out of the way. The werewolf got to me first, and he had the thick arms of someone who could do some damage if I let him. So I got right to the "not letting him" part. I vaulted over his head and flicked out a kick to the back of his skull, sending him sprawling to the sand. Then I pounced on his back, grabbed his left wrist, and pulled his arm back until I heard the unmistakable *pop* of a shoulder dislocating. I left Fuzzy screaming on the sand and stood up just in time to see Faerie Ninja almost on top of me.

He threw a dizzying array of kicks faster than any human could react. Good thing for me, I'm not human, and even better for me that my normal sparring partner is the most badass vampire in history. When you get your ass kicked on the regular by Dracula, you learn to anticipate an opponent's moves before they even know what they're going to do next. I took one punch to the jaw, then a kick to my right thigh, then I retaliated with a feint at his head, an uppercut to his jaw, and a knife-edged chop to his throat. I finished him off with a punch right to his forehead that I'm pretty sure left an imprint of my knuckles on his cerebellum.

That left the real threat. Not the demon. Not really. The bigger threat was that the demon would recognize me and blow my cover. Not all demons have been around since The Fall, and most of the really powerful ones wouldn't be stuck in Tier Two, but it was definitely possible that this was someone I'd killed before, reconstituted into a new body, and returned to Earth to wreak more havoc.

The demon and I circled each other like two cats vying for the same mouse, each measuring the other and looking for an opening, a weakness to exploit. I had the distinct feeling that whoever made the first mistake was going to have a really bad afternoon. Turns out my mistake was made several heartbeats earlier, when I dislocated the shifter's arm but didn't render him unconscious.

Because just as I thought I saw an opening to go after the demon, two hundred pounds of fur, fangs, and halitosis slammed into my back, driving me to the dirt and sending all my breath out in a *whoof!* I tried to roll, but Fuzzy had me pinned, and as he clasped his jaws lightly around the back of my neck, I heard the demon chuckle from ten feet away. I tapped the ground, signaling surrender, and the were-wolf hopped off me to sit on his haunches and stare at me, tongue lolling in a doggie grin.

"Nice one," I said. "I forgot that your shoulder would be fixed as soon as you shifted. Well played."

He shifted back to human form faster than almost any were I'd ever seen, and walked over to me, hand extended. Like most shifters, he had no sense of modesty, and his junk was just swinging in the breeze as we shook hands. "Thanks. Good job on the arm bar, yourself. If I was anything but a were, that might have ended my night."

"I'm just glad he didn't bite off any of our parts," said the Faerie Ninja, joining our impromptu circle of mutual admiration. He held out a fist, and I pounded it, then looked over at the demon, who hadn't come any closer.

"Don't worry about him," Ninja said. "He's just here for the bloodshed. He keeps moving up and down the tiers looking for new people to eviscerate."

"What do you mean?" I asked, honestly a little confused.

"He'll win a few fights, then throw a fight right before Tier Five so he doesn't have to fight to the death. I think he just likes to hurt people."

Well, that didn't narrow the field on what kind of demon he was, but it definitely meant he was the one out of this bunch I had to watch out for. So naturally, he was the one I got "randomly" paired with on Wednesday night. Yay, me.

16

I stood on the sand, looking across at the closed door, waiting for my opponent. I wore a different collar this time, one that didn't cut off my access to magic but limited how much I could draw or expend in one go. Living in NASCAR country, it was like someone had put a restrictor plate on my power. I didn't like it, but I seldom needed to draw on all my juice to take out a demon.

The bigger problem was going to be beating him without killing him. Demons weren't known for their willingness to surrender, and I wasn't known for my restraint. I knew who I was facing because the first Tier Two bout had been streamed to my room and I got to see the jovial werewolf pummel the absolute shit out of the Faerie Ninja. He'd put on a hell of a show, shifting at the blink of an eye every time he took a serious wound. That kind of speed was beyond what I thought lycanthropes could manage and made him seriously scary. When your opponent heals whatever you throw at him, it makes for a difficult night.

So now I stood with my Docs in the sand as my unknown demon made his appearance. He hadn't participated in any of our sparring sessions, so I had no idea how strong or fast he was. I, on the other hand, had tussled with Faerie Ninja and Wolf-Boy for three days, so he'd gotten a good look at my moves. At least, at the moves I wanted him to see.

The ring announcer's voice boomed over the Colosseum. "Ladies and Gentlefreaks, get ready for your final second-round fight of the evening. Remember that these fights are weaponless, and the fight stops when one of the competitors submits or is unable to continue, as judged by our medical staff."

Said medical staff was watching on a video monitor backstage because they were all human, at least as far as I could tell, and had zero interest in getting their faces scorched off by an errant fireball, proving that they were among the more intelligent and cautious entities in the entire building.

"Combatants may not use any weapons they did not bring into the arena with them, so please do not throw anything over the barricade. It will result in your ejection from the Colosseum and may cause your fighter to be disqualified. All betting on this fight closes in one minute. Now, the moment you've been waiting for. Please welcome the longest-tenured gladiator in Colosseum history—Abraxar The Murder Machine!"

The crowd went mild. There was some applause, but not much more than for my entrance. I guess they just weren't as into the matches where there was little potential for them to watch someone die. Vultures. That all changed when Abraxar stepped onto the sand and grabbed at his face, ripping it in half and continuing to pull. He took great handfuls of flesh in each hand and just kept pulling, revealing his true shape underneath.

Well, shit. He was a goddamned Reaver Demon. They're fairly low-level, but vicious motherfuckers, with long scythe-like forearms, legs hinged backward to give them incredible leaping ability, and an extended mouth full of razor-sharp teeth. I'd fought plenty of them before, but I usually had a pistol in hand. He extended a disgustingly long forked tongue and licked the last scraps of skin from his muzzle and swallowed.

"Yummy," he said, his voice amplified over the PA system. I looked around for hanging mics before realizing there was probably a mage somewhere playing sound engineer. "I wonder what you taste like, little human?"

"Too bad you won't find out," I said, calling power and flinging a half dozen balls of purple energy at his face. He dodged, but one clipped his shoulder and drew a longer hiss, this time of pain. I intentionally had gone all hand-to-hand in my sparring sessions, since I figured I'd need some kind of ace in the hole when I faced this jackass.

Reavers are quick, mean, and nasty. They're smart in the same way a velociraptor is smart—high-tier predators but not much for thinking outside the box. Their normal tactic is to overwhelm an opponent with superior strength and speed, but if you can keep one off-balance, you'll probably be okay. So it was no surprise when he charged me, taking three quick steps and leaping twenty feet across the sand to land right on top of me.

It was surprising to him when I wasn't standing there waiting on him, though. I poured on my own enhanced speed and managed to be ten feet away when he slammed into the ground, and I cut loose another round of energy spheres, these aimed right at his back. No, I have no moral qualms about shooting a bad guy in the back. I'm not fucking Wyatt Earp, and I firmly believe that if Earp had been fighting a demon, he'd have much rather shot one in the arse than look it in the eye. All six of my blasts smacked into Abraxar's spine, and he went face-first into the sand.

He didn't stay down long, though, flipping to his feet and whirling on me, his scythe arms flashing through the air in a lethal dance of pain and dismemberment. He charged me again, this time staying on the ground, his arms wide to cut off my escape. But I kept on flipping the script on him, this time driving forward myself instead of trying to dodge. I spun up a purple shield around my right arm and wove a spike of pure force out from the center of it.

Abraxar saw his imminent impalement coming and stepped aside, slashing across my back with one razor-sharp arm. Fire exploded across my ribs and spine, and I could feel the poisonous ichor searing my blood. Some Reavers have evolved or created poisonous claws for themselves, and I'd gotten lucky and found one of those in Abraxar. My legs went numb instantly, and I sprawled on the sand.

That was the only thing that saved me from being cut in half by his follow-up stroke, and I had to use my elbows to roll myself over to keep from getting stuck to the floor when he slammed a claw down right about where my liver had been. Now I was lying on my back, staring up at something that looked like a Predator had sex with an H.R. Giger nightmare, and he was grinning down at me.

"Time to die, human. I think it's time for me to ascend to the Main Event." He raised both arms over his head, ready to bring them down through my chest and rip me to pieces. So much for not fighting to the death.

Too bad for him I heal fast and had scrapped with enough Reavers over the decades to have a slight resistance to their venom. I swiveled my hips to bring both legs around his left knee and flipped onto my stomach, toppling the demon and leaping to my feet in one smooth motion. Okay, smooth-ish. Maybe smooth-adjacent. Okay, I probably looked like a drunk giraffe playing Twister, but I got to my feet before the demon managed, and I kicked him in the jaw, earning a satisfying *crack* for my efforts.

My back still hurt like a motherfucker, and I was definitely moving a step slower than normal, so I knew I needed to bring this fight to a close, and fast. I didn't want to kill him and break the rules because I didn't know if that would keep me stuck in Tier Two, drop me back down further away from the Main Event, or get me killed by an overzealous security guard. I also didn't know what the collar I wore could do other than dampen my magic. For all I knew, I was trapped in an old Rutger Hauer movie and some dickhead in a control room could blow my freaking head off with a twitch of their thumb.

So I didn't kill him. I stomped on both knees, breaking them with magically shrouded Doc Martens, but I didn't kill him. I snapped both his scythe arms off at the wrists and jammed them into the dirt like I was planting a flag on the moon, but I didn't kill him. I hoisted him up by his broken jaw, wrapped my right hand in green energy, and punched him halfway across the arena where he lay broken and unconscious, but I didn't kill him.

Then I stood on the center of the ring, looking up at the control booth where the announcer grinned down at me, and shouted, "I guess I have to ask this again. Is he fucking incapacitated enough yet?"

The crowd was totally into the show now, and as we waited for the announcement of my victory, I heard them start to chant "Mur-ray, Mur-ray, MUR-RAY!"

When the announcer finally picked up his mic and bellowed "Your winner, moving on to Tier Three...MURRAAAAAAY JAAAAAAAAMES!" They went fucking nuts. I felt a little twinge of worry because I was starting to see why people did this shit. It was *fun*, having a bunch of people chant your name, and not because they want to see you executed.

17

My new room was a little closer to the arena and about twice the size of my last one. This time I actually had a bathroom, with a door that closed. Sort of. It was one of those sliding pocket doors, with anything resembling a locking mechanism removed, but it afforded the illusion of privacy, at any rate. And there was a bathtub. A big-ass bathtub with jets. And after getting pummeled by a fucking Reaver demon and getting sliced almost in half by poisonous claws, I needed some hot tub time. I wouldn't have minded an ice bath, but since I wasn't a first-round draft pick, I figured the trainer's room would be off-limits to me. At least until I beat some other asshole's face in.

"The crowd really liked you tonight," Pete said, walking into the room ahead of me. He pulled a remote out of his pocket and pointed it at the ceiling. "Cameras and mics are off now. Nobody can see or hear us but me. Who the hell *are* you, man? There's no way you're some random drifter, not taking out Abraxar like that. He's shredded Alpha weres with those claws, but you didn't even slow down when he tagged you. How did you do that?"

I wanted to trust Pete, I really did. He looked so goddamned earnest, like an Eagle Scout beaming with pride at his latest merit badge project. Or whatever Eagle Scouts get proud about. I wasn't born in America, remember? And when I was growing up, it was a little more…Dickensian than running around in short pants collecting patches for our sashes. But I didn't. I couldn't. I don't trust many people, and I don't let many people get close. It's probably a character defect, but it's a character defect that has kept me, and Luke, alive for a long time, so I think I'll keep it.

"I fought a Reaver once about five years ago. I think I was in Texas. Maybe Oklahoma. I wasn't exactly following a GPS at the time. But the last one really messed me up, and I learned a spell to give me a bit of a shield against its poison then. Abraxar counted on one drop of his venom to completely incapacitate me, and when that didn't work, it made him easy pickings. Relatively speaking."

I could tell by the look on his face that Pete didn't buy it, at least not completely. But that's the thing about magic—it's ninety-five percent art and maybe five percent science. So unless someone knows the exact spell you're crafting, and knows how to watch what magic does in the invisible ends of the spectrum, they can't tell for sure if you're full of shit or not. So Pete couldn't call me on my bullshit, he just knew he smelled it.

"That's cool, man. Turning your defense into offense is slick. But how are you so strong and fast? You didn't test for any fae genetics when we ran your blood, but you're way faster than a human should be."

Ran my blood? Fuck. If there were samples of my DNA somewhere, I had to make sure I got those back before I brought this whole place down around their ears. I'd left plenty of blood splattered around plenty of crime scenes over the years, but to my knowledge I'd never had anything run where it could be labeled and tied directly to me. That could be dangerous. If some shadowy branch of some shadowy government somehow found out that I had a sliver of demon soul inside me, they'd want to put a lot of very large needles in very uncomfortable places and run very invasive tests on me to figure out how to create demon-infused human weapons.

Shit, I didn't trust the non-shadowy agency of the government I *worked for* with that information. Becks knew, of course, and her boss, Paranormal Division Director Keya Pravesh, but I trusted Becks with my life and soul, and Pravesh had her own secrets to hide from the higher-ups, so we had a little mutually assured destruction working for us there.

I snapped my attention back to Pete, who was waiting for an answer from me. "I don't know, Pete," I said. "I don't know about all that DNA stuff. I just know that when I started out, I had to cast spells on myself to enhance strength, speed, and endurance. Over time, I had to refresh the spells less and less often, so maybe pouring the same magic into my body over and over again changed me somehow. You know magic, dude, it's all about intent and willpower. I poured enough of myself into those spells over the years that I guess they just kinda…stuck?"

"Shit, makes as much sense as anything, I guess," Pete said, with a broad grin that didn't quite make it to his eyes. He was holding something back, and I couldn't tell if it was his decision, or if he had orders. Either way, I was probably right not to trust him completely. Although, if you're the prisoner, it's always a good idea not to trust the guards. They have one job, and keeping you happy isn't it.

"I think I'm gonna clean up and soak in that tub now, if that's cool," I said, peeling off my scrub top. It was crusty with a mix of dried blood and sand, and had several rips in it. "Think I can get a new change of clothes? These are hanging on by a thread."

"Oh yeah," Pete said, pointing at a small dresser. There was no mirror, because you don't give prisoners things that can be turned into a weapon in half a second, but there were some toiletries on the top, along with a belt. "There's real clothes in there. We kinda guessed at the sizes, but we went up and down a little in the pants and the shirts. It's basic stuff—t-shirts, jeans, sweats—but it's all clean. And there's a six-pack of assorted beer in the fridge." He pointed to a dorm fridge beside the dresser. "I'll be back at seven tomorrow morning to walk you to the mess hall. Have a good soak, man. Good fight."

With that, Pete hustled out of the room and I untied my Docs and peeled out of the rest of my disgusting clothes. They'd been pretty good about providing fresh scrubs every day, but I'd still coated them with a thick layer of sweat, blood, and fine sand tonight. I stood under the steaming shower for a while, letting the heat soak into my muscles, and reached out to Becks.

You there, babe?

Yeah, I'm here. Glad you're okay.

A little banged up, but you should see the other guy.

I can. I'm in your memories, remember? I could almost feel her laughing in my head.

Yeah. Listen, it's gonna take me at least a couple more weeks to get to the bottom of all this. You finding out anything on your end?

No more bodies have appeared, so whoever lost the last Main Event must have been someone that didn't leave a corpse.

Or they're getting better at hiding them. No Main Event tonight, so there shouldn't be any deaths. Next big fight is Saturday, and I'll move up another bracket.

There's five brackets, right?

Yeah. I need to win two more before I fight in a Main Event. Any luck on figuring out where the fuck I am?

I've got a couple of ideas. There aren't many places in town big enough for the kind of operation you've described, so we're looking to outlying areas like Pineville, Concord, or Matthews.

That tracks. There's still some undeveloped land up by the speedway. Not much, though. The chunks of North Charlotte and Concord where the racetrack was had grown up a lot in the past decade.

So we've narrowed it down a little, but I can't get enough of a fix on your signal to narrow it down any. It's like your thoughts are being bounced off a bunch of different satellites or something.

Weird. Well, I'll let you get some sleep. Now that I've washed most of the blood off, I'm gonna soak in a tub of scalding water and let my muscles recover.

Wish I was there to wash your back.

It's hard to blush across a telepathic link, but somehow my fiancée managed to bring it out in me, along with some other awkward responses to the thought of her washing my back, among other things. *I wish you were here, too. Love you.*

I know. She tamped down our connection and I filled the tub, sinking all the way up to my chin. There were a lot of questions still rolling around in my head as the heat soaked into my battered body. Where the hell was this place hidden? Who was running it?

I had a pretty solid suspicion that the shadowy "Boss" I'd met a few days ago might be the day-to-day manager, but I was pretty sure the real power lay elsewhere.

How much could I trust Pete? I liked the kid, but at the end of the day, he worked for the people running an underground fight club for cryptids, not all of whom were here voluntarily. That made him sketchy at best, and a murderer at worst.

What was I going to do when it came time to fight to the death? I'd killed a lot of people—human and cryptid alike, but could I murder somebody for the entertainment of a bunch of bloodthirsty assholes? Or would it be self-defense because if I didn't kill whoever I got matched up against, they would definitely kill me. Sometimes life was easier when I was just a berserk killing machine ripping Nazis to shreds all across Europe. At least then I knew the assignment—see a Nazi, kill a Nazi. This whole "conscience" thing was a real pain in the ass.

Those thoughts were all tumbling through my head like psychotic squirrels when the heat, the fatigue, and the relaxation of the soak all combined to pull me under into a deep, dreamless sleep.

18

That sleep lasted about three hours before I woke up, everything pruned as a motherfucker, with my back hurting all over again from falling asleep sitting in a hard-ass bathtub. I drained the tub, showered again to loosen up my muscles, dried off, pulled a thick comforter over my naked body, and sprawled across the plush queen-sized bed for another few hours.

I felt a lot better when I woke up the second time, around six in the morning. I took another shower, this time to mostly wash the sleepy off, and got dressed. They did pretty well with sizes, so I grabbed a pair of jeans and a black t-shirt, and was just looking through the mini-fridge for something to eat when Pete knocked on my door, waiting all of half a second before entering. I guess my promotion to Tier Three came with some privacy, but not really.

"Ready for breakfast?" he asked, beaming. I don't trust people that are happy in the morning, but for all I knew, Pete was some kind of weird fae that didn't sleep, despite his claims of humanity. "I forgot to tell you that you have unrestricted access to the mess hall now, so you don't have to eat in your room. Breakfast runs until ten, then lunch starts at eleven. Dinner is from five to midnight, but there's always some food available if you get peckish in the middle of the night."

More reason to think he might be a faerie. Nobody says "peckish."

"So my door isn't locked?" I asked. If there was an opportunity to snoop around unescorted, I was sure as fuck gonna take it.

"Oh, it's locked, but if you flip the red switch by the door, someone from security will see the alert and open the door for you." So much for snooping. I can cast a glamour to make me invisible, but I'm not good enough at illusion to make it look like I walk to a dining hall, fix a plate, and eat, all while I'm really sticking my nose somewhere it's not supposed to be. That's some David Copperfield shit right there.

Yes, David Copperfield is a real wizard. So is David Blaine. Criss Angel…not so much. "Okay, so if I don't need an escort to mealtime, why not just send me a message? Why come yourself?" I asked.

"One, I kinda like you, Murray. You've got a little bit of an underdog vibe, and that's something people like to root for. But not everybody. So I wanted to be there while you got the lay of the land around the other upper-tier competitors. And two, I'm hungry, so I thought I'd grab you and show you around the mess while I get myself some grub. Kind of a kill two birds with one stone thing."

Okay, that made sense. He wanted to keep an eye on me, he wanted to make sure that I didn't get murdered my first breakfast with the other kids, and he wanted a snack. I could understand all that. "Okay, but I have a really important question before breakfast?"

"What's that?"

"Is the fucking coffee decent? Because if it's instant, I might murder somebody."

The coffee was decent. The mess was about a third of the way around the circle of rooms from my dorm, at least as far as I could guess from our walk. It seemed to be nestled under the bleachers at the far side of the arena from where I entered for my fights, although I still had no real sense of the scale of the building. The Colosseum itself was a flat oval with steeply raked sides leading to several rows of seating, but I couldn't tell how much space might be under those risers. All the dorms/cells that I'd occupied were arranged on the opposite wall, but I had yet to see any corridors branching out to what might be an exit. Maybe we were underground and the only way out was up the bleachers? I promised myself I'd work on that mystery after I found some food.

The breakfast spread was set up cafeteria-style, with eggs, bacon, sausage, grits, assorted fruits, different types of cereal and yogurt, and even an omelet station. I got a cheese omelet with bacon, some fruit, and some home fries, then sat at an unoccupied table. I'd looked for a seat with my back to a wall, but those were all taken when I arrived. You put a bunch of hungry predators in a room and you aren't going to find a lot of people willing to sit facing away from the door. We've all watched the same movies, after all.

I'd just taken the first bite of my grits when a lanky man in his twenties put his tray down and sat across the small table from me. All the tables were metal picnic benches, and they were all bolted to the floor, a wise design choice when everyone in the building was there to beat the shit out each other. "Mind if I sit?" the newcomer asked, dropping bonelessly down onto the bench.

"Go for it," I said. "Murray." I extended a closed fist.

He bumped knuckles with me and said, "Anthony. I'm fae. Summer Court. You?"

I put on my best Hagrid impression and said, "I'm a wizard, 'Arry."

Anthony chuckled and took a bite of some sort of melon. "They feed us a lot better here than at Oberon's basic training. I swear, sometimes I think he wanted us to exist on honeysuckle and sunbeams. You Tier Three?"

"Yeah, just got promoted."

"I figured. I haven't seen you in the mess before. They save the good food for those of us who make it to Tier Three. Or who start here." He jerked his chin at a pale man sitting alone with a large glass of red liquid on the table before him. Every once in a while he'd take a long drink, letting a tendril of blood run down the side of his mouth. Vampire. And an old one, given how energetic he seemed this early in the day. Vamps don't have to sleep during the day. I've seen Luke go for a week without closing his eyes when we've had to, but it's not ideal for them.

I didn't recognize this bloodsucker, but I instantly disliked him. His eyes scanned the room constantly, not just looking for threats, but looking for weaknesses, too. He wanted to find something he could exploit in the arena, which was smart, but also felt kinda shitty. People should be able to at least eat without watching their backs. But apparently that wasn't how this place worked. And the whole blood trickle thing? That was just showing off who he was and how tough vampires are. Drinking blood freaks out most people, but I was willing to be good money that no one in the dining hall qualified as "most people." So that just made it ostentatious, and an ostentatious vampire is pretty quickly a dead vampire in most environments.

"You missed a spot, Maris!" a thickly muscled man from the next table called to the vampire, and he and his friends all laughed like they'd told the funniest joke ever.

I looked at Anthony. "What's this shit about?" I pointed to Vamp and Muscles. "They got beef?"

"Yeah, sorta. The vampire is called Maris, and the guy with muscles on top of his muscles is an Alpha were from Hungary named Yannis. They fought in Tier Four last night, and Maris left Yannis laying in a pool of his own blood. He didn't even drink it, which Yannis took as an insult."

"He didn't take ending up on the floor bleeding like a stuck pig as an insult?" I asked. Wounded pride—the downfall of more Alphas than silver or wolfsbane. Which works on all weres, not just wolves, by the way.

"I'm sure that didn't help his mood," Anthony replied. "And neither did getting bumped back down to Tier Three. Yannis is looking to win out, and losing to Maris, and not even on a Saturday night when the betting is good, doesn't help his chances."

I cocked an eye at Anthony, and he went on. "The amount of money wagered on your bouts is what determines how easy or hard your fights are. It's not rigged per se, but if you're a shifter with a lot of money bet on you to win, you get a tougher fight, or worse odds.

And a percentage of everything wagered on a fighter is held in escrow for when you leave, so if you make it all the way to the Main Event and leave as a champion, you're pretty much set for life. You probably don't have enough to buy your own island, but you could live comfortably for a long time."

"Anybody ever make it?" I asked. Pete had already told me that he'd never seen it, but maybe Anthony knew some gossip that didn't make it to the staff.

"Not all the way through," he said with a shake of his head. "But when you make Tier Four, you get a choice after every match. You can cash out and take whatever your cut of the wagers is, or you can keep fighting and try to become a Champion."

"Ever seen anybody cash out?" I asked, a suspicion starting to form.

"Oh, yeah. Just last week a shifter that had been here for almost two months, bouncing up and down between Tier Three and Four won his Four match and opted out. He said he was tired of fighting all the time and missed his old life, so he took the money and left. I hope he's happy. He…never seemed like he liked the fighting all that much."

Sounded like Willy, the dead shifter whose body on the golf course had put this whole thing in motion. "How did he get started with the fights? He get shanghai'd like I did?"

"Not at all. It's pretty rare that anybody who's conscripted actually wins a fight. Usually you guys are just picked up, get your asses kicked in an opener against some Tier Two weenie who lost his last fight, and then you get dumped in an alley with a hundred bucks in your pocket. But Will got into betting on the fights, lost more than he could afford to lose, and started fighting to pay off his debt to the house. He was doing good, too, but you could tell his heart wasn't in it. I knew he'd take the out. He wasn't a killer. The Main Event scene was never going to work for him."

"What about you?" I asked. "You a killer?"

"Nah, I'm a lifer, man. I fight on Tier Four one week, lose, fight Tier Three the next, win, then back to Four for another loss. I don't want to kill anybody, either, but I like the fight. And I'm a faerie. I know as long as they don't kill me, I'll outlive all these idiots anyway, so as long as I'm young, I might as well have some fun, bust some heads, and eat for free. Plus this way, I don't have to do whatever shit duty Oberon wants to make me do as punishment."

Okay, now I was intrigued. "Why would Oberon want to punish you?" As someone who the King of Summer absolutely fucking *hated*, I was always interested in hearing from another party on Obie's shit list.

"I might have banged one of his maids," Anthony said, dipping his head in mock embarrassment.

"I thought faeries weren't into the whole monogamy thing?" Certainly none of the ones I'd known back in my Studio 54 days had been.

"They aren't, but Oberon looks at his maids as more his property than his servants, so in his mind, I may as well have slept with Titania herself. Not that I would ever—" He held up his hands as if to stave off any possible offense. I waved his protests aside with a strip of bacon. The cooks in this joint were really good. The bacon was that perfect shade of almost burnt.

"I get it. You would never dream of besmirching her Royal Hotness in such a way. Plus, you're scared she'd rip off your junk and stick it on her mantel alongside all her other former lovers' equipment."

"You've heard that story, too, huh?"

"Everybody's heard that story, bud. At least everybody who deals in magic and might ever encounter a faerie." I added that last part as I realized that not everybody had probably heard that story, and even fewer had seen the evidence with their own eyes, but that's a story for much later. "I get it. Titania's hot, but so far off limits as to be on another plane of existence."

"Exactly," my newfound friend agreed.

Titania's hot, huh? Becks chimed in, reminding me yet again that there was a perennial hitchhiker on my dirtiest thoughts. *I think this is another conversation we're going to have when you get home.*

Losing in the Main Event gets more appealing with every conversation I want to avoid, I replied.

Oh, no, Harker. You don't get off that easily. If anybody murders your ass, it's gonna be me.

Or him, I thought, looking up at the shadow that had just fallen across our table. *Gotta go, babe. I think it's time for the obligatory fight in the prison mess hall scene.*

The heavily muscled were called Yannis stood glaring down at Anthony. "You talk too much, Tony. Tell too many stories. I shut you up now." He talked like a cliche of a Russian mob goon, but from the look on Anthony's face, he had the skills and strength to back up his threats. I guess it really was time for the fight in the dining room. I shoved the last of my bacon in my mouth as Tony stood up, palms out to try and defuse the situation.

I knew I was about to get in a fight, but that was no reason to let good bacon go to waste.

19

I stood up and got my legs clear of the picnic bench before looking up, and up, and up at Yannis. Not only was he packed with muscle, he was pushing seven feet tall, too. It was like somebody from Central Casting decided I shouldn't fight anyone my height or smaller lately. "Hey buddy, no need to make a mess in the mess hall. Get it?"

My fake laugh got no more reaction than my dad joke. Tough room. Of course, given that most everybody in here was competing in the supernatural edition of *Bloodsport*, that tracked. Yannis just glared at me for half a second, then seemed to dismiss me as irrelevant and focused back on Anthony.

"You tell new guy I am pussy. That makes me look bad. Now I rip your head off and shit down your neck," the wall of muscles with a mouth said, his lips twisted into a snarl.

"You ever seen anybody do that?" I asked. "Because I have. It's way more disgusting than it sounds, and that's a high bar. So why don't you give Tony one good slap across him overactive mouth, then go back and finish your brekkies with your pals over there. We don't need to get blood and entrails splattered all over everybody's eggs, do we?"

That got his attention. The big wolf turned his glare fully on me, and I could see this was a glare that cowed men's souls, as it were. I mean, normal men who haven't had a sliver of demon wrapped around said soul since birth. To me it just looked like another overgrown shithead making weird faces at me while his nostrils flared. But I'm not easily cowed.

"You want to die in his place?" Yannis asked. "You want me to shit down *your* neck?"

I raised both hands in a sign of supplication. "Trust me, big guy, I do not want anything to do with you shitting, either down my neck or anywhere else. I'll go so far as to say I have less than zero interest in any part of your digestive system, your asshole, or anything in between. I just want you to fuck off so I can get another one of those yummy parfaits. I'm a sucker for granola and yogurt with the little chunks of fruit in them."

This obviously confused Yannis. I was neither cowering in fear nor bowing back up to match aggression with aggression, and the predator side of him, which seemed to be like ninety percent of his makeup, was baffled. I have that effect on people. Snark is my superpower. Along with strength, speed, durability, healing, and magic—you know, my *actual* superpowers.

But confused predators only react in one of two ways. They either attack, or they flee. And with a dining hall full of people he'd have to fight soon watching, Yannis's flee reflex was pretty well suppressed. Which I'd expected when I first opened my mouth. I knew there was going to be a fight, and I knew I was going to get dragged into it. At least this way, I could control when the violence popped off.

And pop off it did. Yannis didn't bother going over or around the table to get to me. He just reached down and yanked the table up, shearing the aluminum legs off from the bolts holding them to the concrete. He tossed the whole thing over his shoulder without looking, and a couple of other fighters had to scurry to get out of the way. Neither of them had the presence of mind to save their literal bacon, I noticed.

I didn't have much time to feel smug about my culinary reflexes because in one big step, Yannis loomed over me, panting and flaring those nostrils. I might not have any interest in his asshole, but I was giving serious thought to poking a couple fingers up those noseholes and pulling him around by the snout. And this was in his *human* form.

Not for long, though. He immediately went into a half-shift, growing another foot and packing on even more muscle, if that's possible. His face elongated, and his nostrils grew even larger, another thing that stretched credulity. I stopped worrying about his nose at that point and focused on his throat instead.

Namely, I focused on putting my fist in it, wrapping my right hand in a glowing shield and punching Yannis right in his Adam's apple with magically enhanced might. That kind of explosion of pain in the middle of a transformation does one of two things to a were—it either reverse their shift entirely, leaving them curled up in agony for several moments in their human form, or it pushes the shift all the way to their full animal form, where they lose all sense of humanity and become a snapping, snarling death machine with no real sentient thought, only knowledge of pain and hunger. It's a lot like throwing a lycanthrope back to their first turn, and it's really mean. But either a helpless human or a mindless wolf is better than dealing with a fully focused half-wolf, who has the best traits of both human and animal. And hey, I might get lucky and punch Yannis back into a sobbing human curled up on the floor choking and blowing snot all over the place.

Spoiler Alert: I did not get lucky.

Second Spoiler Alert: Yannis was a really goddamned *big* wolf. Like, he was a *Game of Thrones* dire wolf-looking son of a bitch. And now he was right in front of me, with a sore throat, a bad attitude, a lot of fucking teeth, and one enemy in his sights: Quincy Fucking Harker.

I looked for Anthony, but he was ten feet away, brandishing one of the legs of the picnic table at a trio of fighters who didn't look all that enthused about attacking me in the first place. "I'll hold these guys off, Murray! You take care of Yannis. I got your back, buddy!"

Great. He had my back. I wasn't worried about my back. I was worried about the giant fucking wolf in front of me. Until it wasn't in front of me anymore. Suddenly, faster than even I could see, Yannis sprang at me, knocking me flat on my back and sending me skidding across the floor of the mess. I was going to need another shower and a change of clothes if I lived through this.

I got my shield-wrapped left arm between Yannis's jaws and my throat, then pressed my right palm against his chest. *"Forzare!"* I said, pushing my will out through my hand and sending the wolf flying off me.

Well, it would have sent the wolf flying off me. Except he had a death grip on my left forearm, and a wolf has the grip strength of your average shop vise. So he flew, but I flew with him. Right about the peak of our arc, Yannis opened his mouth enough for me to wrest my arm free, which let me control my fall just a tiny bit.

Okay, that was bullshit. I wasn't in control of a goddamned thing, but I got lucky enough that when Yannis landed on another picnic table, crushing it like a Budweiser can against a frat boy's forehead, I happened to land on his big fuzzy belly instead of any of the aluminum shrapnel around us. This was not the time to see if the good boy wanted belly rubs, and besides, as I've recently learned, I'm a cat person, so I put both hands on his midsection and repeated the spell, this time sending myself into the air on purpose, and flipping over to make an almost perfect superhero landing.

And I swear I would have stuck that landing if my back foot hadn't landed in somebody's discarded yogurt, sending me skidding across the floor on my knee and making me think about parfait again. I still managed to get to my feet before Yannis, who was wriggling around in a twisted heap of metal trying to get free.

I stalked over to my downed foe, planning on knocking him unconscious with one good punch and leaving him to shift automatically and then heal, when someone blurred into motion to stand between me and my quarry.

Maris. The vampire who had beaten Yannis and sent him down to Tier Three. "I cannot allow you to kill him while he is in this condition. It would be uncivilized."

I was confused. Like, sincerely confused. Here was the guy who'd beaten this shifter to within an inch of his life less than twelve hours before, telling me that killing him would be uncivilized? Ignoring the fact that I didn't plan on killing Yannis, who was *this* asshole to tell me about being civilized? I was willing to take that shit from Luke because he was actual nobility and, despite his odd diet, one of the most well-mannered beings I'd ever encountered, and that includes all the Archangels. But this prick?

"We're indentured servants forced to fight for the amusement of a bunch of rich pricks. What's so goddamned civilized about that?" I asked. "I mean, seriously, it's like we're in a low-budget remake of *Gladiator,* only this sequel could use more Pedro Pascal."

Maris cocked his head at me, a gesture so familiar I almost laughed out loud. Luke does that same shit to me all the time. That thought made my blood freeze. If he had Luke's mannerisms, and I didn't know him, then he might be an old vampire.

Like, *really* old. Like before Luke met my parents, old. Like, from back in the old days in Eastern Europe old. Like, old enough to be powerful beyond all fucking recognition old. If this guy was more than a couple centuries old, he might be able to take out everybody in the room without breaking an ever-so-slightly bloody sweat.

"Nevertheless," Maris said. "I will not allow you to murder Yannis while he is senseless. He is an honorable fighter, for a dog." And the way he said it, it made sense. Yannis couldn't help that he was never going to be able to beat Maris, because he was a lesser species. Just like me.

Yeah, that didn't fly so well with me. I'd been there for a pompous little asshole talking about a whole chunk of humanity being a lesser species before, and it didn't end well for him. But not before he and his asshole friends killed something like eight million of those "lesser" humans all across Europe. I hate that kind of racist bullshit when it comes from humans, and I hate it even more when it's speciesist bullshit coming from guys who have lived long enough to know better.

There was still too much of a restriction on my power to summon my soulblade, and that would give away too much of my power anyway, but I had more than enough juice stored up to make my eyes glow red, wrap my fists in glowing orbs of power, and give Maris a really impressive death glare as I said, "I'm not planning on killing him, just knocking him out so he'll shift and I can go get a shower. But there's not a goddamned thing keeping me from changing my plans and adding vampire to the menu. So why don't you put your aristocratic nose back where it belongs—out of my fucking business."

I didn't even see the slap that sent me flying backward, but I definitely felt it. And I sure as fuck felt the impact as I slammed against the far wall, impacting the concrete with my shoulders first, then my stupid, stupid head. I tried to reach out to Becks and apologize for not letting her be the one to kill me, but the doors burst open and a dozen guards streamed in, including a very annoyed-looking Pete, all holding some kind of remote control in each hand.

"That's enough!" Pete yelled, holding his right hand over his head, finger on a red button. "You all know that if we press these buttons, your collars explode. There might be one of you that can survive with your head separated from your body, but we will make sure that your survival is very short-lived, and very painful. So stand the fuck down!"

Shit. Now I really needed to remember the name of that Rutger Hauer movie.

20

Concussions suck. Even if you're really strong, and even if you recover way faster than a normal human, smacking your head into a cinderblock wall after flying across a room rings your bell like a motherfucker. And I got the whole damn menu of symptoms—nausea, dizziness, light sensitivity, difficulty focusing, more nausea, crippling headaches, and worse, inability to use my magic.

Not that it mattered much because the guards dialed up my collar until I could barely heal and sense Becks, much less cast anything. So I basically lay in my bunk for a couple days, getting off every once in a while to crawl over to the toilet and puke, then curl up in the floor of a shower in a futile attempt to make my head feel better. Anthony brought me plates from meals after the first day, once I could keep a little bit of solid food down, but I didn't catch so much as a glimpse of Pete until Saturday morning when he slammed my door open and flipped on all the lights, making me groan in pain and setting my guts a-roiling all over again.

"Rise and shine, pookie bear!" he called out at the top of his lungs. If I could have moved, I would have murdered his freckled ass.

"Fuck off," I croaked, pulling a pillow over my face.

"Time to heal up, dickhead. You've got a fight tonight."

"I've got a concussion, you asshole," I muttered.

"Not for long," Pete said. I heard a soft *click*, and in half a heartbeat, all my magic came rushing back. And I mean *all* my juice. For the first time since I woke up in this place, I could not only touch all the magic around me, but there were no restrictions on how I used it. I could feel Becks like she was in the next room, and as I tentatively poked at my abilities, I could feel my soulblade hanging out in the ether beside me, just waiting to be formed into three feet of flaming retribution. I briefly considered summoning it and shoving it up Pete's ass, but not only would that not get me the answers I was looking for, I still had a blinding headache and a gut that felt like I'd spent the last week drinking well drinks at a Tijuana dive bar.

Pro tip: don't do that. Even if you've got a magical constitution and the stamina of a horse, don't drink Tijuana well drinks for seven days straight, even if it's to win a bet. Odds are, if you survive, you won't remember what the bet was for, and if you do, you'll realize that it wasn't worth the dysentery.

Harker, are you okay? Becks asked. *You've been kinda fucked up for days now.*

Yeah, I hit my head. A lot. And they blocked my magic. But I'm better now. How's it coming getting a fix on my location? There can't be too many places this size in Charlotte.

There aren't, but we don't really know if you're in Charlotte. You were unconscious for a while, so we've had to expand our search out to about a hundred-mile radius. You could be in Greensboro, Columbia, or anywhere in between.

Fuck. Okay, keep working it. I think I'm gonna have to fight tonight, and I expect it's gonna suck. I kinda pissed off the bosses getting into a fight in the dining hall the other day, so this is probably going to be some kind of punishment bout.

You, piss off an authority figure? Quelle fucking surprise, Babe.

Yeah, love you too.

Her tone turned serious. *Be careful, shithead. I do love you, and we haven't found you yet, so stay alive until the cavalry can get there.*

Yes, ma'am. I sent her a mental image of me saluting and tamped down our connection so I could focus on the grinning ginger in my dorm room. I took the pillow off my head. "That helps," I said, pulling power in and pouring it into the injuries to my brain. "Couldn't have done that shit forty-eight hours ago?"

"We could have, yes," Pete said. "But the Boss thought you might actually learn something if we let you suffer a little bit."

"Little does he fucking know," I said.

"That's the argument I made, too, but he's the Boss. You've got the rest of the day to heal up, then it's into the ring with you tonight. And it's going to be a *good* one."

Well, that nasty little grin sealed it—this was definitely a punishment bout. My money was on either Yannis getting to gnaw me a new asshole for embarrassing him in the mess, or Maris getting to play with me like a cat toy for a while before he left me half-drained and completely shattered in the middle of the sand. Neither one was appealing, but I just sucked it up and smiled at Pete.

"How long do I have to get ready? I could use another shower and a change of clothes."

"It's ten in the morning, so you've got all day. You'll have unfettered access to your magic until an hour before the bell, so you can heal. Then you'll get shackled back down to Tier Three levels for the fight. You're still Tier Three, so it's incapacitation of surrender, except for this fight, surrender is not allowed. You will fight until one of you can no longer compete. And the audience will decide when you can't continue. So knocking your opponent out might not be enough. They're going to want to see blood, and a lot of it."

"So you assholes can just change the rules whenever you feel like it?" I asked. "That's bullshit. What about the guys who are here voluntarily? Doesn't that kinda fuck them?"

Pete looked at me like I was a particularly stupid first-grader caught eating paste. "You don't think the guys who volunteer for this shit are here to cause as much chaos as fucking possible? Come on, Murray, don't be obtuse. The guys like Maris are here for the mayhem; they love this shit. It's losers like you with some kind of fucking moral compass that think things should be fair. Everybody else knows that fair is bullshit."

Wow. This was a new Pete. I guess when he had to threaten to detonate every collar in the lunchroom, he decided that kind, gentle Opie-Pete wasn't working and he needed to go full on tough love. Only without the love. "So no more smiles and pats on the back, huh? All business from now on?"

I thought I saw a flicker of sadness dance across his face, but then it was gone. "It's always been all business, Murray. Every once in a while I try to make people believe that somebody in power gives a shit about them because there are some fighters who perform better that way, but most people here don't give a shit about a carrot. For most of you fuckers, all stick is the way to go. I thought you might be different, but then you had to go and pick a fight with Maris. Can't have anybody damaging one of our biggest draws, not that I think you had a snowball's chance to hurting the vamp anyway."

"Don't sell me short, dickhead," I growled. "I had him right where I wanted him."

"Standing over you while you counted the birdies spinning around your concussed ass?" Pete asked with a snort. "Here's some breakfast," he said, tossing a pair of takeout containers on the floor and pulling a Coke can out of his cargo pants. "Eat up. You're gonna need it." Then he spun on his heel and left me to my food and my shower, in that order.

He was right, I needed all the energy I could consume just to heal myself, and I powered through what felt like half a dozen scrambled eggs, at least half a pound of bacon, and about eight sausage links before I stopped instantly burning every calorie I put in my body to heal. By the time I licked the Styrofoam containers clean and sucked the sides flat on the Coke, I felt almost like myself again. I was still weak from lying in bed for days, but I could move my head without wanting to puke and I wasn't in any serous pain.

I took a shower, pulled on some clothes, noting that my previously tight t-shirt hung loose on me after burning so much body fat to heal, and did some light stretching to loosen up my muscles. I moved from stretches into a few easy katas, then did about thirty minutes of yoga before sitting on the floor to meditate, draw in enough power to keep my batteries topped off once they throttled my magic again, and tried to rest.

I left my room for lunch feeling much better, but the dining hall was almost completely empty. I asked one of the servers what was up and was told that most fighters had been eating in their quarters since the big dustup. I'd seen enough of those walls for a while, so I picked out a prime spot where my back wasn't exposed and tucked into a huge plate of fried chicken, mashed potatoes, and mac and cheese. It was good mac and cheese, too, not the stuff out of a box. I mean, *Hawkeye* was right, boxed mac and cheese is delicious, but this shit was off the hook.

I was just contemplating not if I was getting dessert but how many desserts I was going to get when a massive shadow fell across my table. I looked up into the mournful face of Yannis, the wolf who had been trying to murder me just a few days earlier.

"May I sit?" he asked.

I nodded, and he put down his tray and lowered himself onto the bench opposite me. This left his back completely exposed to the entrance and most of the room, so he was taking a massive risk doing this, a fact that was not lost on me.

"I must apologize to you for Thursday morning," Yannis said, in one of the most surprising conversational openers I've experienced in my ridiculously long life.

"It's cool," I said, in that kinda mumbly was dudes talk when they know they're supposed to say something but have no goddamned idea what they're supposed to say.

"No, it is not cool," Yannis insisted. "I should not have threatened Anthony. My pride was wounded from losing to Maris, and I behaved poorly, causing everyone to suffer. This is not how an Alpha should behave to a lesser creature. I am sorry."

I decided to let the whole "lesser creature" thing slide because he really was trying to apologize. Besides, Becks had been trying to get me to not beat the ever-loving fuck out of people at the slightest hint of an insult. She's trying to get me to move from "toxic masculinity" to "slightly incapacitating masculinity." I'm not sure how well it's working, but I was also pretty sure I was going to have a hell of a fight in a few hours, so getting into a scrap with Yannis would almost certainly burn energy I didn't have to spare.

So I just said, "I accept your apology. Not sure I accept the concept that I'm a lesser creature, but I'm willing to concede that point in the interests of not spilling my macaroni." I held out a hand.

Yannis shook it, although he looked a little confused as he did so. "Murray James, you are a very confusing man. I think I like you, and I will be sad if I have to kill you someday soon. I will do it, but I will be sad."

And that's about as good as it gets when you're trapped in a cryptid fight club where vampires and werewolves fight to the death once a week. At least if he had to kill me, he'd be sad about it.

21

Eight hours later, I was pretty sure whoever I was about to stand across the arena from would not be the least bit sad if they managed to beat me to a bloody pulp. And honestly, I wouldn't be all that sad if I turned them into a red smear on the sand, either. Now that I'd been awake for a while and had kept down two whole meals without painting the inside of my toilet with mac and cheese exiting the wrong direction, my slightly less than toxic masculinity was demanding I get out of my room and beat the shit out of somebody. It had been like three whole days since I kicked anyone's ass, after all.

Pete came by to escort me to the ring, but he was still a lot more surly prison guard than the genial goofball he'd been masquerading as before my fight in the dining hall. It seemed that the guy who led me to the indoor death fighting pit wasn't actually my friend. I would have to find some way to bear up under the weight of the crushing disappointment. "Who am I fighting?" I asked.

"You'll see."

"Still pissed at me for getting in trouble with the Boss, making it look like you don't have your people under control and thus getting you in trouble with the Boss?" Maybe twisting the needle in the guy with the keys to my cell and the remote for my neck bomb wasn't the brightest move, but it was pretty irresistible.

"Still pissed at you for putting me in a position where I had to clean up your puke and blood off the floor of the mess hall," Pete replied.

"Okay, that I'm actually sorry about," I said. Pete looked at me, and I shrugged. "Look, if you got a time out because I refused to be a good little gladiator, then tough shit. But cleaning up my puke? That must have been nasty. I'd had a *lot* of bacon."

Pete actually grinned a little at that. "Took me all day to get the smell of bacon barf out of my nostrils."

"Pretty sure it took me two days to get the *actual* bacon barf out of my nostrils, so you got off easy in that regard," I said.

He laughed, and some of the tension eased. Which I really needed, because I didn't want his thumb slipping on my boom collar at the wrong moment. Which would be *any* moment, by the way. We reached the door to the arena, and I caught a wicked grin on Pete's face.

"Have fun," he said as he pulled open the door and shoved me in. Going purely by the grin, I decided that maybe all was not forgiven after all.

I stepped onto the sandy floor and got my bearings just as the announcer finished shouting my name, and my heart sank as I looked across the ring at my opponent. Anthony. Yep, the faerie warrior that I'd stood up for in the cafeteria was the guy I now had to beat the shit out of to move up the ladder.

Mother*fuckers*. I wracked my brain for a good out, then decided, *fuck it*, and chose the path of most resistance.

Becks, if you can hear this, turn down your pain receptors because I'm about to get my ass kicked. On purpose this time. I'll explain later. Love you.

I tamped down our connection before she could respond, if she even could. I could definitely feel some barrier to my magic, albeit less than in my last fight. They wanted me to have access to more power to fight Tony, because that would up the chances of me hurting him seriously and really head-fucking myself. Assholes. This whole place was full of assholes, and I promised myself then and there that I was going to bring the whole place down around their fucking ears if it was the last thing I did.

"I'm sorry, Murray," Anthony said, walking across the sand and extending a hand. "But we've gotta fight, or they'll send in somebody like Maris to take us both out, and if we piss them off any more, they might not stop him before he kills us."

I shook his hand. "Nah, I get it. They're all assholes, and one of these days, I'm going to make them pay. But tonight, we'll put on a show." I let go of his hand and stepped back, but not fast enough. Anthony shifted his weight onto his back foot and clocked me on the jaw with a wicked fast snap kick.

I danced back, shaking my head to clear the cobwebs. There weren't any, really, but Tony didn't need to know that. It had been a *good* kick, and it didn't look like it had cost him any real effort. Anthony was skinny, so the power in his legs surprised me. He was about my height, with short-cropped dark hair and a neatly trimmed beard, and was built like a distance runner. Which is to say, he looked like a stiff breeze would blow his ass away. But he kicked like a Tae Kwon Do black belt, and he had impressive reach. Fucking faeries, man. You never can tell what they'll be like just looking at the cover.

He came in again, feinting low with kicks, then springing forward with a big overhand punch that I barely blocked. But blocking the big punch left my midsection open to three quick body blows that had me dancing back again. This guy was good, and he was mixing up his style enough that his moves were all hard to counter. He threw kicks, punches, and elbows, and I hadn't managed to land a strike yet. Not that I was trying all that hard.

I wanted to lose. I was here on a case, and that case didn't involve kicking the shit out of someone who had the potential to become a friend if we both survived. Anthony was in it for the cash, so if I could improve his value to the Boss while not dying, I was willing to give him the "W" and spend a few extra days eavesdropping in the mess and the exercise yard.

But I still had to avoid getting my goddamn head taken off with one of his kicks, so when he threw a couple of thrust kicks toward my midsection, I knew a big roundhouse would be coming for my face, and this time I decided to be somewhere else when his foot shot through the space where my head had been. I ducked, and when I stood up quickly, I stuck my fist right into his solar plexus.

His dropped to his knees, gazing for air, and I laid him flat with a palm strike and moved over to wrap him in a sleeper hold. "Chill out, asshole," I whispered while our heads were next to one another. "I'm trying to give you the win, but I'd really rather not get concussed again in the process."

I felt him nod, then he slammed an elbow into my ribs. I let go of my hold and scooted backward on the sand to get some separation, only to look up and see him leaping across the ring to throw a big honking Superman-style punch at my face. I rolled out of the way, but he stayed with me, peppering me with kicks and jabs. He wasn't putting his full force behind them, but they still did some damage.

"Don't go easy on me for my sake, Murray. I can take you out all on my own," he hissed as we scuttled across the ring. The audience was starting to get restless as we grappled, wanting to see more flashy magic and claws, and especially wanting more bloodshed. I needed to make this look good, and so far, I was getting my ass kicked for real and we weren't even putting on a good show. In short, my whole plan was sucking.

Time to shift gears. The next kick Tony landed, I oversold, flopping completely onto my back and lying there like he'd knocked me out. He got to his feet and came over to me to deliver a coup de grace, but when he got within a couple feet, I kipped up and slammed a magically enhanced punch right into his solar plexus. I made sure to pour a little extra magic into my fist so it would glow purple with the punch.

Anthony flew back a few feet and I let out what I hoped sounded like a horrifying war cry, but probably sounded like a constipated lion, and I charged him, head down and arms outstretched. Tony took the hint and leapt over me, landing on my back and driving me to the floor. I felt a rib crack and let out another yell, this time more genuine and definitely higher pitched.

Fuck. That really hurt, and it made it a lot harder to focus on any casting. Good thing most of my magic is the "blow shit up" variety rather than the "intricate spell weaving" variety. But even fireballs take a certain level of focus, and that's hard to manage when it feels like someone is stabbing you in the side with every breath. Anthony must have heard the crack as well because all his attacks focused on my torso. Kicks, punches, even shots to my face that made me double over backward to avoid them—everything put more strain on my screaming midsection.

It was all I could do not to unleash on him and win the goddamned fight fair and square, although I was only about sixty percent sure I *could* win with a broken rib against a completely healthy opponent who matched me speed for speed and strength for strength. I called power and started flinging balls of purple energy at Tony, but he dodged them with barely a blink. I tossed some to explode in the dirt in front of him, but he just leapt over the shower of sand and pressed the attack.

He's good, I thought. *I'm gonna have to ask him exactly what he did for Oberon before he got canned because most of the fae I've fought weren't this skilled. Except for the...*goddammit. Except for the faerie knights. The elite fucking fighting force of the magical realm. Faster, stronger, and better trained than pretty much any other group of warriors in any world because they combined physical gifts with centuries of training time. No wonder he thought he could beat me in a fair fight. He could.

I've beaten faerie knights before, but that was with all my magic, home field advantage, a battlefield of distractions, and a little bit of creative manipulations of the rules of fair fights. In other words, I cheated. Now I'd let myself get a broken rib by taking it easy on a guy who could just kick my ass legitimately. Sometimes I'm just a fucking idiot.

And this fucking idiot needed to get this shit over with before I took any more serious damage, so the next time Anthony threw a kick at my face, I zigged when I "should have" zagged, stuck my forehead into his foot, and spun away into the darkness, unconscious before I hit the sand. My last thought as I faded out was *well, at least I lost...*

22

I woke up in my room, with a massive headache, dry mouth, and as I looked in the mirror after grabbing a shower, a truly impressive array of bruises. The best one was on my back, a perfect outline of a foot along my ribcage that hurt when I touched it, hurt when I moved, it hurt when I breathed. Hell, it hurt when I thought too hard. I started getting dressed but stopped after my jeans to catch my breath. Broken ribs suck.

Are you okay? Becks asked. *It feels like somebody kicked the shit out of you.*

That's because somebody kicked the shit out of me. I threw my last match, because I liked the guy, but halfway through giving him the win, I realized he was a goddamned faerie knight, and I was barely fifty-fifty to beat him on my best day.

So you let somebody kick your ass who could probably kick your ass anyway? That was dumb.

You're not wrong, I replied. *It wasn't my best decision. And now it sounds like I'm going to pay for that bad decision. Gotta go, babe. I think I'm getting called to the principal's office.*

Love you, Becks said. *Don't do anything else stupid.*

No promises. I tamped down our connection as the footsteps I heard outside my door slowed and Pete came in.

"The Boss wants to see you," he said. He was back in Stern Pete mode, a face he'd been wearing most of the time since my fight in the cafeteria.

"I guess he's not going to offer me a raise, huh?" I said, wincing as I pulled a shirt on.

"Not so much," Pete said, gesturing for me to precede him out the door. "Are you healed?"

"No," I replied. "Probably going to take a couple days. If I can stay out of trouble, I can use a spell or two to speed things up and be ready to go by the next fight." Assuming there *was* a next fight. I couldn't be sure the Boss wasn't going to toss me out right then, which would leave me with no more idea where the fight club was than I'd had at the beginning. And with a busted rib and a shitload of bruises to go with my lack of anything useful. I needed to stay inside, no matter what. As long as my next fight wasn't a death match, I was going to have to win it.

We stopped at a door I hadn't seen before, about halfway between the arena and the mess hall. There were no signs anywhere, just a plain door with an unadorned brass knob. Pete knocked, and the Boss called out "Enter."

Pete gestured at the door, and I went inside. This was my first good look at the Boss, not that I had any illusions that he was actually in charge. He was a manager, taking orders from whoever was really running the show, a guy who *might* show up for the big fights on Saturdays, if that. But anything I learned from this douche would put me one step closer to the real boss. I just had to convince him that I still wanted to fight, I just didn't want to fight Tony.

He was a big guy, probably six-three or four, but it was hard to really tell with him sitting down. Thickly muscled, with big hands that looked like they'd seen a fair bit of hard use. He had short red hair, an almost military-tight buzz cut, and a long handlebar mustache. Frankly, he looked a lot like an actor off *The Walking Dead*, but more muscular and with a soul patch. He wore a polo shirt that was about one anabolic steroid away from splitting every seam, and he leaned on his elbows with a disapproving look on his face.

"Mr. James, what am I to do with you?" He had a little bit of a brogue, and I pegged him for first-generation Irishman. He'd been in America a while, but no more than twenty years. Probably came over as a teen, if I had to guess his age.

"Well, I'm shit at canasta, but I play a pretty mean game of checkers," I replied. One of these days I will learn not to mouth off at the boss bad guy. Today obviously was not that day. I didn't have high hopes for tomorrow, either.

To my surprise, he laughed. It wasn't my worst effort, but usually the middle management villains are so hyped about keeping what little power they've managed to scrabble their way into that they can't find the humor in anything but suffering. This guy was either secure in his position, or had a shred of humanity left in him. I was putting my money on Column A.

"That's pretty funny," he said. "Have a seat. Water?" He held up a bottle.

"Sure," I replied, then caught the bottle he tossed at me. I cracked the seal and took a long drink. "So…I lost."

"You did."

"Am I fired?"

"Not even a little bit." Okay, that was off script.

I took a drink of my water and sat silently, waiting for him to explain. He sat silently waiting for me to ask for an explanation. The joke was very much on him. I'm over a century old, so I've built up a decent stock of patience, and I knew that I could literally sit in the office waiting for him to grow old and die without aging a day, so it was going to be his move, no matter if the power dynamic dictated that I be the one to ask for more information.

We played chicken for almost a full minute before he chuckled again and leaned back. "You're never going to ask, are you?"

"Nope."

"I like you, Murray James. You're funny, you're a good fighter, and you know how to play to the crowd. I think you're hiding something, probably a lot of somethings, so I don't trust you even a little bit, but I like you."

"Well, since you've all been such founts of fucking information since I got here, I suppose it's a little unfair that we haven't braided each other's hair while I told you about my favorite color and who in homeroom I have a crush on, but that's just the way it goes sometimes," I said.

"What do you want to know about our little operation?" he asked.

"Where the fuck am I, for one. Who's really in charge, for another. And how can I get in a bet or two on myself, for a third," I ticked my questions off on my fingers, expecting to have exactly none of those questions answered.

The Boss held up three fingers of his own, folding them down as he answered. "You're in the Colosseum, but you knew that already. I'm in charge enough for you, and you'd better hope you never meet my boss, because he'll scare the balls off a donkey just lookin' at him, and fighters aren't allowed to bet on their own fights until the higher tiers, and even then only on themselves, not their opponents, on account of we can't have some asshole throwing a fight just because he thinks he'll make more money losing than winning. Which brings us to today."

"I didn't bet on my fight," I said.

"But you did throw your last fight." There was no question in his voice, and I didn't bother lying.

"Yeah, not that I needed to. Tony was just screwing around until he laid me out regardless. He was playing with his food. I couldn't beat a faerie knight in single combat without at least a Desert Eagle, and only that if I had cold iron rounds." It stung a little to admit that, but even my ego has its limits. Oberon's knights were badass motherfuckers, and at full strength, I might be able to take one out, but not without depleting all my stored power and a little more besides.

"He was that, wasn't he?" Boss chuckled. "Still and all, I'm here to make fights, and to make interesting fights, and that show you two put on was boring as all fuck. Because of you. Now, I'm not busting you down to Tier Two, because you're too strong for that shite, and it would just make for another boring scrap. You're obviously here to climb the ladder and make some real money, so I'm giving you one more Tier Three fight. But we're going to add a little something to make it more interesting. This time, you fight two on one."

I thought for a second about the guys I'd seen in the mess and did some mental calculus. If I had my full strength, I could probably take out any two of them at once, as long as none of them were secretly super-warriors like Anthony. Regular paras, used to winning through their strength, speed, and reflexes, are actually easy, if you know the limits of their abilities. It's the ones who pair all those physical advantages with training, like Anthony, who make life difficult.

"Okay, that sounds fine," I said.

"Yeah, I thought you'd think that." He pulled out a keyboard drawer and tapped on it. I immediately felt my connection to Becks, and my magic, thin down to the barest sliver. "That's why I'm also throttling your magic. You're a lot more powerful than we thought based on your Tier One fight, so to keep it interesting, we're going to send you in against a couple of Tier Three guys with just enough magic to keep you alive."

He leaned forward, all geniality gone from his face. "You fuck with my fights, you fuck with me. And trust me, Murray James, no matter how much of a funny fucker I find you to be, you do not want to fuck with me."

I leaned forward, mirroring his posture, and stared deep into his eyes. With my magic tamped down, I didn't have to worry about my soulgaze frying his brain, so I could stare at him like a normal person. "How many times did you have to practice saying 'funny fucker' before you could manage it without getting tongue-tied?"

His eyes widened, and after a second or two of frozen time, he burst out laughing. "Oh, Jesus Christ on a pogo stick, you are a fucking *riot*, Murray. I hope they don't break your jaw when they kick your ass, because god*damn*, you are hilarious! Now get the fuck out of my office and get some time in the yard before Saturday. Because I guarantee it's going to be a fight, and an entertaining one as well. Just...maybe not so entertaining for you."

23

It was a boring few days between fights. I ate, I worked out, albeit not much until my ribs healed, and I slept. I also read, finding out the day after my little tete-a-tete with the Boss that there was an expansive digital library and a dozen e-readers available for fighters. A more tech-savvy hero than I would have figured out how to hack the building's wi-fi with it and send a message out to Becks with my location encoded in it, but I'm more the "blow shit up" guy than the "sit in a chair and figure it out" guy. I might have stolen that last line from Bubba, but it holds true regardless.

So I read, and I recuperated, and I ate most of my meals with Anthony, who felt a little bad about nearly decapitating me with a kick. But just a little bad. The morning after our fight, we met for breakfast, where he claimed that he knew his own strength well enough to have just knocked me out, but confessed that he was glad I wasn't a normal human because that probably would have resulted in my skull flying ten feet away from my shoulders. I told him I was also glad he didn't literally kick my head off, and we had a pleasant breakfast.

So I was bored by the time Pete came to fetch me for my next fight, this one a Saturday night bout, so the crowds were larger and the money wagered far more significant. So far, I didn't have a good sense of who I'd be facing, but I was hoping for at least one of the new paras that had just been promoted from Tier Two. One guy was a shifter that looked scared out of his noggin anytime anyone looked at him cross-eyed. I couldn't fathom how he'd made it past Tier One, much less anything else. If I had to fight two on one, I really wanted him to be part of the two. Then it would be more like a fair fight.

I followed Pete into the arena, and the roar when the door opened to let me in was deafening. I'd been in the audience for some massive concerts, and the decibels that slammed into my chest when I stepped onto the sound was like Live Aid, Farm Aid, and pretty much every Kiss concert ever, all rolled into one. I literally staggered back with my ears ringing before I could get myself under control. Pete put a hand between my shoulder blades and shoved, mistaking my sensory overload for reluctance.

I staggered a step or two into the arena and barely heard the clang of the door behind me. I looked around for my opponents, and just as the ring announcer bellowed "Murrrrraaaaaay James," my heart sank. I got the dance partner I wanted in the skittish were fresh from Tier Two, but I also got one of the opponents I least wanted to face—Yannis, the wolf I'd pummeled and embarrassed in the dining hall. He stood grinning at me, then gestured to the smaller were and began to shift.

Seconds later, I was looking at a massive half-man, half-wolf creature that stood nearly eight feet tall on his back legs, and had enormous hands tipped with claws like razor blades. Beside him stood his far less imposing partner, who would be dangerous nonetheless. New guy wasn't a wolf at all, explaining his smaller stature, but a were-bobcat. Tufts of fur sprang all around his neck, and elongated canines extended down over his short muzzle. If I was being honest, he looked about as intimidating as the Rum-Tum-Tugger from *Cats*, but I knew from past experience that were-bobcats were fast and their claws were needle-sharp. He wasn't going to be a pushover, but Yannis was definitely the biggest threat.

But like all good generals, Yannis sent his subordinate in first to test the enemy. His method of delivering orders was to kick the bobcat in the ass with one massive furry foot, sending the little were down to all fours, where he dashed across the sand and sprang straight for my face.

Not being a complete moron, I moved my face, and the rest of me, to one side, slamming a shielded fist into the cat's ribs. If I could incapacitate him quickly, I could turn my attention to Yannis, and maybe not get my ass completely kicked. Bobcat spun off his flight path at my punch but did that annoying cat thing where he twisted in midair and landed on all fours, then launched himself at me again, this time in a blind fury. Now I was beginning to see how he'd won a couple fights—sometimes you can get by on rage when you don't have training or skill, and this kid definitely had some berserker shit going on.

I threw up a quick shield and caught the were on it, dropping to one knee as his body weight slammed into me. He clawed my shield and hissed at me in his fury, but I just shifted my arms, twisted at the waist, and slammed him to the ground. The air rushed out of him in a *whoosh*, and his eyes crossed momentarily. I dropped my shield, slammed a fist right between his eyes, and watched as he went unconscious. Mission accomplished. Now I could focus on Yannis.

Except Yannis had already focused on me, and reminded me half a second later what I'd learned the hard way in the mess hall—motherfucker was *fast*. He was on me before KitKat's eyes had even fluttered closed, wrapping both massive arms around me in a crushing bear hug. My ribs screamed in protest, and Yannis leaned down to my ear.

"You embarrassed me in front of the other fighters. Now I embarrass you in front of everyone."

I would have been way more concerned if it hadn't been such a stupid thing to do. Bear hugs can be crippling if you have a significant power advantage over your opponent, but there's one thing you have to be really careful about. So I did exactly the thing you're never supposed to let your opponent do when you've got them in a crushing grip—I slammed my skull backward into Yannis's face. At least I didn't bite his nose off.

It wasn't quite as good as if he'd been fully human because his elongated snout was more over my shoulder than directly behind my head, but a broken orbital socket still hurts like a son of a bitch, and that's what I gave my fine furry friend, courtesy of my thick noggin. Luke always tells me my head is my best weapon in any battle. I don't think that's exactly what he means, but I'll give him credit anyway.

Yannis dropped me, and I fell to all fours in the sand. I spun around and threw three quick punches, one to his left knee, one to his right knee, and one right up into the center of his gut. Yannis dropped to the sand, unable to decide what hurt worse, his face, his knees, or his solar plexus. More fortunate for me, he was too confused to shift into full wolf, which would have healed him and made me start all over again on the kick his ass plan. I hopped to my feet, stepped back, and punted him right in the jaw. Usually, when I'm at my full strength, a move like this will stand my opponent completely up before they fly a couple feet back and sprawl on their back. It looks really cool. Except I wasn't at full strength, and Yannis in his half-shifted form weighed at least four hundred pounds, so he just kind of hopped up onto his knees, then fell to one side. I figured I'd take what I could get.

I raised my arms to the screaming crowd, expecting to hear the door open and the ring announcer call my name, but instead I got slammed in the back with a goddamn furry ball of rage and claws. Apparently Bobcat hadn't been knocked quite as silly as I'd hoped and shifted to his feline form to keep going after me.

And go after me he did. He knocked me facedown in the sand, and my back erupted in pain as he shredded my shirt, then my flesh, with his claws. I felt his jaws close around the back of my neck and knew this was how bigger cats killed their prey, with one sharp shake to snap the mouse's spine. If I didn't get my shit together, I was dead.

Good thing for me I'm smarter than the average field mouse. I didn't have my full complement of magic, thanks to the collar, but I had enough for this dickhead. I pressed both hands flat on the ground and, through gritted teeth, shouted, *"Forzare!"* We both flew up into the air, but I was the only one prepared for it. Bobcat let go with a sharp yowl and pushed off me with all fours to land several feet away, looking around in confusion.

I scrambled to my feet before he could attack again, feeling blood sheeting down my back from his claws. I cast my eyes to one side, where Yannis lay unconscious, shifted back to human as he passed out, and thus now completely healed. If he woke up before I dealt with Hello Kitty here, I was seriously fucked. I was bleeding too much to take them both on, and the furball in front of me didn't seem to be playing to incapacitate.

He sprang at me again, and this time I called up a disk of energy along my left arm, then cast a shield of fire on top of it with a cry of *"Fuego!"* When Bobcat smacked into my shield, I was instantly assailed by the stench of burning fur, and my ears rang with the howl of a scorched werecat. He sprang off me as fast as he'd leapt at me, and I saw him begin to shift back to his half-cat form to heal.

That didn't bode well for me, so I decided I should probably stop it. With prejudice. I flung a ball of pure force at his feet, forcing him to leap aside or be blasted into next week. Then another, then another, until I'd chased him across the entire arena with glowing purple spheres of power, pinning him to the far wall. He snarled at me and started his shift again, but with nowhere to run, there was no chance he could transform in time. He was no Yannis, who shifted faster than any lycanthrope I'd ever seen or heard of. It took him several seconds to begin his transformation, which gave me plenty of time to close the distance between us and wreath my right hand in crimson fire.

"Yield," I said, putting a little magic in my voice to be heard over the crowd noise. I held my flaming fist over my head and glared down at the shifter.

He snarled back at me, continuing his shift. He swiped at me with his claws, but the change was upon him now, and his motor functions were hampered by the snapping and cracking as bones lengthened and tendons reattached.

"Yield!" I called again as the crowd started chanting "Kill, Kill, Kill!" These were some bloodthirsty pricks. If I could find out who they all were, I was going to go after them as well as the dickheads who ran this place.

Bobcat was almost shifted to his mid-form now, and he snarled at me again, making a feeble slash with his claws as I stepped closer.

"Okay, dipshit," I said softly as I stepped within arms' reach. "I tried." I looked to the crowd again, and for a third time, much louder, called out one word. "YIELD!"

Bobcat was in his half-man form now and lashed out at me with his claws, but I was ready for him. Even bleeding from dozens of scratches along my back, I was more than a match for one were-bobcat, even fully healed by his shift. I let my fire wink out, stepped inside his slash to block it with my left arm, and laid a massive, magically enhanced punch on the side of his jaw, slamming the back of his head into the wall and crossing his eyes. I threw three or four more punches as he slid down the wall until he collapsed in a heap, unconscious.

Sometimes you can win a fight with pure youthful adrenaline and rage, but most of the time the older fighter will kick your ass because he knows how to kick ass and has been doing it longer. At over a hundred years old, I'd been kicking ass longer than almost anybody in the building, and as the shifter's eyes rolled back in his head, I made sure the lesson was hammered home. Pun fully intended.

I turned to look back at Yannis, but he was still on dream street. Both my opponents vanquished, I strode to the center of the ring and looked up at the luxury boxes, knowing the Boss was either in one of those or watching on a monitor somewhere. I turned in a circle as I called out to him and the crowd, "Is that the best you've got. Come the fuck on, bring me a goddamned *challenge!*"

Then I stalked over to the door, which opened at my approach, and walked out leaving nothing behind me but two bloodied opponents and thunderous cheers from the psychopaths in the audience.

24

The next day, you would have thought I was Leonidas coming back from the wars, the reception I got when I walked into the dining hall for breakfast. It was like the parting of the Red Sea when I walked up to get my plate, with half a dozen badass cage fighting cryptids and paras stepping aside to let me have my pick of the best bacon. And if you don't think a bunch of apex predators stepping aside to let a skinny dude get to the bacon first is a big deal, you really need to reevaluate your relationship with our lord and savior—pork.

I loaded up my plate and headed over to a perimeter table, where I usually sat with my back to a wall, but Tony waved me over to a round table in the center of the room. I sat down next to him, and he gestured to the other hardy few willing to sit without any architecture guarding their backs in a room full of killers.

"Guys, this is Murray James. He's the one I told you about. He almost kicked my ass, and last night he took out Yannis *and* the random new kid in the same bout," Anthony said by way of introduction.

I looked at the three others sharing our table. One was an enormous man, nearly seven feet tall and well over three hundred pounds, with muscles peeking out from under his muscles and a glare on his face that could stop a clock. I couldn't tell what kind of creature he was at first glance, and he was so damned ugly and mean-looking I didn't want to stare. I figured if I had to fight him, I'd figure it out then. Next to Ugly was a whip-thin rat-faced guy who kept twirling his silverware like it was a pair of throwing knives. He was twitchy, like he couldn't possibly sit still, but the dexterity he showed with his utensils made me think he'd be really dangerous with sharper implements. Last was one of the few women I'd seen in my time at the Colosseum, and she was as striking as she was terrifying. Her face was all sharp angles and hard planes, with eyes that bored into your soul. I pegged her as a vampire, and an old one at that. She was not someone I wanted to tangle with because I wasn't at all sure I could beat her without killing her, and I was here to save lives, not spend them.

"Murray, these are the Tier Four and Five fighters. Well, and us, of course. With your win last night, you made Tier Four, and I…"

"You made your bones when you kicked my ass," I replied with a smirk.

"Yeah, pretty much," Tony replied.

"So you lot are the baddest asses on the playground?" I asked, trying to keep my sarcasm under control and failing.

"We're good enough at what we do," Lady Murderface said, giving me a smile that might have seemed sweet if it wasn't also incredibly bloodthirsty.

"What about Maris?" I asked. "Tight-assed vampire? I thought he was a big deal here, too?"

The wall of muscles spoke, and it sounded like someone grinding two boulders together. "Maris fell last night. He will not be having breakfast."

The way everyone at the table didn't look at him, it was pretty obvious that Muscles was responsible for Maris missing a meal, and maybe all his future meals. If this meathead was able to take out a vamp of Maris's age, then he definitely had something more than brute strength going for him. If my guess was right, Maris was several centuries old, and vampires don't live that long without a blend of power and strategy.

"So what's everybody's name?" I asked, putting on my "first day of school" manners. I didn't give a shit what they were called, but I did want to have some idea of which one of them I was facing if I needed to scrap with one of them in a Tier Four fight.

"I'm Eleanor," the vampire said, holding out a hand for me to shake. I did, and she pulled me in close, licking my ear as she whispered, "Don't trust anyone. Especially me." I pulled back and wiped my ear dry as I felt Becks laughing inside my head. Apparently the Boss had dialed down the blocking tech in my collar after I won last night.

"My name is Steven," said the squirrelly little were. "And she's right." He jerked a thumb at Eleanor. "Don't trust her. She's shifty as fuck."

"And you're not?" Eleanor asked, one eyebrow climbing to the sky.

"Oh, I'm totally shifty," Steven replied. "But I *look* like the untrustworthy fuck that I am. You look like a centerfold, and guys think too much with the little head, so I figured I'd better warn Flounder here about you."

"Flounder?" I asked. "What is this, *Animal House*?"

"I don't know what that is, pal," Steven said, reminding me that I'm a walking antique. "But you're the new fish, so you get to be Flounder. Win a fight up here in the nosebleeds and we promise to pretend to give a shit what your real name is."

"What about you?" I asked Muscles. "Or should I just call you Muscles?"

"I don't care what you call me," the wall of nigh-humanity replied. "But my name is Janik."

"Okay, Janik. Good to meet all of you. I guess sitting in the middle of the room is a flex, showing everybody else that you're too badass to worry about getting jumped?"

"Kinda," Steven said. His voice was as twitchy as the rest of him, with a Joe Pesci tone to him that made me expect him to say some kind of cliche mobster shit at any moment. "Plus it's closer to the froyo bar for refills, and we get all the sprinkles."

Changing the subject, I looked around the mess hall. "Where's Yannis?" I asked. "I figured he'd be up by now barking about a rematch."

Everyone got very quiet, and for a long moment, nobody met my gaze. "Yannis died of his wounds sometime in the night," Tony said, moving some eggs around on his plate.

"What?" I asked. "That's bullshit! I didn't hit him hard enough to kill him, and besides, he'd shifted before the fight was over. He was healed. There was…" I let my words trail off as everyone continued to avoid my gaze. "Oh. He lost too many times, didn't he?"

"Yannis was a moron," Eleanor said, venom dripping from her words. "He talked too much, fought too poorly, and bled too easily to be a champion. He should have quit when he was given an out, but now…"

"Fuck," I said softly, pushing my own eggs around the plate. "I didn't know. If I had…"

"What?" Anthony scoffed. "Like you would have thrown the fight. That whole thing was a setup. They put a pain in the ass like Yannis in there with a pain in the ass like you, and an expendable new guy who didn't have any fans yet. If the new guy won, he'd be sitting here loving life. If Yannis won, he'd still be over there with his back to the wall, except you'd be dead. But you won, and Yannis is dead. So either way it's one less pain in the ass for the Boss to deal with. That was always going to be the deal—one asshole dead, and two left to bleed for the crowd."

"You sound awfully bitter for somebody who's still sitting here fighting twice a week," I said, keeping my voice down. I wasn't sure how much surveillance there was in the dining hall, but I was certain there was some, and I was just as certain I didn't want us being overheard.

"My lord Oberon commanded me here, so I am here until I fulfill my mission or am slain," Tony said.

"I thought you were here because you banged the wrong one of Oberon's maids?" I asked.

"That's how I was selected for the mission," he replied. "But it is a mission nonetheless. So I must carry it out, or never return to Faerie."

"And what is your mission, exactly?" I asked, munching on a strip of perfectly crisp bacon. There were privileges to being a badass. But I was very curious about Oberon sending one of his knights to the mundane world, even a knight he wanted to banish. I'd run into the king of the Summer Court a while back when he tried to unleash a biological weapon to destroy pretty much all of humanity, and I wanted to know if genocide was still on the table for him.

"I am to determine if there are warriors worthy of joining his army," Anthony said.

Alarm bells started ringing in my head. "Is he planning an invasion or something?" If Oberon was moving against this world, I was going to have to abandon ship and call in some heavy reinforcements. I don't know much about Faerie, but I know there are a buttload of different magical creatures there, and most of them could turn humans into sausage without batting an eye.

"Not of this plane," Tony replied. "We cannot exist apart from the magics of Faerie indefinitely. Attacking this world would be pointless for him. I believe he has designs on expanding the boundaries of Summer, either by attacking the Shadow Realm, or moving on Winter."

I felt some of the tension flow out of my shoulders. I did *not* relish the thought of a battalion of badass Anthonys staring at me in full arms and armor. "Well?" I asked. "You find anybody yet?"

The whole table chuckled, and I realized they thought I was applying for the job. I held up both hands in mock surrender. "Not me, bro! One, you kicked my ass while barely breaking a sweat, and two, I don't like mushrooms on my burger, much less going through rings of them to travel to a magical realm. I'm just curious, is all."

Tony smiled at me and said, "I have my eye on a few people, but I will only be allowed to return home as a champion, so I must first defeat one or more of our tablemates. Then I can decide if anyone is worthy to fight alongside King Oberon's banner with me."

The others at the table didn't seem offended at the idea of squaring off against Anthony. In fact, they all kinda looked excited at the prospect. I was definitely sitting with a bunch of people who liked to kick ass for ass kicking's sake. That's never been my thing. I fight when I have to, but if I throw down, it's usually to defend someone who needs my help. Or if someone impugns the dubious honor of my family. But there was a lot more of that when I still thought I was human. I got in a *lot* of fights over Stoker's book when I was a kid. Something about a kid in a newsboy cap calling my mom a fang-sucker was guaranteed to get me seeing red.

I was lost in thought, dwelling on my misspent youth, when an unfamiliar bell rang. Everyone got up and carried their trays over to a conveyor along one wall, and I followed. "What's going on?" I asked.

"Communal exercise time," Anthony said. "Happens once every couple of weeks. I think the boss likes to throw a bunch of idiots into a pot of boiling water just to see what floats to the top. Lower tier fighters get to challenge higher tiers for their spot, so keep your eyes open."

"You think they'll come at me?" I asked.

"You're the newest Tier Four. They've seen you a little, but I'd put good money on there being at least three or four mid-level guys willing to try themselves against you."

"Great." I didn't feel much like a fight, but knew I'd need to keep my reputation intact or I'd never figure out what the fuck was going on in this place. So far, I'd found a fight club and seen that there was money being wagered, but hadn't figured out why they were kidnapping people to fight and how they stayed under the radar. With audiences the size they were drawing, how had I not heard about this place sooner? No, I needed to stay in at least a couple more days. Now that I was among the top tier of fighters, I hoped I could get more intel. And to get more intel, I needed to stay at the top of the rankings.

Which meant that whoever wanted to dance with the Reaper in the playground was about to get a serious ass whooping.

25

When I stepped into the arena, all eyes were on me. The alpha dogs I'd been having breakfast with all peeled off to their own corners of the yard, selecting weight benches or pull-up bars with a good view of the crowd. I just walked over to a nearby wall and leaned against it, waiting. I figured it wouldn't take long for someone to feel frisky and want to test themselves against the new guy. I didn't expect it to be the shifter I'd pummeled into oblivion less than twelve hours before.

Bobcat looked none the worse for wear after me almost giving him a traumatic brain injury the night before, and he held up both hands as he walked up. "I don't want no shit, man," he said.

I didn't reply. He stepped to me, it was on him to make the first move, either by throwing down or saying what he wanted. He shuffled his feet a little and looked slightly embarrassed, like he didn't know how to spit it out. How this guy ended up in a fight club I couldn't fathom. After a moment almost as awkward as a teen rom-com, he spoke again.

"I just wanted to say good fight, man. No hard feelings or nothing." He still didn't meet my eyes, but he stepped closer and held out his right hand. I took it and gave it a shake.

Which was when he clamped down on my hand with his shifter strength and threw a punch for my throat. So much for no hard feelings. I slid my left foot back, shifting my body sideways and feeling his fist rush by my neck, then I shot forward, ramming my elbow into the bridge of his nose, shattering it and causing blood to gush down his face like a crimson waterfall. He tried to let go of my hand, but I wasn't quite ready to give him an escape. I slammed three more quick lefts into his face, then released his right hand. He took a couple of shaky steps backward, putting him at the perfect distance for me to lay him out cold with a big roundhouse kick.

I don't do too many flashy kicks, because most of the time it's better if I either stay close to my opponent and beat the fuck out of them, or stay very far away from my opponent and blast them with fireballs. But I was surrounded by a dozen or so lower-tier fighters who wanted to move up by stepping on my carcass, so I figured a little razzle-dazzle would deter the more sensible among them.

Three. I managed to deter three. Apparently "sensible" isn't a word often used to describe paranormals and cryptids who volunteer to participate in unregulated fight clubs. Although it's probably not used to describe human cage fighters very often, either. There's nothing sensible about voluntarily getting your head kicked in on the regular.

There's even less that's sensible about standing in the middle of a dirt-floored arena and letting a bunch of cage fighters jump you, so I retreated to put my back to a wall, hoping to limit the number of idiots I had to tangle with to a reasonable number.

"I got next!" called a voice from the back of the pack, and a skinny Black man with narrow features and long dreadlocks charged at me. I braced myself to meet his attack, but he dropped into a baseball slide a couple feet in front of me and kicked up a plume of sand into my face. I coughed and wiped my eyes, but he was on me, raining down punches and kicks like the second coming of Bruce Lee. He even did the weird vocal noises Lee used to make in his movies, which defeated the whole purpose of kicking dirt in my eyes. What good is it to blind somebody when you're just going to announce your location a second later?

I dropped to one knee to cover my head and vital organs, and called power to wrap a shield around myself. My power was still at full flow, as strong as it had been ever since I woke up, so I was able to use some of that energy to heal my bruises, and the rest to keep from getting any new ones. After a couple seconds of rapid blinking, my vision cleared, and the next time Dreadlocks came in, aiming a kick at my skull, I stood up and grabbed him by the ankle.

He was not a large man, maybe five-eight and a hundred fifty pounds, so I wrapped both hands around his ankle and snatched him up into the air. I turned around in a circle twice, then released him like I was at a Highland Games, sending his scrawny ass flying across the arena and taking down three spectators like I was picking up a spare at my bowling league.

I channeled a little power into my eyes, making them glow purple, and looked at the gathered morons who wanted to step to me. "Next," I growled, kinda hoping no one would want a piece of me.

I shoulda known better. This time they didn't bother trying to play King of the Mountain and take me down one by one. This time four of the assholes rushed me all at once. A big hairy motherfucker with biker tats and a beard you could hide a family of mice in came at me from the left. Next to him was a wiry little Asian dude with a shaved head, twirling a pair of long knives and grinning like he knew the punchline to a joke no one had told yet. Then there was a milque-toast-looking ginger with freckles on his freckles, a hairstyle right out of Riverdale High, and a feral grin like he wondered what my liver would taste like. A pair of long fangs poking out of his smile told me that the first vampire had entered the chat. And finally, rounding out the Four Horsemen of the Assholepocalypse, came a spectacularly obese man with stringy black hair, a patchy beard that looked like a shag carpet with mange, and fists the size of softballs. He didn't look like he could fight worth a fuck, but he definitely looked like it would be work to get any damage to his vital organs, on account of all the lard armor he was coated in.

"Okay, fuckers," I said, letting a wild grin dance across my face. "Let's dance."

I bent my legs slightly and sprang straight up, shoving power through my feet to give me extra lift. I'd been magically handcuffed for days, so I might have overdone it, shooting better than ten feet straight up. I spun around in the air and cut a flip that I hoped looked as cool in real life as it did in my head, and dropped behind the Asian guy with the Ginsu fetish. I punched him in the center of his back, adding a little extra magical *oomph* to it, and heard the matchstick sound of ribs breaking under my knuckles. I grinned as he dropped to the dirt with a shriek. One down.

Archie the Vampire whirled around and leapt for me, but I flung up a shield and he slammed into it like something out of a *Tom & Jerry* cartoon. He actually slid straight down my shield, and I shoved my magically shielded right hand into his mouth as he lay gasping in pain. A pair of quick snaps of my wrist, a shriek from the writhing vampire, and I dropped his fangs onto the ground next to him. Two down.

Biker Tats was almost on me by then, and I held up my blood-streaked fist, calling power to wrap it in purple magic. "You really want to?" I asked, letting more power flow through my eyes. He decided that Tier Two (or Three, I neither knew nor gave a shit where he fought) was good enough for him and backed away, holding both hands up in surrender. Three down.

That's when the meat bulldozer hit me from behind. The problem with fighting fat guys isn't that they're fast, because they usually aren't. It's not that they're strong, although when somebody deadlifts four hundred pounds just getting off the shitter, there's gonna be some muscle under all the flab. No, the problem in fighting lardasses like the one that bowled me over into the dirt is that once they start moving in any direction, they're almost impossible to stop. And when you've got a body that could generously be called skinny, and used to raise money for undernourished children at worst, you just don't have enough mass to stop an object that size once it gets moving.

So I didn't. Lardass ran into me, then over me, and all I could do about it was groan and swear. Now I'm *very* good at swearing, but I've practically never won a fight on the basis of my profanity alone. I usually have to hit somebody, and I have to hit them in a vulnerable place. And when the guy I've got to hit is wreathed in a couple hundred pounds of personal insulation, there aren't very many vulnerable places. And I certainly can't reach them when I'm lying face down on the floor.

I've fought massive opponents before, human and otherwise, and they usually have similar fighting styles. Their plan usually goes something like this: knock me down, step on my back, step on my back again, and if I'm still breathing, belly flop on top of me until I die. Fortunately, I've managed to thwart the latter parts of this plan for a lot of years. Unfortunately, I end up getting knocked down and stepped on a lot. And this time I'd already spent a good bit of my magical reserves kicking the shit out of half a dozen other assholes. So I didn't have all that much left in the tank for this dipshit.

But I had some juice left. Not a lot, but some. And I'd be goddamned if I was going to go out squashed in the dirt like an overzealous grasshopper. So I took a gamble that he'd reflexively try to stomp on me with his right foot and rolled to my left. That put his foot slamming down right beside my elbow, with me wedged in between his ankles looking up. Not exactly where I wanted to be, but definitely in a spot where I could lock on a vital target barely needing to aim. I raised my arms up straight in the air and pointed my palms at his balls, then shouted, "*Fuego!*" at the top of my lungs.

Yeah, I threw a fireball at Fat Boy's taint. Not my proudest moment, but goddamned effective. Purple flame streamed from my palms into his crotch, and his shrieks sounded like someone was slaughtering an entire farm of pigs right over top of me. As this giant piggy went *wee-wee-wee* and started running around in circles, I rolled to my feet and looked around the room.

The gathered fighters were staring at me with their mouths hanging open, and silence fell across the crowd. Well, silence except for the whimpering of a corpulent asshole trying to put out the purple flames dancing across his nutsack. Every eye was on me as I looked from face to face, trying to see who wanted the next piece of me.

Turned out who wanted the next piece of me were the guards, because the door slammed open and four guys in body armor sprinted in to surround me. Pete followed them, looking disappointed and more than a little disgusted. "What the literal fuck, Murray? They just wanted a little scrap."

"I don't do little scraps. I either fight, or I don't fight. And if I fight, I win. Got a problem with that?" I snarled.

The guards backed up a step at my tone, but Pete just shook his head. "Come on," he said, turning around. "We gotta go see the Boss. Again."

I guess I was in trouble for getting in a fight at the fight club. Doesn't seem fair, does it?

26

M r. James, you are very quickly becoming a pain in my ass," the Boss said as Pete escorted me back into his office. I felt a little like the naughty kid getting dragged into the principal's office yet again, except in my case it was the head-master's office, but no matter which side of the pond I was on, it always ended up the same—the naughty boy got bent over the desk and his ass swatted with a paddle. Good thing I'm no longer what anyone would consider a naughty "boy."

"Yeah, I have that effect on people," I said, plopping down in one of the chairs in front of the big desk. I figured I'd go ahead and sit down, in case somebody got any bright ideas about paddling. Some people are into that, but it's never been my particular kink, and I sure as fuck wasn't interested in any of the dudes in that office.

"I didn't say you could sit," the Boss said, his tone icy.

"I didn't ask," I replied, my tone not giving a shit. I was getting frustrated. I'd been here two weeks, and I didn't feel any closer to figuring out who was behind all this than before I ever set foot on the Colosseum sand. Part of me didn't care, because that part of me was enjoying all the violence, but the reasonable parts of me missed Becks, missed my life, and missed knowing that the people I was beating the shit out of were the bad guys, at least as much as my bent-to-fuck moral compass could define a "bad guy."

"Look," I said, leaning forward and putting my elbows on my knees, "you and I both know that you're not calling all the shots in this operation. You might be the Boss in this building, but you're a middle manager at best. You don't get to execute me, at least not without approval from someone higher up the food chain than you, and you haven't had time to get that approval. So you didn't bring me in here to put a bullet in my skull. You brought me in here to bitch. Well, pal, I've been bitched out by better men, and *way* better women, so let's just put that shit on the back burner, pour a couple glasses of that fine Irish whisky I know you've got tucked away in one of those desk drawers, and have ourselves a wee dram before you get on with what you really want to say to me."

The Boss stared at me for a long moment, before bursting out in laughter. "Now I know why you never walk sideways, Murray James! You couldn't stand the clanging as those colossal brass danglers you got between your legs slam together!" He did indeed pull a bottle of whisky out of a drawer, set two glasses on his desk, and pour two fingers of amber liquid into each of them. I reached for one, and his hand snaked out lightning-quick to wrap fingers tough as steel cables around my wrist.

"You're right, lad. I can't kill you without permission from the owner of this here fine establishment, but that doesn't mean I can't make it so you die in your next match. You've proved yourself the master of handicap matches, winning a couple of those already, but let me tell you this, and know I tell you true—you put one more fucking foot wrong with me, you do another goddamned thing to make my life more difficult, and I will make sure you end up as the first man into a battle royal this weekend that will make *The Hunger Games* look like a Ping Pong tournament. Do we have a fucking understanding?"

The look he gave me wasn't even a little bit angry; that was what made it scary. In fact, the grin never left his face, but it never touched his eyes. This was a man who never met a rule he couldn't twist to his own devices, and one who was very willing to sacrifice me and anyone else on the pyre of his own self-interest. And that, not his authority, was what made him dangerous. This guy had the intelligence to manipulate the rules to fit his needs, and the moral flexibility to not feel even the least bit bad about it. That is not a man to fuck with unless you know you're the one doing the fucking.

I held his gaze, and it was like staring into the eyes of a cobra. He looked deep into my soul and didn't flinch, which is not something many mortals can manage. After a long stare, I nodded. "We have an understanding."

He let go of my wrist, leaned back in his chair, and sipped his whisky. "Good. Glad to hear it. Now what the fuck am I supposed to do for my fights on Wednesday? You just put most of Tier Two in the hospital with your little stunt."

"Well, Boss, if they weren't ready for the champ, they shouldn't have stepped in the ring," I said, sipping my own drink. It had a nice burn to it, going down smooth as glass and setting a nice little campfire in my belly. The Irish make good liquor, but most of the best booze comes from the UK, if I'm being honest. And I try never to lie about alcohol. Except tequila. But all good tequila is laced with magic, so it doesn't really count.

The Boss laughed and poured himself another drink, then put the bottle back in his drawer before I could help myself to one. Asshole.

"Be that as it may, I now have to shuffle some things around for the midweek fights. Normally I would have you tangle with one of the Tier Three fighters as a tune-up for your first Tier Four fight this weekend, giving the audience a look at your skills to determine how much to wager on or against you. Unfortunately, you just took out most of the Tier Three fighters I would have paired you with, so I must adjust the fight card accordingly. So I will give you a choice."

I raised an eyebrow. "A choice? I didn't think this place was much on democracy."

"It isn't, but as I mentioned, you are becoming a pain in my ass, so it behooves me to keep you at least moderately happy with your lot in life here. So I will give you a choice. You can participate in a first-blood Battle Royal against all the unpaired fighters in Tiers Two and

Three, where you will have plenty of opportunity to showcase your skills, albeit against less challenging opponents, or we can offer the crowd something they may actually be interested in seeing—a rematch."

There it was. He assumed that I'd want to kick Tony's ass to get some of my own back after being embarrassed last week. And if I was somebody who actually gave a shit about building a reputation in his little club, I would want exactly that. Problem was, I kinda *liked* Tony, and now that I knew his deal, I also knew that he might be the most dangerous opponent in the entire place. Not just because faerie knights are incredibly strong, fast, and well-trained, but also because I liked him. And since I liked him, I would be inclined to pull my punches, which would get me dropped on my ass again and sent back to Tier Three. That wouldn't get me any closer to the top of the heap and wouldn't get me home to Becks any faster. This little ass-kicking summer camp was fun, but two weeks away from my fiancée was starting to wear on me. I missed my cat, too.

"How about a different idea?" I asked.

"What do you have in mind?"

"Who's your Main Event guy for this weekend?"

"My *guy* for this weekend isn't a guy. This weekend's Main Event will be one of you top-tier fighters squaring off against Eleanor. This will be her fifth Main Event. If she wins this Saturday, she retires as a Grand Champion."

"But you haven't decided who gets a shot at her yet?"

"Not yet, no."

"Then let us fight for it," I said. I started ticking off names on my fingers. "Me, Janik, Steven, and Anthony square off, and the last one standing gets the shot at the baddest chick in town. Don't do any other bouts with top-tier fighters, just a four-way dance to see who gets a shot at the brass ring. It'll probably go a lot longer than most of your one-on-one fights because people will make and break alliances mid-match, so you can get the same excitement from the crowd with fewer fights, and probably even more betting, because the line on who wins a four-way brawl will be tighter than a solo bout."

Bossman closed his eyes for a moment, considering my proposal, then nodded. "Not a bad idea, Mr. James. Not a bad idea at all. Yes, I think a Number One Contender's Match seems like exactly the way to fill out the card, and build excitement for this weekend. But I think we may need to insert an element of randomness into the match."

I didn't say anything, letting him cook on whatever idea he had in his twisted little noggin. A small smile flickered across his face, and he leaned forward, his arms on his desk.

"Yes, Mr. James, we'll have a Battle of the Contenders. But every two minutes, an additional wild cryptid or paranormal creature will be set loose in the arena. So you won't just have to vanquish other fighters, you'll also have to defend against monsters. Very hungry monsters, who find human flesh to be something of a delicacy."

Great. Not only did I talk myself into a fight against not one, but three incredibly dangerous pit fighters, this sadistic assclown just added monsters into the mix. And not a Bubba in sight. With my luck, I was going to be the one with my hands full of Sasquatch schlong by the time all was said and done.

27

I wasn't the most popular dude in the Thunderdome the next couple of days, as each of my Tier Four cohorts thought they should have an uncontested path to fighting Eleanor in Saturday's Main Event. I didn't bother telling them that I was saving their asses. I studied Eleanor with my Sight, and she was one badass vampire, and then some.

See, Eleanor wasn't just a vampire, she was also a mage. In talking with Luke, I learned that if someone who had aptitude for magic was turned, they didn't lose their ability to sling spells. No, they kept their magic, and added speed, agility, stamina, and an almost unmatched healing ability to it. And some peculiar dietary restrictions, but it wasn't that much of a drawback, unless you were addicted to sunbathing. Or a vegan. And from what I could tell, Eleanor had been around longer than the concept of vegans had existed.

I asked him once if that was my deal, if I could use magic and some of the vampire traits that I had, but the explanation was so convoluted with its combination of magic, demonic possession, and science that my eyes glazed over before he finally landed on "I don't know" as an answer. What I did know was that Eleanor and I weren't the same, but

I probably had the greatest chance of surviving against her out of any of the top-tier fighters.

So I ate my meals alone for the next couple days, worked out alone, and hung out in my room alone. Just me and the voice in my head. At least the voice in my head really belonged to someone else and wasn't a hallucination.

If I was, I'd be the hottest hallucination you've ever had, Becks said into my skull.

I grinned. *You're damned right.*

Can you win this fight, Harker? There's three of them, and only one of you.

Yeah, but it's every man for himself, so it's not like they're going to gang up on me or anything.

Are you high? Of course they're going to gang up on you. From what I can eavesdrop, they're pissed *at you. Except for your buddy Tony, who's all bound up in his honor and knighthood stuff. Those other two would like to rip your head off and shit down your neck.*

That seems to be a popular metaphor around this place, I replied.

What I'm saying, Harker, is don't fuck around with these guys. They're at least in the same ballpark of badassdom as you, or they wouldn't be in the top ranks with you. And Janik and Rat-Faced Steve are going to get in there, make some kind of bullshit temporary alliance, kick the ever-loving shit out of you, and then fight each other to see who gets to die to the vampire chick on Saturday.

You talk like you've seen this kind of fight before, I said, chuckling to myself.

I grew up watching the Royal Rumble. *I know the script. So don't screw around, keep your head on a swivel, and be ready to bust out moves you haven't let them see before. Because if you don't, you're gonna get hurt. Bad. Or worse.*

We're not supposed to fight to the death tonight, I said.

Yeah, and nobody's ever accidentally *died in a cage fight.* It's amazing how sarcastic someone can sound when you're communicating mind-to-mind.

I'll be careful.

You better. Because if you get yourself killed, I'll kick your ass.

Love you, too. I tamped down our connection because I could hear Pete's footsteps in the hall outside.

He pulled my door open and stuck his head in. "You ready, Murray?"

I got off my bed and rolled my head from side to side, loosening up my muscles a little. "Yeah, let's do this thing."

The four of us stared across the sand at one another, nobody wanting to be the first one to commit to an attack. We all knew that we had less than two minutes before some monster was going to be set loose on us through small doors set into the arena walls, but we also knew that whoever charged first gave away their strategy, and thus a little bit of an edge. As long as no one knew where you were planning to strike, they had to defend against every angle. So nobody moved. And nobody moved. And then nobody moved a little more.

Finally, I just said, "Fuck this noise," and called across the sand, "Tony, let's dance!" Then I sprang halfway across the arena floor in one massive leap, landing in a perfect superhero pose half a second before Anthony dropped out of the sky in front of me. I lashed out with one leg, trying to sweep his feet out from under him, but he vaulted forward over me into a crisp handspring, then spun on his hands like a breakdancer, throwing kicks at my face.

I dropped flat onto my back, then rolled back onto my shoulders into a nip-up, but Tony got there first. I stuck the landing, but as my body snapped forward, I slammed into a waiting fist and my feet went out from under me. I flopped onto my back without even an iota of control, but had the foresight to call up a shield and spin that over myself to deflect the elbow that came crashing down onto my magically defended sternum. I focused my will and pushed the shield outward from my body, flinging Anthony into the air, and scrambled to my feet.

Janik was there, moving faster than anyone with that many

muscles had a right to, and I barely ducked a fist the size of a Christmas ham as he swung a punch at my face. I grabbed his wrist and used his momentum against him, flipping him onto his back and giving him a stomp to the gut that took his breath and left him writhing on the sand for a few seconds.

I looked around for Tony, but saw him tangling with Steve, who'd traded in his dining hall cutlery for a pair of fighting knives that he whipped around with blinding speed. Anthony dodged every strike, but Steve seemed to get faster as they danced. Left momentarily without a dance partner, I glanced over at the doors where I expected the monsters to come through, only to see it sliding closed behind the biggest goddamned rattlesnake I'd ever seen.

Now I've traveled a lot of the world, and I've been to some deep jungles, some remote mountains, and some places that the maps don't even show as places. For most of my life, I thought I knew every monster in the world, and until a few years ago when I found out that dragons are real, I'd seen nothing to disabuse me of that notion. But nowhere in my experience did twenty-foot rattlesnakes exist in the same world as me, and I was pretty goddamned happy about that.

And yet, here one was, slithering across the sand with its rattle sounding like a goddamned percussion section, heading straight for Tony's unprotected back. Anthony was still tangled up with Steve the Knife Festishist and wasn't going to have time to turn and deal with the snake before it sung foot-long fangs into his ass. And while I wanted to beat all three of these guys, I didn't necessarily want to kill any of them, and Tony less than most.

So I fireballed the snake. I'm not proud of my moment of bullshit heroism, going against my plan of "every asshole for himself," but I did it. I called up power, swirled it into a glowing orb of purple flame, and sent it streaking across the arena to hit the snake right between its beady little snake eyes.

Tony saw the fireball heading his way and spun to the left, earning himself a gash along the ribs from Steve in the process, and just before he let out a profanity-filled tirade in my direction, he happened to glance over and see enough dead rattler to make an entire snakeskin tuxedo lying on the ground. He mouthed a "thanks" in my direction, right before his eyes went wide and he opened his mouth to yell.

I didn't turn around, didn't wait to hear what Anthony was trying to tell me, I just leapt forward, trying to put as much distance between me and what I assumed was a recovered Janik as possible. It wasn't enough. The musclebound asshat caught me by one ankle as I jumped, and slammed me into the ground like Hulk did to Loki in the *Avengers* movie. Then, because apparently Mark Ruffalo is his hero, he picked me up and did it again. And again.

But I'm not Loki. Or any kind of Norse deity, and I'm also a little stouter than Tom Hiddleston, so when he picked me up to slam me to the turf a fourth time, I decided enough was absolutely fucking enough, and I summoned my soulblade. The flaming white blade of pure mystical energy came to life in my hand, and I lashed out blindly, hoping to keep from getting used as a blunt object for the rest of my possibly short life.

I didn't see what I cut, but I flew a good ten feet across the arena before crashing to the ground and rolling to a stop. Lucky for me the soulblade winked out of existence the second I let go of it, or I probably would have gutted myself on my own weapon. I struggled to my feet, trying to poke my ribs back in place, and looked back at Janik.

"Oops," I said, staring at the muscle-bound screaming man across the ring from me. Blood spurted between his fingers as he clapped his left hand to a huge gash in his right shoulder. Apparently with great muscles comes great blood flow, because a great amount of blood was flowing out of his upper arm. I didn't even know there was that much blood *in* an arm. Well, Janik was out of the fight, so now it was time to concentrate on Steve, Tony, and whatever critters the Boss sent out after us next. One down, and...many to go?

Anthony and Steve were going at head other hammer and tongs. And seriously, these are like the least intimidating monster names ever. Even WWE does better. At least they came up with "The Boogeyman," although they also put the belt on a white guy named John almost twenty times. But really, after vanquishing a muscle-bound bruiser named Janik, now I was supposed to fight…Tony and Steve? It felt like a rewatch of *Civil War*. All I needed was for one of them to say they could do this all day.

And frankly, it looked like they both *could* do this all day if they needed to. The faerie knight and the were-rat had obviously sparred together a lot because they knew all of each other's moves and counter-moves. Whenever Steve slashed out with his blades, Tony leaned back just enough to get out of the way, but never so much that he overbalanced and couldn't respond with a quick punch or kick. It was kinda like watching a masterclass in close-quarters combat, except for the fact that I either had to tip the scales, or fight the winner. And I wasn't completely sure I could take either of them in a fair fight.

Good thing the Boss didn't give a shit about fair, then, wasn't it? As I stood off to one side of their lethal waltz, trying to find the perfect spot to cut in and reduce my number of opponents by one, two doors opened in the arena walls. Apparently as the number of fighters dropped, the number of monsters was going to increase. Fantastic. I could only hope it wasn't going to be another goddamned snake.

So of course as soon as I saw what it was, I wished it was another goddamned snake. This time it was a pair of monsters converging on us from opposite sides of the arena, and at least one of them was going straight for Tony. It was a little bastard, but I knew this was one situation where size definitely didn't matter because the three-foot tall hunch-backed creature with a sickle in each hand and razor-sharp teeth was grinning as it charged the faerie knight, eager for a nibble on some royal seelie ass.

If its appearance didn't give it away, the blood dripping from its crimson newsboy hat certainly would have. This was a redcap, a fae monster with a taste for blood, and the more the better. Legend said that its hat wasn't actually red when it was first acquired, but that the monster dipped it in the blood of its victims so often that it was permanently dyed. And it was streaking across the sand at Tony's unprotected back.

Just as I readied myself to jump in and help a guy who I would have to then try to beat the shit out of, I remembered that there was another door, and probably another monster. I whipped my head around just in time to meet the fist of a massive Torment demon, all eight feet tall and literally bulletproof of him. I turned my head enough that the first punch didn't catch me square, but the follow-up shot to my ribs lifted me off my feet and dropped me to my knees. I was spending way too much time in this fight staring either at the dirt or the lights, but before I could solve that problem, I had to not get my ribs staved in by the massive foot swinging at them.

I caught the demon's shin under my arm, getting a good grip on the beast's leg, and stood, throwing the demon off balance. It dropped to its back on the sand, and as its other leg came up, I tucked that under my other arm and started to spin. It took a few revolutions before the centrifugal force kicked in and floated the eight-foot-tall demon off the sand, but after a few high-speed spins, I was able to let go of the beast's ankles and send it sailing. I got good air, sending the demon a good twenty feet before it slammed to the dirt, but I had barely a second to catch my breath before a flicker of light drew my attention, and I got a shield-wrapped arm up barely in time to send one of Steve's throwing knives clattering away.

I glared at the smirking were-rat, who gave me a "had to try" shrug before turning back to Tony, who was now dividing his attention between Steve and the redcap, who had eyes only for the faerie knight. I held no illusions about that, though—the second Tony went down, the redcap would be after another target. They're the Tasmanian Devils of Faerie—complete psychopaths that exist only to shred anything in their path. If Anthony went down, one of us would have to deal with the redcap, but we'd be doing it without the expert in kicking faerie ass.

But for now, I had a Torment demon to deal with. Now, Torment demons are like the offensive linemen of the demon world. They're huge, strong as fuck, and almost impervious to pain. They have some magic resistance, and they're completely immune to mundane weapons, but the biggest problem, aside from their strength, speed, razor-sharp claws, and general hunger for blood and agony, is their healing. They can heal from almost any injury, so usually you only get one shot to kill them. And the time for my one shot was fast approaching, as the demon I'd flung across the ring was now on his feet and hauling ass back in my direction, looking even more pissed off than before, if that was possible.

The last time I tangled with Torment demons, I'd had a whole team of superfriends by my side. This time, I had just my power, my wits, and a few new dirty tricks I'd learned in the past half a dozen years. One of those dirty tricks involved, coincidentally enough, sand and the application of a fuckton of heat to it. I stretched out my arms at the ground in front of the charging demon, called power, and shouted, "*Fuego!*" at the top of my lungs. Fire streaked from my palms to the sand, turning it to glass and trapping the demon in mid-stride.

For about half a second. I didn't expect a full-grown Torment demon to be stopped by essentially a set of glass ankle bracelets, and it wasn't. What I did expect was a sheet of glass to coat the ground in front of me, splintering with the first step of the demon's heavy foot. Which happened. I also expected to be able to grab one of those splinters and wrap it in my own magic, which also happened. Then I took my improvised sword and, dropping to one knee to give me a stronger base to strike from, swung the magically imbued shard at the onrushing demon's midsection, slicing it neatly in half right above its bellybutton.

That Newton guy was pretty smart because the demon in motion definitely stayed in motion, even though its brain was no longer communicating with its feet. The demon took two full steps before it got the message that it was now two halves of a demon instead of one whole, and fell to the sand in a messy *splat* of entrails, organs, and blood.

"No healing from that, bitch," I said, tossing the shard of glass to the ground and turning to look at the trio of Tony, Steve, and the redcap.

Except it wasn't a trio anymore. Steve was lying on the ground screaming and clutching his knee, and Tony had two of the were-rat's knives buried in the redcap's eye sockets. As I watched, he dropped the fae creature's corpse to the sand, wiped his blades on the monster's pants, and turned to me with a grin.

"Ready for a rematch, Murray?" he asked, tossing the knives aside and raising his hands in a guard position.

"You could always just concede," I replied, calling a shield around my left forearm and rolling my head from side to side. I was low on mojo after turning ten feet of sand to glass with magical fire, but I knew that the only way I'd beat a faerie knight in a clean fight was if he had both hands tied behind his back in cold iron shackles.

"Where's the honor in that?" Anthony asked, closing his eyes for a moment. When he opened them, he was arrayed in his full armor, somehow having summoned it through the Colosseum's defenses.

That's just not fucking fair, I thought. *I have to spend magic like it's water dealing with a Torment demon, and he blinks his eyes and ends up wearing full plate armor.*

You're right, Becks' voice came in my head. *It's not fair. But when have you ever given a single solitary shit about fair? Suck it up, Buttercup, you've got a fight to win and a faerie's ass to kick. Now take off your fucking skirt and go be the badass motherfucker you claim to be!*

As motivational speeches go, it was pretty goddamned good. I summoned my soulblade, expanded my energy shield to cover my whole body, and saluted Anthony with my blade. "Let's dance, motherfucker," I said, letting a grin slide across my face.

I could barely see Tony's matching grin through his helm, then he leapt at me with a battle cry, covering twenty feet in a single bound. I didn't try to jump up and meet him, because like Tom Petty said, coming down is always the hardest goddamned thing. I just watched him fly, judging his descent carefully, then stepped to the side and slashed at his midsection with my flaming sword.

He blocked my slash, and the ring of enchanted steel versus magical blade was nearly deafening, drowning out the roar of the crowd for a moment. Then he was spinning, raising his blade in a parry, and striking down at my skull. I couldn't tell if he was trusting me to be good enough to dodge or block his lethal strikes, or if he was just all wrapped up in bloodlust and didn't give a shit if he killed me. It didn't matter, I was in a fight for my life whether I meant to be or not.

I slid sideways and spun, letting my momentum carry me into what would have been a devastating cut across his middle if I'd connected. Of course I didn't, as Tony swung his sword around to block. I pushed forward, trying to bind his blade with mine, but he spun his sword around as he backed away, pulling the hilt from my hand. He grinned as my soulblade winked out of existence, and rushed me, grinning.

"I thought you would know better than to let yourself be disarmed so easily, Murray," he said as he came at me.

"I thought you would know better than to let me call up my soulblade right into your guts," I replied, a wicked grin of my own splitting my face as I did just that. A gleaming three-foot blade manifested in my hand as he ran toward me, and as I swatted his blade away with my shielded left hand, I shoved the entire sword into his chest, letting his momentum carry him onto my blade. I swear I saw the white flames flicker in his eyes as the sword emerged from his back, but it was probably an illusion.

"Well, fuck," he said, sagging against me as he dropped his own blade to the ground. I caught him, banishing my soulblade with a thought, and immediately started pouring power into my wounded… okay, friend probably isn't the right word, but it's as close as anything I've got.

Either way, I threw power at him until the worst of his wounds healed, and I shouted to the ceiling, "A little help in here!"

All the doors in the walls opened, and a team of white-clad minions flowed out into the arena to tend to both Steve and Anthony. I stepped back to let them do their work and shouted up at the luxury boxes, "As if there was any fucking doubt, here's your winner, MURRAY FUCKING JAMES!"

29

S o am I in trouble again for cutting the shit out of Janik?" I asked Pete when he came to escort me to breakfast. I was a little surprised to see him, as he'd mostly stopped playing babysitter a while back. Now the only times he popped by my room was when I'd pissed off the Boss. Which meant that I still saw him almost every day, given my typical behavior around authority figures.

"Nah, the healers fixed him up right after the fight," Pete said. "I just wanted to give you the rules on Saturday Night's fight. The Main Event runs a little different from all the other tiers."

"Wait a minute," I said, holding up a hand. "There are healers?"

Pete looked surprised that I didn't know this. "Of course we have healers on hand. We can't have our best fighters going down with an injury right before a big fight. That would hurt the bottom line."

"So why the fuck did everybody get all bent out of shape when I fucked up the losers in the yard a few days ago? The way the Boss was acting, you'd have thought I tore up a picture of the Pope on live TV."

Pete looked confused, and I was reminded how much older I was than everyone I knew except Luke. I waved a hand in his direction. "Never mind. It's a pop culture reference from before you were born.

But what the fuck, man? Why did I catch so much shit for hurting those assholes if there are healers right here in the building?"

Pete looked at me like I was being particularly dense. "The healers are for top-level fighters. We don't want to waste their energy on the lower- and mid-tier guys. We try to save them for when a big draw gets hurt, like Janik. If he bleeds out, then we're short a Tier Four fighter, which means less money wagered, and maybe even fewer tickets sold. That costs the Boss real money. Some Tier Two dipshit picks a fight he can't win, gets his guts strewn all over the Colosseum, and nobody gives a shit, because he hasn't had time to build a fanbase. It's just like real life, Murray. The stars get all the perks, and the schlubs get the shit."

"So what about you, Pete?" I asked, thinking this might be my opening. "Are you a star or a schlub?" I figured if I could get Pete to break ranks with the Boss, even once in a private conversation, I might have a better chance of flipping him to my side and getting some real information out of him.

He just grinned at me. "Neither. I'm one of the smart ones. I don't fight, and I don't bet on the fights. I just do my job, collect my pay, and stay the fuck out of the arena."

I shook my head, a little disgusted. "Like a drug dealer that doesn't ever sample his own product, just gets everybody in the neighborhood hooked then profits off them."

Pete didn't catch the insult for what it was. "Exactly, my friend. Exactly." He walked over to sit on my bed, since I was currently parked in the room's only chair. Tier Four got me a swanky room, but it was still a glorified cell. A cell with a nice bed, jacuzzi tub, and a bigger TV than I had in my own apartment, but a cell nonetheless. And I still had that fucking collar around my neck, with an explosive charge tucked right against the base of my skull. I've survived a lot in my time, including actually being dead once, but I had my doubts about coming back from a grenade exploding right against my medulla oblongata.

Pete sat cross-legged on my bed and clicked off the TV to make sure he had my full attention. "Here's the deal with the Main Event. It's a fight to the death or to incapacitation. And this time we mean serious incapacitation, the kind your opponent isn't coming back from without major healing magic."

"So basically to the death," I said.

Pete smiled a sheepish smile. "Yeah, it's a fight to the death. I just don't usually say that part out loud in case someone gets squeamish."

"I've been cage fighting against monsters for two weeks so a bunch of rich assholes can get richer while we bleed. I think squeamish went out the window after my second bout," I replied.

"Fair enough. So yeah, you're fighting to the death, and you know your opponent—Eleanor. She's the closest thing we've had to a Grand Champion in a couple years, so the betting is heavy. If you want to place a wager on yourself, the odds are really heavy on the opposite side, so your payoff would be massive." He sat back and looked at me, grinning.

"And if I lose, I'll be dead, so it's not like I can bet on Eleanor and collect, huh?"

"Yeah, pretty much."

"How much cash do I have in my account?" I asked, more out of a desire to see what they had in the coffers at this joint than any interest in placing a wager. I was pretty sure I could take out one vampire, even one as skilled and powerful as Eleanor, but I didn't need the money. I invested wisely in my first century, and I've mooched off Luke for decades, so I'm pretty well set for dough.

"You got ten grand for winning the Contender's Battle Royal, plus two grand for winning the Tier Three fight before that, plus a grand for Tier Two, and five hundred for Tier One. You got docked two grand for losing your first Tier Three fight, but you won that back by beating two fighters in the makeup bout. So you have…" He counted on his fingers for a second, then beamed at me as he said, "Thirteen thousand, five hundred dollars that you can wager on yourself."

"That Battle Royal paid out ten grand?" I asked, a little stunned. There must have been a *lot* of money moving around this place.

"It counted as two Tier Four fights, and those pay five thousand to the winner, so it was worth ten."

"And what are the odds on my fight? I assume they're pretty heavy in Eleanor's favor."

"Oh, yeah," Pete said. "The odds right now are plus one thousand for you to win." Yeah, I was a massive underdog. If they ran their shit like a legit sportsbook, and it seemed like they were, that meant that if I bet a hundred bucks on myself, I'd get back a thousand. So basically a ten-to-one payout.

"Okay," I said. "Bet it all on myself."

"All of it?" Pete looked surprised.

"Why wouldn't I?" I asked. "If I lose, I'm dead, so there's no point in saving anything. I doubt you guys will be looking for my next of kin to give them the money left over in my underground fight club account after you bury me in a shallow grave somewhere."

Pete nodded. "Yeah, that's fair."

I continued. "And if I win, I get a hundred thirty grand and change to keep betting on myself until you figure out a way to kill me off or I retire as champ, right?"

He looked uncomfortable at me pointing out that I knew the deck was stacked, but finally answered. "Yeah, pretty much. Like I said, I've never seen anybody walk out of here as a Grand Champion."

"And I don't just get to randomly retire after tomorrow night, even if I win, do I? That's all bullshit, right?" I remembered some line about walking away after a couple big wins, but I could still feel the collar around my neck and was pretty sure that if I tried to take early retirement, the Boss or his real boss would go all Suicide Squad on me in a heartbeat.

Pete wouldn't look me in the eye, which told me a couple things. One, that he knew I was right, and two, that there might still be a decent person in there. Maybe I did have a chance at flipping him to my side and helping me shut this whole shitshow down. "No, you don't. If you beat Eleanor, the Boss is going to keep you here until you lose. After a couple Tier Five fights, there's just too much money to pay out if you walk away, so nobody gets to walk away. Sorry."

"Don't be sorry for me, pal," I said, standing up and cracking my knuckles. "Feel sorry for Eleanor and the next four assholes I have to beat to get out of here. Now let's go get some breakfast. Daddy needs bacon."

The rest of the week was light training, loading up on bacon and pancakes like I thought I was a dying man getting my last meal, and talking to Becks about how we were going to bring this whole place down. The biggest problem we were having was that they still weren't quite sure exactly where I was. We'd narrowed the search down to a five-mile radius north of the city, so somewhere around Concord or the speedway was the best guess we had. Not exactly perfect GPS coordinates.

So I studied Eleanor in our training time, but I could tell watching her that she was holding back, not showing all her moves in the arena. I didn't blame her because I was doing the same thing. Problem was, I *had* shown off my best moves when I fought Anthony and the others to get the chance to fight Eleanor, and now I was going to face off against an old, powerful vampire who'd spent the last several weeks destroying all comers in cage fights to the death. And my magical tattoos were almost completely depleted, so the only mojo I had was what I could build up normally. The power I usually stored in my ink was pretty well drained, which meant I was going to be heading back down to Atlanta soon for another eight-hour session of painful needlework. Assuming I survived the weekend.

Tony spent a few hours training with me, doing his best to mimic Eleanor's speed and strength. The problem was, very few creatures are anywhere near a vampire's speed, and the older the vampire, the faster they get. Fortunately for me, I've been practicing combat with what I assume is the oldest vampire in the world ever since I was old enough to get in any scraps more serious than a schoolyard brawl, so I knew how to anticipate and punch where the monster was going to be, not where they are. But I couldn't tell Tony that, and I didn't mind the workouts, so I pretended to be a little worse than I am, and he pretended not to notice me sandbagging.

But eventually, Saturday night rolled around and it was time to fight. I loaded up on breakfast, then had a very light lunch, not wanting to feel all bogged down when the bell rang. Also not wanting to shit myself in the middle of the Colosseum if she caught me with a stout punch to the gut. There are few things worse than fighting with your pants full of homemade chocolate syrup.

I waited until the early fights started, then reached out to Becks. *You there, babe?*

I'm here.

Any better idea on where I am?

I think so, actually. We might be able to get to you within the hour. Luke's been out ever since sunset chasing leads, and he just texted me an address and told me to meet him there as soon as I could. So I'm rounding up whatever reinforcements I can find and heading up the highway to what I hope is your location.

Reinforcements? I thought Glory and Faustus were still...I dunno, doing whatever redeemed fallen angels do.

They are, Becks replied. *But I've got a few people willing to lend a hand. I don't want to get your hopes up, but if things go the way I've planned, we should have enough firepower on our side to shut this place down completely.*

Good, because I'm ready to end this bullshit and come home.

You miss me, sweetheart? She somehow managed to make her mental voice sound both snarky and saccharine-sweet at the same time.

Hell yeah, I do, I replied. *I'm definitely not cuddling up to Anthony the Faerie Knight or Eleanor the Vampire at night.*

Well, don't get dead, and you can cuddle up to me in a few hours.

That's all the motivation I need. See you soon. Love you.

Love you too. Now go kick ass.

We cut our connection down to a trickle so I wouldn't get distracted by her thoughts, and she wouldn't get distracted by me bleeding, and I geared up for my fight. I had a fresh pair of jeans, one of those skintight Under Armour kind of shirts that's like yoga pants for your upper half, and my Doc Martens. I wanted to stay as light as possible, and since the Boss continued to turn down my request for a flamethrower in my matches, I didn't need any kind of holster.

Pete opened the door, and I followed him down the hall to the arena, noticing how everybody got out of my way and nobody met my eyes on the trip. I was a dead man walking to them, and nobody wanted to acknowledge their own mortality by being the last one to speak to me. Except Tony. He stood by the door, a bruise growing on his jaw from his own bout, which he'd obviously won, given the fact that he was standing.

"Good luck, Murray," he said. His face was grim.

"You don't look excited about winning," I said.

"I am not. If you lose, then someone I might consider a friend dies."

I got it then. "And if I win, you have to fight me next and only one of us gets out of that alive."

"Exactly."

I leaned in and gave him the one-armed bro hug, and as my head neared his, I whispered, "Stay on your toes. I don't plan on losing, and I don't plan on killing you in a week, either. So pay attention and when Plan C comes along, jump in."

He pulled back, a confused look on his face, but he nodded. "Good luck, Murray."

"Thanks, bud." And I stepped up to the door, waiting on my cue to enter.

Pete pulled the door open, and I stepped out into a darkened arena. I took about five steps forward, then a spotlight hit me. I've got enough of a sense of the theatrical to stand still, with my head down as the ring announcer spoke into his microphone.

"Ladies and Gentlebeasts, please welcome to the ring the newest challenger to our four-time champion Eleanor the Red. Remember, if she wins tonight, she becomes a Grand Champion and her name will be etched forever onto the Wall of Heroes in the lobby. But before that happens, she has to get through one of the most electrifying combatants we've ever seen here in the Colosseum. He is the nightmare walking, he is the random chromosome, he is the beast that walks out of the valley of the shadow of death. Please welcome tonight's challenger…MURRAY JAMES!!!"

I raised my head and threw my arms in the air, letting multicolored streamers of magic flow out of my fingertips to cascade all around me. The crowd went nuts, even though I knew damned well not a one of them had bet more than the price of a lunch on my winning. But I didn't give a shit. Becks said she was on her way, and I'd been fighting vampires since before I fought Nazis, so all I had to do was hold on long enough for the cavalry to arrive, and we could shut this place down. Then all I needed to do was some good old-fashioned detective work, follow the money, and find the asshole making paras and cryptids fight to the death for the amusement of a bunch of rich asshats.

As the applause for me died down, "We Will Rock You" came over the loudspeakers, and the whole crowd started stomping and clapping in unison. *Stomp-stomp-clap, stomp-stomp-clap.* Freddy Mercury's voice split the air, and colored beams of light played all across the sand as the house lights went out again. Just as the chorus kicked in and all the attendees started screaming in unison, the lights spun faster and faster until they all flashed white and focused on the figure standing a hundred feet away from me on the other side of the arena.

"AND NOW, please welcome back to the arena your champion, the sanguine mistress of mayhem, the blood-drinking battering ram of brutality, the death dealer, the soul stealer, the one and only… ELEANORRRRR!!!"

If I thought the crowd was nuts after my intro, they went

completely unhinged at this shit. There was screaming, there were flowers thrown, and there were proclamations of undying love and proposals of marriage. It was like Taylor Swift and the Beatles all showed up for the same party, with Elvis driving their limo.

I looked across the sand at Eleanor mugging for the crowd and kinda felt bad for her. She didn't seem all that awful for a centuries-old creature that legit has to murder people to live. And she had no idea that she was standing across the ring from the guy mama vampires tell little baby vampires stories about to get them to behave. She thought I was Murray James, kinda goofy wizard who got lucky a few times and she was about to rip into little pieces for the entertainment of the one percenters.

She had no fucking idea what she was in for.

Unlike all the other bouts I'd been in at the Colosseum, this one had a bell. An actual bell, like we were in a legitimate sporting event or something. I didn't know there was a bell, but I wasn't going to move before Eleanor did because the last thing I wanted to do was to give anything away to an opponent that dangerous. So even though I was a little caught off guard when the bell rang, at least it didn't interrupt me trying to make some kind of fancy attack or something.

Eleanor, on the other hand, absolutely knew there was a bell coming, and the second it rang, she launched herself at me. Apparently, she had zero interest in making a good show of things, and knew she wasn't getting paid by the hour, so she wanted to get this shit over with as quickly as possible. And with most opponents, just rushing at them from the left at full vampire speed would get the job done. I bet she'd ended more than one fight in the first few seconds, leaving her opponent with his throat in her teeth before the sound of the bell faded.

But I wasn't any opponent, and I wasn't watching her hands, or her feet, I was watching her eyes. So when the bell rang, and her eyes flicked to her right, I knew the attack was coming from my left. I sprang back about six feet, letting her pass through the space I'd recently occupied, then diving at her from behind when she stopped, confused. I tackled her around the waist, driving her face into the sand.

Normally I retain enough of my Victorian/Edwardian upbringing to be loath to strike a woman, but when the "woman" hasn't been human since before we invented the telephone, I give my chivalry a rest. So I drove her into the ground like an NFL linebacker and slammed an elbow into the back of her head. Vampires are just as susceptible to concussions as humans, and the best way I know to negate their speed advantage (other than decapitation) is to rattle their noggin enough that they're too dizzy to run at top speed.

But they also heal even faster than me, so any damage I did would repair itself in minutes, if not seconds. And a concussion doesn't make someone weaker. Eleanor got her hands underneath her body and shoved upward, sending me flying into the air to land flat on my back. But she wasn't fast enough to catch me in midair and rip my head off, so I had half a second after I slammed into the sand to roll up onto my feet and block her slashing strike at my midsection.

I glanced at her hand, seeing a gleam of metal, and saw that she had on blade-tipped gloves. Not quite a dime-store Wolverine, it looked more like cat's claws, only metal. Yet another reason I didn't want to let her get her hands on me. I kicked at her face, and she stepped back, easily avoiding my shot. But I didn't want impact, I wanted separation. I called power and flung three-inch spheres of pure energy at her, driving her back again and again.

Then I called up my soulblade and grinned at her across the floor. "Let's dance."

The feral smile that crept across her face matched my own, and she said, "Indeed, Mr. James. Indeed."

I almost outed myself right then, knowing that I could get a few seconds' advantage by telling her who I really was, but at the last instant I remembered the exploding collar around my neck. Probably shouldn't out myself as the Reaper until we found some way to make sure nobody could blow my head off with a garage door opener.

Eleanor leapt high into the air, her metal claws extending as she did and making me second guess my assessment that she wasn't a Wolverine clone somebody ordered off wish.com. I watched the arc of her leap and spun a quick glamour around myself, making it appear that I was standing perfectly still waiting to strike, when actually I stepped three feet to the left and readied my sword for a slash that would cut her in half the moment she landed.

Except you don't get to win four Tier Five death matches by being stupid. Eleanor must have realized something wasn't right in me just standing there, and instead of landing in a strike, dropped all the way to her belly as my blade whistled right over her head. She spun around and kicked my feet out from under me, making it my turn to slam into the dirt. Again. My hands flew open on impact, making my soulblade vanish, and I brought them together in front of me, spinning a shield of energy over my chest to deflect the claws coming for my entrails.

Eleanor's hands slid off my shield and she slammed into me, driving the breath from my lungs again. She wasn't very big, but solidly muscled, and she managed to drive a knee into my crotch as she scrambled off me. Even through my shield, I felt that shit. I rolled over and hopped up, whipping my head around to find her again, only to feel lines of fire blaze across my unprotected back as she got in a good slice.

"Fuck!" I yelled, profanity being a scientifically proven pain reliever.

"Too slow, Murray," she almost purred in my ear. "Time to die." I felt her hot breath on my neck and bent sharply at the waist, getting my carotid out of the way in the nick of time. Vampires can't drink from me and get any nutrients, on account of my weird part-vampire DNA, but an opened artery would still kill me in seconds, and dead is usually dead, whether I'm food or not.

I kicked backward, slamming my heel into her crotch and lifting her off the floor. That loosened her grip enough for me to break free of her, leaving bloody furrows from every fingertip along my arms and shoulders, but giving me that blessed separation again. I spun around, put both palms out, and shouted *"Forzare!"* channeling pure kinetic energy at her to blast her across ten feet of sand. Eleanor, as much a showman as a warrior, turned her backward momentum into a flip and landed, sliding across the floor in a perfect Black Widow pose.

"Poser," I said with a smirk, channeling my inner Florence Pugh. Then I called more power and shouted *"FUEGO!"* Fire streaked from my fingertips in ten narrow bands, cutting off the side-to-side escape routes. Eleanor shrieked as a tendril of flame burned her left thigh, and sprang straight up again, apparently deciding that the best way to avoid getting burned was to murder the one throwing fire at her.

She wasn't wrong. I dropped my flamethrower act and called my soulblade, slashing at her throat the instant she landed. She tried to block with her claws, but I don't know if even adamantium could stand up to pure focused magical energy, so I sliced off four claws on her left hand, along with the tip of her middle finger. She screamed and dove at me like a pissed off bloodsucking missile, abandoning all thoughts of playing to the audience and trying to just straight murder me. I dodged her rage-filled leap easily and said, "What's wrong, Ellie? Surprised to find a real challenge?"

She turned her dive into a roll, continued forward onto her feet, spun around, and leapt at me again. I dropped my magical sword and spun sideways, catching her in the midsection with a massive kick. She let out a *whoof* and crumpled around my foot but was too much of a warrior to let that stop her. She bent double but wrapped both hands around my thigh and stabbed me through the meat of my leg with her remaining claws.

Now it was my turn to scream and drop to the ground, more in an effort to shake her loose than in real pain, although there was fucking plenty of that. I needed to get her off my leg before she severed my femoral artery and ended the fight with the wrong person still standing. She rolled away from me and got to her feet, grinning.

"Who's found a challenge now, Murray? Now who's dripping their precious lifeblood onto the sand as he stares across the sand at a true apex predator? Now who's the one without any smartass comments, just the horrible knowledge that his death is staring him in the face?"

Yeah, that was pretty much me. But I couldn't let go that easily. Not only because I knew I'd used my one Get Out of Hell Free card, but also because I hadn't cracked the case yet. I didn't know who was behind this shit, and I didn't know how to stop them from serving up cryptids and paras to be slaughtered for the entertainment of a bunch of rich assholes. No, it wasn't time to die yet. So I didn't say anything, I just put my head down and charged, wrapping my left arm in a shield of pure energy and slamming into Eleanor, knocking her claws aside and throwing punch after punch at her ribs.

She just stood there, chuckling. I hammered fists into her midsection for all I was worth, and she just took a dozen of my strongest blows, then backhanded me almost out of my Docs. I flew several feet and spun to the dirt, spitting blood. Eleanor took two steps and kicked me in the ribs, sending spikes of agony through my chest and the sickening sound of snapping twigs through my ears. I couldn't scream, because I couldn't draw in a deep enough breath. But as I rolled over from the force of her kick, I kept rolling and staggered up to my feet.

"Stubborn," Eleanor said, her eyes glinting with predatory glee. "I like that. The fight makes the blood taste sweeter." She sprang into the air again, this time landing behind me, but I was ready. I knew that trick, so I spun in place and threw a punch that would have shattered her orbital socket if it connected.

Too bad it didn't connect. She moved her head barely an inch and my fist slammed through nothing but air. My guts erupted in fire as she drove her remaining claws into my middle, tearing even more flesh as she withdrew. She nailed me with an uppercut as I looked down at the four neat round holes gushing blood out of my abdomen, and I flew back to flop on the sand again.

I wanted to lay there and just bleed. I'd given her all I had, and she was too tough for me. I'd fought Luke for years, but he'd always been holding back, assuming I'd never face a foe with all his power and speed. But I thought I had it all scouted. I thought I knew how to kick ass, how to outsmart and outfight anything. Hell, I'd gotten one over on *Lucifer*, for fuck's sake. But now I was about to bleed out in the sand in an underground monster fight club, and nobody I cared about even knew where I was.

Well, fuck it, I thought. *Everybody dies alone.* But if I was going to die, and it was looking more and more likely that I was, I wasn't going to do it on my back. I rolled over, slowly got to my hands and knees, expecting every second for Eleanor to come rushing in and punt my skull right off my shoulders. But she hung back as I struggled to my knees, then one knee, then finally to my feet.

I turned to my right, spat blood onto the sand, and used the last of my stored energy to call up my soulblade, flickering now in my weakness. I was probably going to die, but goddammit, I was going to die on my feet.

Then with three words, everything changed.

On your left.

Becks knows that *Avengers: Endgame* is one of my favorite movies, and that the moment where Falcon flies through the portal to save Captain America's ass is one of the greatest movie moments I've ever seen. So when I heard those words in my head, I knew the cavalry had arrived, and it was time to tighten the straps on my shield and get the fuck back in the fight.

Glad you could make it.

Sorry about the delay. Traffic was a bitch. But we hacked into the building's system and got the collars turned off. You can stop fucking around with this bitch now and show her who she's really messing with.

You got it. And thanks.

I love you, asshole. Now end this, so we can go home.

I locked eyes with Eleanor and did the most terrifying thing an opponent can ever do when you're in a fight for your life. I smiled at her. I straightened up, pouring a little extra mojo into my leg to knit the flesh back together, and I smiled at her.

"Oh, I've found a challenge, Ellie," I said, using magic to amplify my voice so everyone in the building could hear me. Eleanor froze, completely dumbstruck by the change in my demeanor. Where a second ago I'd been focused and dangerous, but on the back foot and bleeding, now I stood before her grinning like a psychopath. Something had shifted, and she had no idea exactly what it was.

"But you have no fucking *idea* what you've found." I reached up to my throat and pulled at the collar. The metal resisted, but I poured a little extra magic into it, and it sprang open. "You see, my name isn't Murray James. James was my brother, who died a long time ago. And Murray? That was my mother's maiden name. Before she married my dad and took his surname. My real name is Jonathan Abraham Quincy Holmwood Harker, and I'm the son of Jonathan Harker and Mina Murray, nephew to Lucas Card, aka Vlad Tepes, aka Count Fucking Dracula."

"But you can just call me Reaper."

That's when the screaming started.

3 2

Now, I can be pretty scary sometimes. I'm frequently grumpy, perpetually snarky, and occasionally murderous. But the screaming in the middle of the underground bloodsport arena wasn't for me, even with my declaration of my true identity, which did have the intended effect of making Eleanor the vampire get even paler, which is a hell of a feat when your opponent doesn't make their own blood anymore. No, the screaming was because just as I made my grand pronouncement, the doors of the arena blew open from the outside and a stream of federal agents and werewolf bikers stormed the place.

At the same time, both doors of the arena blew off their hinges and flew inward as parts of Team Harker, along with my old friend Saint (who apparently was now my friend and not just a werewolf biker gang leader who frequently wanted to gnaw on my liver) stormed in from one direction as literally every fighter in the building stormed in the other.

The cheap seats emptied quickly, as people just dropped to their knees with their hands in the air. Those were almost all humans, and they didn't have a whole lot of interest in fighting cryptids themselves, just watching us fight each other. The luxury boxes were a little more interesting, as there were some private security guards who got overly enthusiastic for a few seconds, until the first lycanthrope ripped out the first throat. That had a chilling effect on the resistance.

None of this bled onto the arena floor, though. That chaos was all mine. Mine and Becks' and Luke's. My own personal Avengers stepped up beside me as I tried not to look nearly as beaten down as I felt, while a couple dozen paranormal cage fighters arrayed themselves across the sand at me, hurling insults, invectives, and threats in my direction. I let them go on for a few seconds while the cops and bikers corralled the spectators, then finally bellowed, "SHUT THE FUCK UP!" at the top of my lungs.

They did. I actually froze up a little, so stunned was I that everyone actually shut up. Then I remembered that I had shit to say. "Yeah, I'm Quincy Harker. No, I was never just a hapless goofball trying to win money fighting. No, I'm not sorry I lied to you all. Yes, I'm shutting this shit down right the fuck now. No, that's not up for debate. No, I don't give a shit if you were having fun beating each others' brains out. And no, they weren't ever going to let you leave with a bag full of cash. If you won your fifth main event, they were just going to send you to a farm upstate, or to the glue factory, or whatever stupid fucking metaphor you want to use for taking you out back and murdering the fuck out of you. And if you think I'm lying, go get Pete or any of the other guards and beat on them until they tell you the truth."

About half the fighters grumbled, but reluctantly nodded. They knew the score, even if they didn't want to admit it. About a quarter looked like they didn't believe a word that was coming out of my mouth, and about a quarter looked like they didn't give a shit, they just wanted to fight somebody. But the one I was most immediately concerned with looked like she knew the score and still wanted to kill me, and that was the one who had almost managed to do just that— Eleanor.

"I know who you are, Quincy Harker. You're the pitiful half-vampire lapdog of that dried up husk of a monster standing beside you. You used to be terrifying until you lost your edge. But lately you've been more retired than Reaper. You've spent so much time the last few years chasing your own personal demons that you've lost all relevance, and your useless 'uncle' is even worse. Vlad, you used to be a *force*, but now…now, you're just a farce. You may as well wear a velvet cape and decorate a cereal box. You're more mockery than monster, and I'll be happy to slaughter you both right here. The rest of you can have the human. She's barely worth a snack to me."

I'm killing this bitch myself, Becks said in my head.

Not if Luke gets to her first. And I'm not inclined to get in his way, I replied.

I glanced over at Luke, who let a tiny smile flicker across his lips before he took one step forward. "I wondered who was responsible for new vampires being turned right under my nose. None of the vampires I knew of in the region would dare such a thing, and yet new fledglings kept popping up. I should have recognized your little rebellion, Eleanor. You of all my children were always among the most headstrong, but until right this moment I never knew you were *stupid*."

He took two more steps forward, his eyes locked on Eleanor, paying no attention to the chaos in the stands, to the bloodshed in the boxes, or to the other monsters arrayed before him. He only saw Eleanor, and having been the subject of his laser focus more than once, I knew for a fact that she could no more move than a deer caught in headlights. "You are old, Eleanor, and powerful. You have lived nearly three centuries clinging to the shadows, eking out an existence on the fringes of human and vampire society. You have managed to stay ahead of the purges our kind have suffered in many places, all because you have been wary, and wily, and occasionally wise."

He never stopped moving, never varied his pace. He just took one step after another until he was right in front of the badass female vampire who had pushed me to my very limit. "But tonight, you have stepped out of the shadows and into the spotlight, and in doing so, you have made a grievous, and fatal, mistake. You nearly killed my nephew, the closest being to a son I have ever had, but that is not your final error. You have made new vampires right under my nose without my permission, but that is also not your worst mistake. You have challenged my authority and insulted me in front of many of my subjects, but that is not the reason you shall not walk out of this arena tonight."

He was right in front of Eleanor now, close enough that he could reach out and touch her. And he did, running his fingers along her cheek almost lovingly. "No, your fatal mistake was in challenging me. In questioning my authority over the vampires of this city, and in fact this *world*. That cannot stand, and I long ago learned that disrespect of that magnitude must be dealt with swiftly, and decisively. And thus I shall."

"You shall what, old man?" Eleanor said, spittle flying from her lips in her rage. "What are you going to—"

Her words cut off as Luke's hand flashed out and wrapped around her throat. He lifted her up into the air, never taking his eyes off hers, and shook her. That's all. He just shook her from side to side. Once, twice, three times, and we all heard the *crack* as her neck snapped. Luke stared at her as the life fled from her eyes, then he dropped the body to the sand and looked around the assembled cryptids and paras.

"Would anyone else like to challenge Count Dracula? I expect that your fame would eclipse anyone here should you manage to even land a blow against me, much less actually survive the encounter."

Nobody seemed in a hurry to step to Luke. But a roar from the back of the pack galvanized them into action, a dozen of the crew rushed us at once, and the melee was on. Oh well, at least he tried.

Notable in *not* charging forward to kick my ass was the one I was most worried would be able to do just that—Tony. The faerie knight calmly walked over to one of the Colosseum walls and leaned against it, sword drawn but point down in the sand, just watching the mayhem. I raised an eyebrow at him, and he just gave me a nod. I guess he wasn't who I needed to pay attention to.

Who I *did* need to pay attention to was Rat-faced Steve, who ran straight at me with a pair of knives flashing in the stage lights over the fighting grounds. He grinned as he took in my battered, bloody body and the way I held my left elbow pressed tight against my broken ribs. He got to within ten feet of me and opened his mouth, probably to make some smartass comment as he slashed open my throat. After all, that's what I would have done.

Except he focused so much on me that he ignored the gorgeous Black woman standing next to me, her MP5 set to three-round burst mode. Becks took one step forward, raised her submachine gun, and put three 9mm rounds right in Steve's face. He dropped to the sand, blood, and very little brain matter spraying out behind him like a Jackson Pollock original.

"He's a shifter," I said, trying to keep my tone as blasé as her execution.

"Silver nitrate-coated hollow points," Becks replied. "New ammo straight from the nerds at R&D."

I looked at Steve, who lay on the ground with half his head gone. "Please tell the nerds I love them."

Yannis was trying to test his strength against Luke, but I only gave that a glance. The big dipshit didn't stand a chance, and six lower-tier fighters converged on me and Becks at the same time, so I needed a little bit of focus. I drew in the very last dregs of magic I had and went back to my old reliable method of destruction—kill it with fire.

"*FUEGO!*" I shouted, holding up my hands and sending six-inch spheres of white-hot flaming energy at the oncoming asshats. I caught a young vampire in the face, turning him into a running, screaming birthday candle. Another slammed into the guts of an onrushing were-bear, causing him to instantly shift to his human form, only to catch another fireball in the face. His body couldn't heal two mortal wounds in ten seconds, so he went down for the last time. My last fireball smacked into a massive woman who looked like a slightly more feminine Yannis, with muscles on top of her muscles. She just shrugged it off, looking more amused than hurt or annoyed by the flames.

Shit.

Becks must have heard my internal monologue, because she yelled, "Duck!" and swung her MP5 around. I hit the dirt, literally, as half a dozen rounds from her submachine gun whistled over my head and slammed into the massive woman. Her bullets had no more effect than my fire, and this was shaping up to be a bad time for our heroes.

Until Anthony decided to pick a side, and for some reason it was mine. He leapt across half the arena floor in one massive bound, bringing his sword up as he did. He crashed down behind the seemingly impervious woman and cut her diagonally from neck to hip, slicing through meat and bone like it was water. I swear, his sword moved through flesh easier than my soulblade, and that thing's made of nothing *but* magic. The monster woman's top half slid off her bottom half, and both chunks fell to the floor with a soggy *splat*.

I looked up at Anthony and nodded. "Thanks. I don't know what I had left for her."

"She was an earth elemental. Not much, I expect. Your magic butter knife would have done it, but it doesn't look like you're in any shape to conjure it right now."

"Yeah, not so much," I said. "As a matter of fact, I think I…" I meant to say, "need to sit down," but some asshole turned all the lights off before I could get the words out, and I passed out right in the middle of the bloody sand.

There was a cat on my chest when I woke up, so I guess I wasn't dead. Pretty sure there aren't cats in Hell. At least, I've never seen any on my trips there. But there was very definitely a large gray ball of floof sitting on me now, and as I took in more of my surroundings, I was in my own bed. Alone, unfortunately, except for Nameless, who once he saw I was awake, jumped off and sprinted out of the room, as if he didn't want me to know he was concerned. Cats, man.

"Did we win?" I asked, my voice barely more than a croak. Unfortunately, Nameless doesn't speak English, and I was alone in my bedroom. I heard voices on the other side of the door, so I threw the covers off and got unsteadily to my feet. My everything hurt, and I was *disgusting*. I had sand caked to my body with sweat, blood, and some bodily fluids that I didn't recognize but probably weren't mine, there were bruises on my bruised spots, and something in the left side of my chest grated when I moved, sending spikes of pain radiating all up and down my side.

I held onto the bed and made my way to the bathroom, hoping that it was Becks and not Luke who'd undressed me. Not that Luke hadn't seen me naked more than once, but it's a little embarrassing when you're more than a century old and your uncle still has to peel your clothes off and help you into bed. No more embarrassing than having him show up and fight your battles for you, but since reinforcements arriving when they did meant I was still alive, I figured I'd let that one slide.

I managed to get to the toilet, without peeing all over myself, and in even better news, I didn't piss blood, so either there wasn't any internal damage, or it had already healed. I sat on the toilet, took a deep breath, and shoved my ribs back into place, biting down on a towel to keep my screams from waking up the three floors below me.

You okay in there? Becks sent across our link.

Hurts like a motherfucker, but I'm not dead, so I'll heal. Did we win?

Oh yeah. Luke and your hot friend Tony went through the rest of those assholes like a tornado through a trailer park after you dropped. I just kinda stood over you and shot anybody that got too close.

My hot friend Tony?

You know, Black, trim, neat beard, dazzling smile, muscles, pointy ears. Hot.

I'm gonna need a lot of booze to get that image outta my head, thanks.

That's what you get for thinking naughty thoughts about Titania. Damn, this woman had a memory like an elephant. I make one remark about a smoking Faerie Queen, and she's never letting me live it down.

Not in a million years, babe, she replied. *You gonna shower?*

Yeah, I need to wash the blood off before I sit on the white sofas. I'll be out in a few.

Try not to pass out. Luke's got some kind of gross whiskey concoction waiting for you when you get done, and I made bacon.

Okay, I'll get cleaned up and we can plan our next move. I stood up, glad for all the grab bars I'd installed when we moved in. I never intended to live long enough to become an invalid, but I had a bad habit of getting beat to shit, and a lot of mornings it was really useful to have things in the bathroom to hang onto. I turned the water on just one notch below scalding and got inside, rinsing off for a minute before I sat on the wide bench and let the double shower heads pour soothing heat onto me.

After about ten minutes, I felt as close to human as I could get, so I cleaned up, toweled off, and went into my room to get dressed. Nameless was curled up on Becks' pillow, and he raised his head a little when I came in.

"Mrowr?" he said, staring at me with way more intelligence than I was used to in a pet. Not that I'd had many pets in my life. As a matter of fact, this might be the first one, now that I thought about it.

"I'm okay, pal," I said, scratching behind his ears. He wrapped both paws around my wrist and nipped at my thumb, not hard enough to break the skin, just kind of a "glad you're home" bite. Maybe I could get used to having a cat.

I pulled on boxer briefs, my most comfortable jeans, and an Avett Brothers t-shirt and walked out into the living room, stopping in the doorway when I saw a faerie knight sitting on my couch. "Tony?"

He stood up, in very much better shape than me after last night's battle, and crossed the room to give me a big hug. "Glad you're okay, Murr—um, Quincy."

"Thanks, pal. And you can call me Q. Or just Harker. Most of my friends do."

"I'm honored to be considered your friend." He pulled back and extended a hand. It felt oddly formal after the big hug, but I shook it, and something in the back of my head clicked, like we'd cemented an alliance of sorts.

"You know being my friend isn't going to do you any favors with Oberon, right? He kinda hates me."

"A lot of people hate you, Harker, usually the most powerful people in any room," Becks said, coming around the kitchen island into the living room with a mug in her hand. She handed me the mug then wrapped her arms around my neck, molding her body up against mine and laying a kiss on me that made me forget I'd ever laid eyes on Titania, or any other woman ever. "Welcome home. Now don't ever do anything like that without telling me first! I had no idea where you were, you asshole!"

"That's my love," I said, smiling and stepping back a little. "All the kisses, and all the ass-kicking, rolled into one." I held up the mug. "What's this?"

"No idea," Becks replied. "Luke brought it over and said you should drink it as soon as you woke up. Then he went back to his apartment and crashed."

I smelled the concoction. Definitely whiskey, and the good stuff, but there was a hint of something else in there, too. But Luke had kept me alive for more than a hundred years by never steering me wrong, and by frequently pulling my ass out of the fire when I got in over my head, so I drank it down.

Fire coursed down my throat, and heat exploded out from my belly to every extremity. It felt like someone had plugged me into a live electrical outlet as power flowed into me, and I knew exactly what Luke had added to the booze—his blood. Luke's blood can turn humans into vampires if they're drained, but for me, someone who already has a sliver of his demon Skyffrax inside me, it was like drinking from the Fountain of Youth, if the Fountain's water was laced with uncut cocaine. My healing powers were immediately sent into overdrive, and all my already heightened senses were super-charged. I handed the cup back to Becks and grabbed the back of a chair for balance.

After a few seconds, I steadied myself and looked around the room. Tony and Becks were staring at me with concern, and Nameless sat on the back of a sofa, licking a paw and smoothing the fur around his head with it. "I'm okay," I said. "Just a little pick me up from Uncle Dracula."

"What the fuck was in that whiskey, Harker? Luke just told me not to touch it because I wouldn't like what it did to humans," Becks said.

"Vampire blood," I replied. "About three drops, if I'm any judge." They both looked at me like I was crazy, so I walked around and sat down in one of the armchairs at the end of the two facing sofas. "Luke and I discovered a long time ago that my blood can heal injuries in humans, although with certain unanticipated side effects."

"Yeah, like you living rent-free in my head, literally, for the rest of my life," Becks said, remembering a time almost ten years ago when I'd given her my blood to keep her from bleeding out on a case.

"Your probably very long life, by the way," I said. "Another side effect. But we also learned that if I take in any of his blood, it has a similar effect on me, except without the mental link, thank all the gods." The idea of my uncle hitchhiking in my head, especially during my years at Studio 54, was not a pleasant one. For either of us, probably.

"So you can drink vampire blood and be healed instantly?" Tony asked. "Why didn't you just take a bite out of Eleanor during your bout and cure yourself?"

"Because she's not close enough to the source," I said. That led to an explanation about how Luke turned by taking a piece of a demon inside himself, and how all the vampires we knew about today were in one way or another descended from Luke, but how I was more closely descended than most of them even though I wasn't exactly a vampire, just the eldest son of two people who got snacked on by vampires, thus altering my DNA somehow. "So basically, I can heal with just a couple of drops of Luke's blood, but I've never found any beneficial effects to drinking the blood of other vampires. At least not in the quantities I've been able to make myself consume. It's possible that if I drained an entire vamp, I could heal, but have you ever tried to drink that much blood? It's *nasty*. Also, dead vampires begin to dissolve very soon after they're slain, so you have to drink them very fast."

"I have questions," Becks said. "But I don't think I want the answers, because the questions are gross enough."

"It was a long time ago, and the experiments were at least as unpleasant as you think they were," I said. I decided it was well past time for a subject change, so I asked, "Did we get the Boss when we shut down the fight club?"

Becks looked chagrined. "No. We didn't get the Boss or any of the handlers. They must have had some kind of escape route pre-planned. By the time we finished up in the arena, and the rest of our team had processed the spectators, anyone in management was gone."

"Well, shit," I said. "At least they won't be running any more fights to the death until they can rebuild and start to get the word out about a new location. But we need to be more on top of this shit. They were running these blood fights right under our noses, and we had no idea. How do we find them before they get a new arena online, and how do we make sure nothing like this happens again?"

"I have an idea for that," Becks said. "But it's going to mean we bring somebody else into our inner circle." We worked for the Department of Homeland Security's Paranormal Division, which was already a super-secret government agency within a pretty secretive government agency. But the fact that I was Dracula's nephew and a real-life wizard was even more secret than *that*, and practically no one outside the room we were in knew that Becks' boss was actually a naga, a mystical half-snake creature in the guise of a human.

"I guess if it's somebody you trust, then I trust them, too," I said. I glanced at Anthony, who raised both his hands as if in surrender.

"Not me," he said, standing and heading for the door. "I'm still trying to get home. I just came by to see if you were going to be okay, so now I'm off to continue redeeming myself with the Queen. The second Titania will let me cross over, I'm back to the Summer Court. This world is way too weird for me." Too weird for the fae—maybe Charlotte's tourism board could put that on a flyer somewhere. Like maybe the Eighth Circle of Hell.

I stood and hugged Tony, then turned to Becks as the door closed behind him. "Okay, who do we have?" I asked, hesitant. I didn't love the idea of bringing anyone new into our inner circle, but ever since Dennis, my last tech guru, had turned into an Archangel (yes, really), we had been lacking in that department.

Becks pulled out her phone and pressed a button. "You can come in now."

Whatever I expected from a Department of Homeland Security Official Computer Nerd/Hacker wasn't what walked into my living room. First off, the picture I had in my head was a scrawny middle-aged man who still had acne, the kind of basement-dwelling pallor that only *Final Fantasy* nerds and vampires have perfected, greasy hair, permanent Cheeto stains on his fingertips, and the social skills of someone who's grown up on a deserted island. I did not expect a tall Asian woman with spiky magenta hair in black leather pants, a BABYMETAL t-shirt, and fingerless leather gloves with a wheeled hard-sided gear case in tow.

"'Sup?" she asked, walking over to me and extending a hand. "I'm Xia. You need a computer genius?"

I took her proffered hand, still a little struck by her appearance. "Harker. Quincy Harker. Good to meet you."

Xia turned back to Flynn and let out a little chuckle. "Does he always do the 'Bond, James Bond' thing when he meets somebody? Because that's kinda cute, but also kinda pretentious."

Becks laughed. "No, usually just when he's surprised. I think he was expecting someone who looked more like they just stepped out of

The Office reruns than someone who looks like they're on their way to a Hatsune Miku concert."

"Miku's more a Japanese thing," Xia corrected gently. "I'm Korean, so I'd be more into BTS or Stray Kids, except I'm obviously a little more hardcore, and less culturally specific." She pointed to her shirt. "Besides, I grew up in St. Louis, so I'm more American Korean than Korean Korean. Where can I set up?"

I pointed over at the dining room table, where Nameless was currently sprawled out keeping an eye on these proceedings. "Will that work? There's an outlet right by the head of the table."

She looked over at the table and nodded. "That'll do for now. Eventually I'll get my whole supervillain lair set up in the empty apartment Deputy Director Flynn showed me, but I've got a shitload of stuff to get delivered before I can have my command center set up." She walked over to the table and scratched Nameless under his chin. "Hi, Kitty. You wanna share the table with me? I'll share my treats."

Nameless just purred in response. Damned cat was a total traitor. The first time I met him, he clawed the fuck out of my leg, my shoulder, and my head. Now everybody he meets is his best friend. Admittedly, he probably saved my life the night we met, so I gave the furry little Benedict Arnold a pass. Mostly.

Xia dragged her case around to the end of the table, flipped it open, and exploded into a whirlwind of activity involving wires, touchscreen monitors, two laptops, a stack of equipment I didn't recognize, and even more wires. She pulled so much shit out of the case that I had to peek inside and make sure there wasn't some kind of dimensional rift in there, but I guess it just adhered to purse physics, where the interior boundaries have no real limit on the amount of shit you can put into a receptacle.

"Um, I guess we'll let you get set up while I grab some coffee," I said.

"Great," Xia said, waving a hand at me absently. "Gimme about half an hour and I'll be up and running. And if you're making coffee, I take mine with four sugars. And cinnamon if you have it."

I glared at her for a second before she looked up at me, smirking. "Fucking with you, boss. Just fucking with you. I loaded up on caffeine before I got here. Oh, and is cursing a problem? I kinda got fired at my last gig for having a potty mouth."

I somehow managed to keep a straight face, which is more than I could say for Becks, who let out a donkey bray of a laugh. "No, Xia, I'd say cursing isn't a problem."

"In fact, it's pretty much a requirement to work on this team," Becks said. She walked into the kitchen and fired up both Keurigs to get some go juice into both of us as quickly as possible. For my part of breakfast, I walked over to the bar and grabbed the Jameson's. If this was how my morning was going to start, my coffee definitely needed to be Irish.

A few minutes later, Becks and I were on my balcony, the sliding glass door shut firmly behind us. I leaned on the railing while my loving fiancée and apparent force for chaos in the universe sat in one of the two metal chairs I kept out here for private conversations or exceptional brooding. If I've learned anything watching Batman movies, it's that if you're going to look down over a city you've sworn to protect, you're going to need a good brooding spot from which to do so. My balcony was great for brooding.

"Where the fuck did you find her?" I asked.

"She's one of the best hackers I've ever arrested," Becks said.

"So you found her in prison?"

"No, I found her on parole. I arrested her six years ago, before I came to DHS. She got out a few months ago and got a job working with the Geek Squad. It was the only computer job she could get after prison."

"So I have an ex-con in my living room?" I asked.

"Oh, get over yourself, Harker. You've broken more laws than you even know about, and your uncle is one of the most prolific murderers in history. Besides, she's the one who hacked into the

Colosseum's network and turned off your exploding necklace, so maybe give her the benefit of the doubt."

"Oh, she's got that and more. I just kinda want to know about the criminal background of the people I let near my cat is all. What's with her getup? She looks like she gets carded buying cigarettes, but if she just got out of prison, there's no way she's as young as she looks."

"She's around thirty, as far as I recall, and I think there might be more to her than meets the eye. I don't have any kind of magic, but something about her feels...different, somehow."

I turned my gaze to the window and opened my Sight. Sure enough, there was an aura about our new computer whiz. It was unfamiliar, but didn't seem malevolent. "She's not completely human, but if she's a demon, it's not one I've ever seen before. She may be some type of Asian cryptid I'm not familiar with, or maybe she just had some kind of dealings with the supernatural that marked her somehow. But you're right, she's not your average K-pop stan."

Becks' eyes widened. "Quincy Harker, you never fail to surprise me. I had no idea you knew what a stan was."

"Not only that, I know the song the term came from," I said. I put on my best Mike Myers voice. "I've got layers, Rebecca. Layers."

"Oh, God," Becks groaned. "Not the *Shrek* quotes."

"My favorite philosopher," I replied. "If you trust her, that's good enough for me. Let's get back inside and see if she's hacked the Pentagon yet."

Becks' eyes went wide again. "Shit, I hope not. She does that again, and I'm gonna be so fired." She sprang out of her chair and shot back inside.

Again?

An hour later, after lots of cursing and a promise from me to upgrade the building's data infrastructure, Xia had something for us. I called Luke over, and he came into the living room in Burgundy silk pajamas with an honest-to-God smoking jacket on, looking like the nobility he used to be, except more like a parody of British aristocracy than one of Eastern Europe's most bloodthirsty warrior counts in history.

"What the fuck are you wearing?" I asked, getting a snort of laughter from Becks.

"I was *trying* to make a good first impression on our new team member, Quincy," Luke replied, affronted.

"You're Count Fucking Dracula," I said, barely suppressing my laughter. "And you come in here looking like the new host of *Masterpiece Theatre*? I don't think you're making the impression you think you're making."

"Oh, he's totally making an impression, Harker," Xia said. "As long as he's going for kinda hot Grandpa Munster, he's hitting the nail right on the head."

Luke turned on his heel and vanished, literally moving faster than the eye could follow. In three seconds he was back, this time dressed more normally in charcoal slacks, black dress shoes, a crisp button-down shirt with cufflinks, and a watch that cost more than a lot of people's cars.

"That's better," I said. Luke didn't reply, just glared at me with a snarl that made lesser men piss themselves. I'd been getting that same dirty look since I was a teenager, so it had a lot less effect on me.

"What did you find, Xia?" Becks asked.

We all moved to gather around the new tech goddess, but she waved us off. "Let's not with the whole crowding the genius thing. I got enough of that in the prison showers. I've patched into the TV so you can all just go sit on the couches and watch my magic."

"How did you patch into my TV?" I asked, looking for the wires.

"You have a smart TV, Harker. I hacked it. Now go over there and sit on the couch like a good Luddite."

"Okay, but if you've changed my Netflix password, I'm going to turn you into a frog."

Becks gave Xia a reassuring smile. "He's joking. He can't actually turn you into a frog. He can throw you off the balcony, though. So don't mess with his passwords. He has enough trouble remembering them as it is."

"Got it," Xia said, and I swear from the look on her face she was making a mental note to go back in and reset stuff the way I had it.

Once we were all settled, the screen on the wall came to life, and Xia started explaining what she'd learned about the Colosseum, who was fighting, who was betting, and who she thought might be the next step in figuring out who was running it.

35

Dangling a skinny banker off an office rooftop by his ankles isn't my idea of a fun way to spend an evening, but I'm willing to bet a whole lot of Luke's riches that it was even less entertaining for the banker. At least, that was my guess based on all the screaming, crying, and pants-wetting.

I'm used to dealing with a sterner class of criminal, I guess. I don't think I've ever met a demon who wet himself at the threat of death. Admittedly, they all just go back to Hell when they're banished from this plane or their meat suit is killed, so they don't have much to fear. Except Lucifer's annoyance, and I can state from experience that he's pretty goddamned scary.

So I was less than pleased when I got a face full of the acrid scent of urine emanating from the crotch of the banker I held some forty-odd stories above the pavement. "Stop pissing," I said.

"I c-can't help it," Piss Boy said. "I-I-I'm scared!" Piss Boy's real name was Jameson Stoller, which should be the name of a spy, or international arms dealer, or at the very least a hedge fund bro, not a mid-level finance nerd covered in his own piss. But this is the world we live in.

"Were you scared when you moved a couple million dollars

around every week for an underground fight club? Were you scared when you helped those assholes launder their money? Money they earned off the blood of innocent men and women? Were you scared then?" I gave him a little shake for emphasis. He was in no danger of falling, not that he knew that. The scrawny fucker probably didn't weigh a buck-sixty soaking wet, which he now kinda was. But since the piss was flowing up his torso on account of him dangling upside down, my grip was secure. I could hold him up there for hours, not that I thought I'd need to.

"Fuck, yeah, I was scared!" he screeched. "Have you met those guys? They're fucking terrifying!"

"More terrifying than me?" I pulled his leg up higher so he could see the grim look on my face. And to create a little distance between my nose and his piss-soaked middle.

"Not right at this moment, no," he admitted. "Please put me down and I'll tell you everything I know."

"Put you down?" I asked, letting a wicked smile dance across my face. "How far down?" I faked like I was going to drop him, and a whole new stink blossomed from his pants. This guy was going to have to replace every stitch he had on before he drove home. Oh well, he shoulda worn his brown pants today, I guess.

"Not like that!" he screamed, and I took pity on him, tossing him back onto the roof. He crumpled to the tarred black surface, weeping, pissing, and shitting all at the same time. It would have been pitiful if he hadn't been helping a bunch of murderous assholes run an underground fight ring that was set up so there were never any winners. But since he was, I was all out of pity.

"Talk, fuckwit," I growled.

"What do you want to know?"

"Names, addresses, anything that can help me find these dickheads and put them out of business permanently."

"I don't know any of that stuff. We did everything via email. I never even went to a fight!" he said, tears and snot covering his face. Better than what was covering a lot of the rest of him, I guessed.

"We've got your emails, shithead. That's how I found you. Now I need the stuff you didn't put in writing. There were at least half a dozen phone calls every week to a prepaid cell phone. I'm guessing that was your connection to the fights?"

"Yeah, that's how I called in, and how I placed my bets."

I paused, confused. "Wait a minute. You said you never went to the fights?"

"I didn't."

"Then how did you know who to bet on?" I asked.

"I just bet the favorites every time. It wasn't really lucrative, but it was safe. And then any time a champion got to their fifth fight, I bet on whoever was lined up against them. I knew the bosses would never let anybody win five fights. That would be stupid. It'd kill the golden goose."

Yeah, stupid. Setting up a fair fight would just be honest gambling, making your money on the vig while the wagers stayed pretty balanced against one another. That's how real sports books do it. They count on enough money being bet on either side to even out, so they make their money on the small percentage the house keeps of every bet placed. It's practically a guaranteed way to make a profit, and why sports books are incredibly profitable. You have to be the world's biggest moron to go bankrupt running a casino.

"So who was on the other end of the phone? Who was taking the bets?" If we could find the phone, which had been turned off ever since we'd gotten that number, we would be one step closer to finding the real boss, not just the Irish asshole who ran things on site. Although I could definitely stand to get my hands on him in the meantime.

"I don't know his real name, honest." I believed him. Usually after you scare *all* the disgusting bodily fluids out of someone, they don't lie to you anymore. He went on. "He told me to call him Pete. He sounded young…"

I didn't catch the rest of whatever Piss Boy said. I was too busy mentally kicking my own ass. Fucking Pete. His whole "nice guy" shtick was an act, and I fucking fell for it. If I hadn't already been totally healed from Luke's blood, I would have checked myself for signs of a concussion, because no way should I have bought anyone's bullshit that totally without a fucking head injury. Except I had.

They fucking played me perfectly. Caught me unawares behind the bar to kidnap me, put me in a shitty cell and made me fight my way out of it so the first person that showed me any sliver of kindness would instantly win my trust, while keeping him close to me through my whole time there so he could keep a fucking eye on me. It was straight out of the How to Stockholm Syndrome Your Captives playbook, and I fell for it. They even had him get pissed at me and then relent a little later. *Fuck.* Now I *really* wanted to find the son of a bitch, just so I could see if it was possible to beat the freckles off somebody.

"Pete, huh?" I asked. "Sounded kinda like Opie from *Andy Griffith?*"

"I guess," Stoller replied. "What's that?"

"The TV show? Are we not in fucking North Carolina? Jesus Christ! Fucking millennials. What do you know about Pete? Something that can help me find him. Where did you meet to get your payout? Or to pay off your losers?"

The banker looked at me like I was a moron. "We…didn't. Everything was done electronically. Through Venmo sometimes, then Zelle sometimes. Once we even used PayPal, but I had to set up an account for that. He didn't use CashApp, like a normal person."

Fucking millennials, indeed. Sometimes I really miss the golden days of crime, when you had to meet your bookie in an alley behind a shady-ass bar and hand over an envelope full of cash. Either way, this was enough information to give Xia a way to track Pete. Hopefully. Worst case, we might be able to get our hands on some of the crew's money and hit them where it really hurt. At least where it really hurt until I found them and showed them what hurting looked like.

"Fine," I said to the piss-soaked banker. "Give me your phone."

He looked at least as terrified at handing over his phone as he had while dangling forty stories over thin air. "What? Why do you need my phone?"

"Because it'll be faster than beating all your account information out of you," I said. "Now hand over your fucking phone."

He patted his pockets, then turned even paler. "I think it fell out of my pocket." He pointed at the side of the building. "When you…"

Goddammit. The hack just got a little harder. "Whatever. Give me your full name and social security number. We can get what we need from that." I made sure Becks could hear the information through our mental link as he recited the info I needed.

I glared down at the terrified little man. "Go forth, and sin no more."

"Huh?"

"Get the fuck out of here and don't do any more criminal shit," I said, laying as much menace into my voice as I could manage while trying not to laugh at the pitiful bastard. He didn't deserve my rage. He was just some hapless shithead that got caught up in shit he couldn't see the bottom of. If I should be mad at somebody, it really should be me for falling for Pete's crap. I felt a little proud of myself for realizing the transference that was happening. It didn't make me any nicer to the little fuckwit, but it felt like some tiny bit of personal growth.

Yeah, Harker, that's what counts. Not developing any level of impulse control, but the realization that the person you're torturing might not deserve it, Becks said. *Maybe next we work on getting you to a place where you don't torture the wrong person in the first place.*

Baby steps, love, I replied. *Baby steps. Besides, I got us the information, didn't I? That's gotta count for something.*

Just get your ass back home while Xia traces this moron's financials.

I turned my attention back to Stoller, who was trying to find a way to sit on the rooftop and not stew in his own filth. "I'm leaving. You wait five minutes and then you can get off the roof. If you try to come down before that, I'll know, and I'll kill you. Understand?"

He nodded, and I whistled the tune to *The Andy Griffith Show* as I walked to the stairs.

36

Xia had about half her "supervillain secret lair" set up in the formerly empty apartment between the unit where Becks and I lived and the one we left cleared out as a "war room" when we needed to have a lot of people sitting around a big table trying to figure out what to do. Which happened more often than you'd expect now that we worked for the federal government. Turns out when you're part of a massive bureaucracy, you need a big-ass conference table.

Xia's place was a dimly lit one-bedroom with a couch along one wall, blackout curtains completely covering the sliding glass balcony doors, and an array of six massive monitors fastened to one wall. She sat at an L-shaped desk in one corner, and there was a long couch by the kitchen as a token effort to pretend people might ever come visit her cave. Luke and Becks were already there with Nameless when I arrived, and Xia looked up from her keyboard at my entrance.

"Oh good! You're finally here. What took you so long? It's the middle of the night, it's not like there was traffic? And why did you stop for twelve minutes on South Boulevard? You were almost here, and then you just...stopped. I was tracking your phone, and I texted you, but you didn't answer. I've been waiting, and I don't like waiting,

Harker." Her words tumbled over themselves like pebbles in a rock-slide, and it took me about ten seconds to actually parse what she was saying.

"I stopped for takeout," I said, holding up a bag. "Wings. The manager owes me a favor after I exorcised an imp that was spoiling his chicken a couple years ago, so he kept the kitchen open late for me."

"Good call," Becks said. "I'm famished. Now that we've got *three* people who either don't have to eat or can't be bothered to remember to buy groceries, there's nothing to eat on the entire floor."

"In my defense, I was trapped in an underground cage fighting ring for like two weeks," I said.

"I keep plenty of sustenance on hand," Luke said. "It's not my fault you can subsist on neither whole blood nor Fancy Feast."

"I just moved in two days ago," Xia said. "But if you got any nuclear face-melting hot wings, I'm all about 'em."

"Dig in," I said. "I got four dozen wings, assorted flavors."

"Garlic Parm?" Becks asked.

"Of course," I replied, handing her a styrofoam container of wings and her extra crispy fries. I pulled out a cardboard container of teriyaki wings for myself, along with some celery, and handed the super-hot ones over to Xia. I didn't expect her to go for the ther-monuclear warhead wings, but I'd gotten eight different flavors, so she was in luck. "What did you find out from Piss Boy's info?"

Everybody stared at me for a second before Xia asked, "Piss Boy?"

"The dude I hung off the roof. I can't remember his name, but he soiled himself in every way imaginable, so I just called him Piss Boy in my head."

"Oh," she replied. "That makes sense. I've been calling him Douche Bro in mine, but given the type of people you seem to run into on this job, that might not be specific enough long-term. By the way, his name is Jameson Stoller."

"Don't care," I said around a mouthful of chicken.

"I get that," Xia said, licking her fingers. "But I saw somebody on some TV show say that details matter in an investigation, and that made sense, so I thought that one might, too."

"Yeah, I watch *Reacher*, too, kid. I like that actor. *Big* motherfucker."

"I'm five-nine and a hundred thirty pounds, Harker. Everyone's a big motherfucker to me. But that's beside the point. Stoller didn't have any direct connection to your guy Pete, but I tracked his phone's movements and his credit card purchases for the last six months, and ran an algorithm to determine—"

I held up a hand. "Xia, I'm sure whatever you did was really impressive to anyone who gives a shit about tech stuff. But I don't. So how about you just say you did nerd shit and found somewhere for me to go."

"Oh." She looked momentarily crestfallen, then smiled. "Okay, I did super-awesome nerd shit that you'll never be smart enough to understand, and I found that every few weeks, Stoller went to the same bar on Sunday at eleven a.m."

"That's early for Sunday drinking, unless he's really into mimosas," Becks said.

"Nobody's that into mimosas," I replied. "They're just the warmup drink, not worth getting up early for."

"Especially since the bar in question doesn't open until noon on Sundays," Xia said.

"Well, how late is it open on Monday nights?" I asked. "And what's the address?"

"I already sent it to your phone and the Suburban's GPS," Xia said with a grin. "Now, did you say you got *four dozen* wings?"

I stuck around the house long enough to get some wings in my belly and change out of my socks and shoes. It seems Stoller hadn't quite managed to miss my feet when he was peeing all over himself. I threw the socks in the trash, but I liked those Docs, so they were gonna have to be cleaned. Once I got my magic fully recharged, I'd use a spell for that.

Some practitioners give a shit about universal balance and not using magic for piddly little shit like cleaning my shoes, but balance isn't something I've ever been very big on, so fuck 'em. I figure if I'm throwing the universe out of whack by not wiping the piss off my boots with a towel, then the universe's balance was way too precarious already. Also, I didn't want to ruin a perfectly good towel with banker piss.

With clean shoes on, I headed out to a faux dive bar in Southend. I didn't bother taking the Suburban because the address was only half a mile from my building, so it was a pretty easy walk. Kind of blasphemous in Charlotte, where people drive to go around the block, but I grew up in London before cars were nearly as ubiquitous as they are today, and I still like getting a chance to stretch my legs a bit now and then.

Plus it gave me plenty of time for a healthy dose of self-recrimination about this whole case. I'd started this shit the better part of a month ago, and all I had to show for my time were a few more dead cryptids and paras, a phenomenal amount of property damage, a couple weeks living in an underground fight club with sweaty monsters who wanted to cave my head in, and a fuckload of self-doubt about my ability to judge character, since I was taken in so completely by Pete's aw-shucks attitude and hapless demeanor. Oh well, at least the odds of me getting to punch somebody tonight were pretty high.

I walked into The Last Ride Bar & Grill around midnight, handing ten bucks to the door guy for a cover charge. Fucking hipster joints, charging an entry fee whether there's a band playing or not. I stuck out like a sore thumb, having left my Harley-Davidson t-shirt, my leather vest with a biker club cut on it, and my chain wallet at home. Or more like I left them at the store, because I owned none of those things. I'd owned a Harley at one point, though, which I figured was more than I could say for three-quarters of the bar's population. Good bike. I think I left it in Boston, but I couldn't be sure. I was really high when I left the city.

I walked up to the bar and passed a twenty over to the bartender. "Harp and information," I said.

"We don't have Harp, and I don't talk to cops," he said. He was the stereotypical biker bartender, about six-six, three hundred pounds easy, with a black sleeveless t-shirt, arms full of ink, a shaved head, and a goatee. I briefly wondered if there was a look requirement for slinging drinks at a biker bar, then decided I didn't give a fuck.

"Then gimme a Guiness. And I'm not a cop." I'm not. I'm a federal agent. Kinda. More like an independent contractor with one client who happens to be the Department of Homeland Security. But close enough to a fed for government work, as the joke goes.

"You're totally a cop," Chrome Dome said, pouring a perfect Guinness, right down to the shamrock in the foam. He slid it over to me. "You stink of cop."

"That's because I'm banging a fed," I replied. "But I'm not a cop."

Hey! Becks protested in my head.

What? I am banging a fed.

Yeah, but you don't have to broadcast that fact.

I didn't say which *fed. Now let me work.*

We're not finished with this conversation.

"See?" Baldy asked. "Totally cop. I bet you've got one of those ear things with somebody talking to you right now don't you."

"No, I don't," I said, turning my head from side to side to let him see into my ears. "I'm a fucking telepath and my fiancée is talking in my head about how much trouble I'm in for telling some rando in a douchebag wannabe biker bar that I'm sleeping with a federal agent. Is that better?"

"You don't have to make up stupid shit, dude. I just thought you were a cop is all."

In my world, the truth is often so much stranger than fiction that I can tell people the absolute facts of a situation and they still won't believe me. "I don't give a fuck what you thought, I just need some information, and I'm willing to pay to get it."

"Well, if it's information worth anything, it's worth more than ten bucks," the bartender said.

"Ten bucks? I gave you a twenty!"

"Eight bucks for a Guinness, two bucks for tip, ten for information. And that's not enough for information."

"Motherfucking hipster bars and their motherfucking hipster beer prices. I guess I'm glad I don't drink IPAs," I muttered, putting two more twenties on the bar. "I'm looking for a man."

"I thought you said you were with a hot fed?"

"Not like that, asshole," I said. He gave me a smirk that said he knew exactly what I meant and was still fucking with me. I pulled out my phone and showed him the photo of Jameson Stoller Xia had texted me. "This dude has been coming in here a lot and meeting somebody. I need to find that somebody."

The top of Baldy's head turned pale. "No, you don't."

"The fuck?" I asked. "I think I know—"

Baldy held up a hand to stop me. "No, trust me. You don't need to find that guy. I recognize your little nerd boy. He's been in here a bunch. And I know who he meets." Baldy slid the two twenties back across the bar to me. "But I ain't sayin' nothing about that guy. He's fucking *scary*, dude."

"Come on," I said. "You work at a biker bar. How scary can one dude be?"

"I work at a fake biker bar in a trendy-ass part of town where most of the people who walk in the door think a fucking Vespa is edgy. But that guy's the real fucking deal. Him and his boys used to be Outlaws before they got kicked out."

The Outlaws were the biggest bad boy motorcycle club in the Charlotte area. They didn't have the national rep of the Hell's Angels, but they were into the same shit. If this guy got tossed out of that club, he might actually be a legit bad guy. "What do you have to do to get thrown out of a one-percenter club?" I asked.

Baldy's eyes kept darting around the bar like he was worried about who might be listening, but he leaned forward and said, "I don't know, I don't want to know, and I'm never fucking asking. I've heard rumors, but it's been everything from sleeping with the chapter president's old lady to sleeping with the chapter president's daughter, then killing the president when he got pissed off about it. But for real—this dude has dropped bodies. He is *not* somebody you want to fuck with."

If only Baldy knew who he was talking to. "I'll take my chances. Just gimme a name, and I'll handle the rest," I said.

Baldy still looked reluctant, although terrified might be the more accurate way to describe him. After a long moment, I slid the cash back across the bar to him, putting a couple of rectangular portraits of Ben Franklin on top of them, and said, "Nobody ever hears where I got my information from, and I promise never to set foot in this place again after tonight." Not that I ever wanted to darken the door of any place that goddamned trendy again.

"Connelly," he said. "Richard Connelly. His boys call him Big Dick."

"Thanks," I said, and turned to leave. Well, at least Big Dick Connelly wasn't lacking in confidence. Now to see if he had information to go with his namesake energy.

37

It only took a couple phone calls to find out where Big Dick preferred to swing, so after giving Becks and the team a heads up on my plans, I rolled over to a far less trendy side of town, out Wilkinson Boulevard where the city's two biggest gun shops vied for attention among the three biggest topless bars. I parked in the Hyatt Guns parking lot, deserted in the middle of the night, and walked across the street to the Hustler Hollywood gentleman's club. I learned a long time ago that if you're likely to get in a bar fight, it's best to leave your car in a different business's lot. That way when your brawl inevitably spills outside, you're far less likely to be shoved through your own windshield, adding financial insult to whatever injuries you might sustain.

The Hustler Hollywood Gentleman's Club bore only a passing resemblance to a club, and none whatsoever to Hollywood, or a place where gentlemen could be found. There were a couple hustlers working the lot, though, offering two-for-one lap dance coupons that I'm sure were totally legit despite misspelling both "Hustler" and "dance." Half a dozen Harleys lined up out front, and the bouncer wore a club cut with "Sergeant At Arms" on his left chest, so I kinda figured I was at the right place.

"Twenty bucks," he said, looking down at me with a cold stare.

"I need to see Big Dick," I replied.

"You got the wrong club, buddy. Swinging Johnson's is across town." He laughed at his own joke, but stopped laughing when I held up another one of the very popular Ben Franklin portraits. I was gonna have to get creative on my expense reports to get this shit reimbursed. Hard to get receipts when you're bribing people, and the government *hates* reimbursing without receipts. Good thing I was sleeping with the boss.

He took my hundred and jerked his head toward the door. "Dick's booth is in the back corner by the stage. Tell Tiny that I said you're okay."

"What's your name?"

"Why do you care?"

I don't mind criminals, and I usually don't even mind the knuckle-dragging leg breakers. But I hate stupid thugs. "Because I can't just tell Tiny that the stupid ugly guy at the door said I'm okay. I need a name for the stupid ugly guy, don't I?"

"I'm not stupid, asshole." At least he didn't argue with me about the ugly part. This dude had a face that looked like somebody dragged him down Wilkinson behind their bike, topped with scraggly brown hair that hadn't seen shampoo since Obama was president. He was fat, with some of the worst prison tattoos I'd ever seen crawling up his arms, and there were gaps where more might once have been, but they had long since fled for more attractive climes. Like a sewer.

"Okay," I replied. "I'll tell Tiny that Not Stupid Asshole at the door said I was okay. Got it." And I slipped past him while he pondered whether or not I'd insulted him again. So much for not being stupid.

I walked into a wall of sound, with bass pounding in my chest as the dulcet tones of the late, great, Janie Lane screamed about his cherry pie. I'm not sure why that song is playing every time I set foot in a strip club, but it's almost like it's a universal law. And I fucking hate hair metal. I liked glam rock. Hell, I got shitfaced with The New York Dolls on the regular back in the day, before David Johansen decided there was more money and better coke in being Buster

Poindexter. God rest all their maligned, abused, drug-addled souls, but those boys knew how to rock. And party. I lost a month after one of their concerts in Newark and woke up under a bridge in Amsterdam with a hash hangover like you wouldn't believe.

The bar was typical cheap strip club decor, with colored lights splashing across the walls and the lights kept intentionally dim around the tables, as much for anonymity as privacy. There was a roped-off section between the stage and a dark doorway with "VIP" over it in pink neon, and a handful of guys seated in a semicircle around one massive dude who I assumed was Big Dick.

The irony of looking for a guy named Big Dick in a topless club was not lost on me, and I figured I needed a little fortification before I started a fight, so I went over to the bar where the prettiest girl in the building, who was also the most dressed, was pulling beers.

"What'll it be? PBR is on special—two-dollar tallboys." She was maybe twenty-five, with red hair and sleeves of tattoos that were way better than the bouncer's. There was a hardness around her eyes that told me she had either a baseball bat or a twelve-gauge under the bar, or maybe both, and she knew how to use them.

"What's your best Scotch?" I asked.

"Shitty," she said. "None of the guys who come in here know the difference between Glenlivet and Wild Turkey, so the boss just fills expensive bottles with crap bourbon. We've got good tequila, though. The guys in the corner like their agave, so the top shelf tequila's real."

"Gimme four shots of Don Julio, then," I said, sliding another picture of Old Ben across the bar. "Keep the change."

"Cop, fed, or cartel?" she asked as she poured the shots.

I knocked back two and raised an eyebrow at her. "What gave it away?"

"You haven't been staring at my tits, so you're here for something besides sex, you sound like you've at least walked past a college once, so you're more educated than anyone else in the building besides maybe me, and you're flashing cash in a way that'll get you killed in here most nights, but you don't look nervous, so you're either packing or you're backed by somebody scarier than Dick and his boys."

"Or both," I said, draining the next two shots. "Fed. And believe it or not, I don't want any trouble. And I don't want to arrest anybody."

"Too bad," she said. "Been a while since I got to put Ethel to work."

"Ethel the bat under the bar?"

"Yeah."

"Is the shotgun named Fred?" I asked.

She smiled, and I liked her. "Yep. Ethel does most of the work. Fred's usually just loud, but when he needs to throw down, he can."

"If I go over there and talk to Big Dick, is he going to give me any shit?"

"Depends on how many of those Benjis you're willing to throw around," she said. "Dick's exactly what his name implies, but he's a cheap dick. If you just want information, five hundred oughta get you out without a fight. If you really want shit to go peaceful, take this bottle with you." She slid the Don Julio over to me.

"How much?" I asked.

"Get me a job interview. I was only working here until I finished my degree at UNCC, and that was a few months ago. So I'm looking for a new gig. Preferably one that smells less like body glitter and bad decisions."

I passed her my business card, which was really Becks' card with her name scratched out and mine scribbled over it. "Call this number and ask for Deputy Director Flynn."

"You mean like the Deputy Director Flynn whose card it really is?"

I like her, said the very same Deputy Director Flynn in my mind.

Me too, I replied. *She might be a good addition.*

Dunno if we want to bring a mundane into our world, Harker.

Yeah, but it worked out alright with you, I said. *And you could always get her a gig somewhere else in Homeland. Somewhere she might not have to fight werewolves on the regular.*

"Yeah, that Deputy Director Flynn. Tell her Quincy Harker referred you to her. I'll make sure she's expecting your call. What's your degree in?"

"Criminal Justice with a minor in Psych. I want to be an FBI profiler someday."

"Well, good luck with that," I said. "But call Flynn. She's good people."

"And good luck with Dick," she replied, then giggled. "That didn't sound good."

No, it didn't, but I was going to need all the help I could get with Dick and the boys he was hanging with, so I carried the bottle of Don Julio over to the rope and looked at the massive biker.

"Big Dick?"

"Who's asking?" This was a different, equally massive biker, again with the shaved head and goatee thing going on. What ever happened to bikers with long hair? Did I miss a TikTok or something?

"You Tiny?"

"Yeah." His voice rumbled, like boulders tumbling over one another.

"The guy outside, said his name was Not Stupid Asshole, told me to tell you that I'm alright. And you should let me talk to Big Dick."

"He lied to you, pal. He's totally a stupid asshole," Big Dick said, laughing. "Bring that bottle over here and you can ask me your questions. But I admit to nothing, and I don't consent to being recorded."

"I don't give a fuck," I said. "I'm not after you, and I fucking hate wearing a wire. The tape always pulls my chest hair off." Then I stepped over the velvet rope into the lion's den. He just didn't know the real predator had just come to visit.

I handed over the bottle of tequila with five hundred-dollar bills wrapped around the neck. "I'm looking for somebody you've done work with."

"How do you know who I work with?" he asked after he made the bills disappear and took a long pull off the bottle.

I pulled out my badge wallet and flashed my DHS credentials. "It's my job to know shit like that," I said. "Now are we gonna do the bullshit dance where you deny, I threaten, we get in a fight, I beat your ass, and eventually you tell me what I want to know, or are we gonna sit here and drink while you tell me what I want to know?"

Big Dick laughed, and his boys laughed right behind him, good sycophants one and all. "You think you can take all of us? You and what army?"

I didn't even lean forward in my chair, one of the overstuffed round-back ones covers in faux velvet that are ubiquitous in low-end strip clubs the world over. "I'm all the army I need, Dicky. I'm the one that shut down the Colosseum a couple nights ago. So yeah, I think I can take you and all your boys here without breaking a sweat."

I heard "Reaper" whispered behind me and let a grin creep across my face. I was finally starting to like that nickname. It opened a lot of doors, as it turns out.

"Okay," Big Dick said, taking another long drink. I noticed his hand shook a little and could hear the bottle click against his teeth as he tried to fortify himself. "What do you want to know?"

"Where to find Pete and his boss," I said. "I know you handled the payoffs to Stoller, so you must have a pipeline to the cash. Follow the stink, you get to the shit. And if you follow the money, you get to the shitheads."

"Why do you want to find Pete and the Irishman?" Dick asked. "You gonna kill 'em?"

"Probably," I said. "Unless they surrender. But the Irishman didn't seem like the surrendering type. Pete, maybe, but that big ginger bastard seemed like he really liked being in charge, and that doesn't make for somebody who has a lot of quit in them."

Dick laughed again but cut off his boys with a wave when they started to chuckle. "You guys can fuck off for a bit. Go polish your chrome or something. And Jerky? That's not a goddamned metaphor. I catch you spanking it in the bathroom again and I'm gonna cut off your thumbs."

His sycophants trailed off and I laughed. "I remember that shit from *Sons of Anarchy*."

"Yeah. That was a good fuckin' show. Now, Pete and Irish. You really gonna kill 'em?"

"Like I said, not if they surrender. If they give up, I'll just throw them into some government prison without a name that doesn't show up on any maps and let them think about their poor choices for the rest of their lives."

"What about the big boss? The guy running the whole thing? You gonna put him in jail, too?"

"You know who he is? Where I could find him?" Now I leaned forward in my chair.

"Nah," Dick said, passing me the bottle. "The boys never let me get that close. Never even hinted at who it might be. But any time I tried to poke around and find out, they looked scared, like he was a real bad motherfucker. Badder than me, and to most folks, that's saying something."

He didn't really look like that much of a badass to me. "Yeah, yeah, you're a tough guy. But where can I find Tweedledee and Tweedledead?"

"We usually meet here when they need to set up a drop for Stoller. I don't know where they live, or where they hang out except at the arena. But I got a phone number. Maybe you can hunt 'em down that way."

"And you'll give that to me out of the goodness of your heart?" If I sounded dubious, it's because I was.

"Nah, I'll give it to you for another five hundred and a promise to get Angie at the bar a gig. I saw you give her a card. She's too smart for this shit, and I'm afraid if she hangs out here much longer, she's either gonna end up on the pipe or on the pole."

A biker badass with a heart of gold? What is this criminal underworld coming to? I handed him another five bills and a promise to help Angie get a job that didn't involve criminals, drugs, or prostitution. Although I couldn't really promise any of that if she actually got a job working for the government.

38

I've already gone into great detail about my lack of love for bookstores, given my parents' guest-starring roles in Stoker's bestseller. But Barnes & Noble is the kind of bookstore I like the least. If I'm going to hang out around the smell of moldering paper, I at least want there to be overstuffed chairs in dimly lit corners, and maybe a shop cat curling up in my lap while I pore over an antique grimoire. I do not want a brightly lit sterile environment filled with people who get all their reading recommendations from Oprah or Reese Witherspoon. They're fine humans, I suppose, but hardly who I want curating my reading list. But if you have no place else to go and escape the world, I suppose a massive Barnes & Noble is good for that.

Or if you're looking for a lycanthropic rabble-rouser who all reports say is in league with an underground fight club manager. Okay, only one report said that, and while "outlaw biker gang leader" doesn't usually top my list of trustworthy suspects, Xia did a deep dive into my old pal Rachelle's financial records and saw a whole lot of cash deposits. So it seemed like she knew a lot more about the underground fight scene in Charlotte than she'd let on at our previous meeting.

So I was sitting in the parking lot waiting on Rachelle's little were-nerd meetup to end so she and I could have a little chat. I couldn't wait inside, thanks to the property damage on my last visit. Federal contractor or not, businesses could still bar me from entering the premises, and this shop had exercised that right the second I left the store last time. Which was fine. I had my cell phone, a dozen new episodes of my favorite true crime podcast *Morbid,* and a flask loaded with twenty-year-old Scotch.

I was three episodes into my podcast binge when my target left the store, fortunately without any of her group members tagging along. I didn't feel like beating the shit out of a relatively innocent shifter tonight. I was trying to save my ass-kicking for people who really deserved it. Like a were-tigress who sold her people to gladiator-style mortal combat. Rachelle definitely deserved an ass-kicking, and I was willing to suspend my natural chivalry and aversion to hitting women for another night. Especially since I've fought were-tigers before. They're *tough.*

I double-checked that my Glock was loaded with silver-tipped hollow points, tucked it into a shoulder holster, and got out of the car, then immediately ducked down as two men approached Rachelle from the shadows of a cargo van. I closed my door quietly and snuck around the back of the car as the men approached her. They stepped into a pool of light and a grin spread across my face.

Jackpot! I said to Becks.

What's up?

Pete the Prick and the Irish Asshole just showed up to talk to Rachelle. Now I can take them all down, figure out who's really behind this shit, and really beat somebody's ass.

Do you ever get tired of beating people up? Becks asked.

I paused. This seemed like one of those questions that mattered, so I stopped to give it some weight. Normally I'd brush it off, what with the whole "getting ready to take down the bad guys" thing and all, but since we can communicate at the speed of thought, I could spare a moment's consideration. This was the woman I planned to marry, so she deserved a real answer.

All the time, I said. I don't like violence. I'm very, very good at it, better than almost anyone I know, but I don't like it. Nobody that's not a complete psychopath likes doing the shit I have to do. I do it because I have the skills, and it needs to be done. There are a lot of people in the world who can't look out for themselves. People who will get stepped on, or run completely over if someone doesn't stand up and say "no."

I've seen that shit firsthand. I've seen what evil people can do to human beings, and it's worse than any cryptid or para out there. Humans are some of the most monstrous beings on any plane of existence, especially when they want to hurt other humans. Throw in the monsters that can't be hurt by normal means, and somebody has to stand up. That somebody is me. I don't fight because I like it. I fight because I can, and because if nobody fights, we end up right back in the fucking Third Reich.

So yeah, I stay tired of beating people up. I stay tired of fighting. But I keep on doing it, because there are people in the world worth protecting, and for whatever reason, I'm the one that was given the ability to protect them. And sometimes the best way to protect the weak is to beat the ever-loving fuck out of the ones that want to exploit them.

There was a long pause across our mental bond, then Becks said, *So what are you waiting for? Get out there and kick some ass.*

I stood up and walked across the parking lot unnoticed despite making no effort to hide anymore. The trio of assclowns was arguing amongst themselves about money, and hiding from the boss, and how they were going to relocate the arena, publicize the fights, and get enough combatants to be back up and running next week. I got about fifteen feet away before I stopped, hopped up to sit on the hood of an F-150, and cleared my throat.

Three heads whipped around, and startled expressions crossed three faces. I grinned. "You know, I kinda expect this level of oblivious from Pete. He's human, or at least he claimed to be human. And I don't know what you are, you Irish assclown, so you might get a pass, too. But you, Rachelle? You're a fucking were-tiger. In a lot of places, you'd be considered the apex predator. And you just let me walk up on you like this, without even noticing that the fucking boogeyman is less than twenty feet away? You should be ashamed. If the were-asshole council found out about this, they'd take away your stripes and make you live on nothing but Meow Mix for a month."

"Fuck you, Reaper," Rachelle snarled, her features morphing as she began to shift. "I smelled you from the second you stepped out of your shitty little Honda."

"And I heard your footsteps from twenty *yards* away, you wanker," Irish added, flashing long incisors at me.

Great. A were-tiger and a vampire. All I needed now was to find out that Pete was actually Oberon in disguise. It was probably going to take me a while to figure out what he was, though, since he was currently sprinting across the parking lot muttering terrified profanity under his breath. So I guess he wasn't King of the Summer Court. That left just two assholes to fight—a were-tiger in her half-shifted form and a vampire charging me with his fangs extended.

I hopped up onto the hood and leapt straight up, letting Irish shoot right underneath me and slide across the truck, sprawling on the pavement. I landed right behind Rachelle, who spun in an instant, claws slashing for my face. Were-tigers are incredibly fast, and even stronger than their natural counterparts, but Rachelle was a city kitty, and she'd obviously traded on her reputation and brute strength to lead her band of misfit weres. She hadn't been in many real fights, so when I ducked under her claws and came up to throw two massive right hooks into her ribcage, she let out a yowl that gave every dog in half a mile nightmares.

I sensed Irish coming for me and sidestepped so he went pinballing off another couple of cars before he could adjust his charge and reorient back to where I stood atop a Subaru smirking down at him.

"That the best you got? I spar with *Dracula*, moron. It's gonna take your A game to land a punch on me."

"I'll show you a fuckin' A game, you fuckin' fuck," Irish snarled, and sprang at me again.

I was impressed. Not with the attack, that shit was elementary at best. But it's not often I find someone who swears more than me, and this idiot vampire was doing a good job in that category, even if he couldn't manage to land a punch. He sailed over the Forester as I dropped to the pavement, and he crashed into the side of a Prius, crumpling the door. I could almost see the little birdies flying around his head as he lay there trying to make his ears stop ringing.

Unfortunately, that meant I took my attention off of Rachelle just long enough for her to clamp her jaws onto the back of my neck, picking me up in her teeth and giving me a vicious shake. This was obviously an instinctive move, since big cats often kill their prey this way before they drag it up into the trees to eat. And it works great in the wild.

On prey.

I'm a lot of things, but prey isn't one of them. This also wasn't the first time this month a were-feline had wrapped its teeth around the back of my neck, so I was even more prepared for it than I had been the first time. Don't get me wrong, it hurt, and I was going to need to visit my chiropractor in the morning, but it didn't do any permanent damage. The same cannot be said for the fireball I launched into the were-tiger's midsection, which set her fur ablaze and made her drop me in order to let out a screech of pain.

I fell to the pavement on all fours, sprang up, and spun around to land a solid kick into Rachelle's ribcage. That cut off her screaming because it hurt too much to breathe. Her eyes glinted gold, and I could tell she was gathering her concentration enough to shift. If she managed that, all her wounds would heal, and we'd be right back where we started from. I made the snap decision that there was only one way to end this fight, and that was permanently.

So I shot her. I drew my pistol from the shoulder rig I wore, and I put two silver-tipped rounds into the side of her head. She dropped like a stone, dead before she hit the asphalt. I watched as her form shrank, then transformed, and then I was looking at the body of a dead young woman who had sold out her own people, people who trusted her to help them find community and safety, to a bunch of dickheads who made them fight for blood and money.

Gonna need a cleanup, I said to Becks. *I just killed the were-tiger.*

What about the vampire? she asked.

I spun around and saw Irish standing there staring down at Rachelle's corpse. He looked at me with terrified eyes and opened his mouth to beg for his life. I shot him right between the eyes. I wasn't in the mood to listen to his bullshit, and I could beat the fuck out of Pete if I needed to find out who the real boss was.

He's down, too, I said.

You okay? Becks said.

I'm not injured.

Not what I asked.

I took a beat. *Yeah, I'm okay,* I said. *Some people just don't deserve to live. And sometimes I'm the only one around to make that happen. That's just the fucking job. I'm gonna scoop up Pete and bring him back to the apartment for interrogation. We'll get the boss's name out of him, then we're shutting this shit down once and for all.*

39

It seemed like only yesterday that I'd dangled a man off the roof of a building by his ankles. Probably because it had been yesterday when I dangled a scrawny banker off the roof of a building by his ankles. Now here I was, contemplating doing it again, only this time off my balcony, which wasn't all that different from the roof, since I live on the top floor of my building. It is a little more recognizable to any passersby, since it would be my apartment, and my building isn't nearly as tall as the bank building I hung Piss Boy off of the night before, so I gave it some serious thought before I hoisted Pete up by his belt and flipped him upside down, walking toward the sliding glass door while he struggled in my grasp.

"Come on, Murray, what are you doing?" he asked, his hair brushing the top of my coffee table. I didn't crack his skull open on the furniture, but only because there might be information inside that gourd that I needed.

"The name is Harker, asshole," I said through gritted teeth. I was inordinately pissed off at Pete for turning out to be one of the assclowns running things at the fight club, and it was totally my fault. I *liked* Pete, and I usually don't like anybody. It keeps things a lot cleaner if I can maintain a consistent level of misanthropy in my life. But I was stuck in a cage, and Pete was the first person there who didn't obviously want to murder me, so I'd let my guard down a little. And he betrayed me.

Okay, yeah, I was totally pretending to be someone I wasn't in order to shut the whole fight club thing down around his ears and send him plunging into unemployment and possible death, depending on how his boss treated loose ends, but I wasn't interested in exploring the inherent hypocrisy in letting someone betray you in an undercover situation and how that created feelings that were totally disproportionate to our actual level of friendship. I was just feeling pissy, not to mention I'd been awake for most of two days hunting these assholes down, and I needed a nap. So I wasn't nearly as charitable as I'd usually be, and I'm not known for my charity.

"Who runs the fight club?" I asked, holding Pete off the ground in one hand as I opened the door. The sticky heat of Charlotte in the spring slapped me in the face, like getting wrapped in a soggy warm blanket.

"Dude, I tell you that, he'll murder me!" Pete's voice went up a notch when he realized how soft the traffic noises were way up here.

"What do you think I'm about to do to you if you *don't* tell me?" I asked.

"I thought you were the good guys? Like, the government or something. You can't kill people!"

I lifted him up until his face was level with mine, albeit upside down. His legs dangled back over my shoulder because of the position he was in, but I trusted him not to try to kick me in the head on account of the whole falling to his death thing. "Are you stupid?" I asked. "Governments kill people all the time. Admittedly, they usually aren't as direct about it as I am, nor are they nearly as precise, but don't think for a moment that I work for the government because they do a goddamned thing to restrain my baser impulses. Which right now, consist mainly of seeing how many cars on South Boulevard you'd bounce off of before you hit the ground. Kinda like Frogger, only messier."

"Dude, put me down and I'll tell you everything. I swear."

I did just as he asked, dropping him in a heap on the balcony. His hands were bound behind him, and his ankles were tied, so there was nothing to break his fall but the concrete, but that was his problem. He should have been more specific in his request. "Okay," I said, kneeling down by his face. "Who's in charge?"

"You're not going to like it."

"I don't like much," I replied. "I'm notoriously hard to buy gifts for. Now. Who. Is. In. Charge?"

"Mort."

Good thing he was already on the floor because that name would have loosened my grip for sure. I'd never considered Mort might be in charge of the whole shitshow, not even in my wildest speculations. It seemed more likely that Luke himself had bankrolled the whole thing decades back and forgotten about it than Mort setting up an underground fight club.

"What the fuck did you just say?" I asked, glaring down at him. I could see a purple tinge across his skin, which told me I had power leaking out of my eyes again. It happens sometimes when I'm not paying attention, and I very much was not paying attention at that moment.

"Mort is the real boss. It was weird at first, having the owner show up in different bodies all the time, but I got used to it after a while. I never let him possess me, though, no matter what he promised. That seemed...I dunno, just weird."

As a hitchhiker demon, Mort moved from body to body at will, usually with express permission from the body's original owner. Some people wanted to know what it was like to be possessed, some people wanted the built-in excuse of "there was a demon inside me" to do awful shit, and some people he just bribed. I'd never known him to take over an unwilling meat suit, but I'm sure it happened.

"*That's* what struck you as weird, Pete? You were helping run an underground fight club for monsters with a were-tiger recruiter and a vampire manager, and a little demonic possession was what crossed the line into weird for you?"

"I grew up around witches and faeries, man. Paras and cryptids were part of my life. But demons? Nah, I never had any dealings with them until I started working for Mort."

"What was the deal? Why did Mort set this place up?" I'd always thought he was content with his place as owner of one of the few real Sanctuaries in Charlotte, and a primo information broker for all things magical and spooky.

"I got no idea, man. I barely know the guy. Jeremiah and Rachelle dealt with him a lot more than me. I was mostly there to handle any fighters that Mort wanted us to pay special attention to."

I paused in my near-steady stream of muttered profanities. "What? Mort wanted you to pay special attention to me? Why?"

Pete shook his head. "Dude, I didn't ask questions. I just did what I was told and cashed my paychecks. I'm stupid, but I'm not stupid enough to ask a demon why he wants somebody to get special treatment in cage matches."

Not the stupidest thing I'd ever heard, honestly. I turned this new information over and over in my head, but it still made no sense. "How long?" I finally asked.

"How long what?"

"How long have the fights been going on?" I asked.

"Right after the pandemic, as soon as things started opening up again. So I dunno, four years or so?"

Okay, so it wasn't something he started as soon as he got to Charlotte, because Mort had been here before I arrived a couple decades back. I thought back to anything that happened around the COVID times that would have made him want to launch a new business venture, but nothing came to mind. "Did he ever say anything around you about why he was running this place? Was there some goal he had in mind?"

"Man, I have no friggin' idea. And honestly, I never cared. There were folks beating down the door to fight, and even more folks beating down the door to watch the fights. We had people flying in on private planes from New York, Chicago, Miami, even some from England and Europe. I heard one time that there was a resort in the

Caribbean that offered our fight trips as a tour for their highest rollers."

The pride in his voice made me want to puke. "You said you grew up around cryptids and paras. How could you want to participate in something like this? People were *dying* in these fights? And that's not even getting into the fact that they rigged things so nobody ever left a winner. How could you do that?"

His pale face flushed under his freckles, and he scowled up at me. "Yeah, I grew up around you freaks. My mother was part faerie, and my father was a witch. My whole life was all about magic, and nature, and being at one with the universe, and all that bullshit. But nobody ever spared a thought for Pete. Poor, useless Pete, with no magic, no faerie glamours, not even the tiniest points on his ears. I wasn't even an afterthought to them, I was *invisible*. Because I was the worst fucking thing they could imagine for their child—*human*." He spat on the last word, a big glob of phlegm right by my shoe.

"I'm sorry they treated you like shit," I said. "I really am."

"Like you give a fuck."

"You're right, I don't really give a fuck. You're lying there whining about being human? About being *normal*? About being able to walk in the sunlight, something my uncle hasn't been able to do for half a goddamned millennium? About being able to look somebody in the eyes without shielding and not be afraid you'd burn out their soul and leave them a drooling husk? I haven't been able to do that since fucking Prohibition, you sniveling little bitch. Your mommy and daddy didn't love you enough? What about all those shifters who have to chain themselves in their basement once a month because they don't have complete control when they're transformed and they don't want to murder anybody? What about the faerie knight I fought beside who may never be allowed to go home, and will just be stuck on this plane, slowly growing weaker and weaker until the separation from his people and his world kills him?

"So no, I don't give a fuck that your parents didn't love you. I don't give a fuck that you're so goddamned insecure that you helped Mort and the rest of your crew commit murder on the regular, slaughtering people who just wanted to try and make a better life for themselves and their loved ones. And I don't give a fuck how big a mess you make when you splatter all over the sidewalk, you pitiful little bitch." And I snatched him back up off the floor by his collar, grabbed his belt with the other hand, and pressed him over my head, ready to send him flying off into space.

"Quincy, stop." I froze at the words behind me. There's pretty much one person who can regularly sneak up on me and calls me "Quincy."

"Why?" I asked Luke without turning around. "You've killed more people than some standing armies. Why do you give a shit if I kill this asshat?"

"Because it affects you more than it does me. I grew up in bloodshed and was a warrior before I was a monster. You are neither. You are a protector, Quincy, and every life you take is one you could not save. I have seen how that affects you, even if you have not. Please do not allow anger to add another red mark to your ledger."

I put Pete down, then shoved him back onto his ass and turned to Luke. He had a look of infinite sadness on his face, and I realized that every body I dropped had a cost to him, as well. "I've killed hundreds, if not thousands of people, Luke. Why say something now?"

"Seeing you in that arena, fighting against nigh-impossible odds, and reveling in the challenge...I was so incredibly proud of you, Quincy. You were fighting for something greater than yourself, for someone other than yourself. You were fighting for the others in the cages, whether they wanted your help or not. That is valiant. That is just. That is honorable. But this?" He gestured to Pete. "This is none of those things. This is power for power's sake. This is killing because you can, not because you must. This...this is what monsters do. If you kill this man, it may feel good for an instant, but the cost to your soul is something you will feel forever."

I opened my mouth, but no words came out. Luke turned, and in a blink, he was gone. I stood there for a long moment, letting his words sink in, letting them really penetrate my consciousness, then I looked down at Pete. I knelt and freed his wrists. "Count Dracula just saved your worthless life. Get the fuck out of here, and do better. Be better. He gave you a second chance. Don't waste it. There won't be a third."

Then I walked into the apartment, leaving all the doors wide open, and went home. I don't know what Pete did, and frankly, I didn't give a fuck. Luke hadn't saved him. He'd saved me. Again.

40

I stood in my living room gearing up to storm one of the few places in Charlotte anyone in the paranormal community, fractured and fractious as it was, considered safe. Mort's Bar wasn't just a place with decent wings and a literally out of this world alcohol selection, it was a Sanctuary. It's one of about three places I knew of where monsters with beefs that would normally have them spilling blood on sight could sit down and talk without worrying that somebody was going to double-cross them. And I was about to throw all that out the window.

Not that it applied to me, anyway. There was literally a sign over the bar stating that the rules of Sanctuary were for everybody *but* me. That went up after Mort's daughter, the half-demon cambion Christy, got killed by one of my enemies. I'd always liked Christy, and between Mort and I, we made sure that the guy who killed her was exceptionally dead, but it didn't bring his daughter back, and it turned what had at one time been a snarky friendship and mutual respect into a relationship balanced on razorblades. Which I guess had finally tipped over into a volcano.

"You think this is because of Christy?" I asked Luke, who sat in an armchair watching Becks and I gear up. He couldn't come with us on this run because we were hitting Mort's in the daytime. There are a fair number of monsters and magical creatures that are weaker or completely nonfunctional while the sun's up, so it was the right time to attack. I still didn't like leaving my heaviest hitter behind. Luke's not just one of the most powerful monsters in the world, he's also one of the oldest, and his tactical mind is second to none. Without him, and with Glory and Faustus still on their re-angeling retreat or wherever they were, I felt a little outgunned before I even left my house.

"I do not know, Quincy," he replied. "It seems the most likely scenario, but he is aligned with the forces of Chaos, so it may be that he simply wanted to, as you say, stir shit up."

"Maybe," I said. "I guess it's a little arrogant of me to think he would have started an entire underground fight club just to get my attention, isn't it?"

"To a certain degree, yes," Luke said, a slight smile twitching one corner of his mouth. "But if it was targeted at you, he definitely chose a method which was certain to separate you from any backup, at least for a while, and to attack you at a point where you are particularly vulnerable—your sense of duty."

I put down the Glock I'd been about to slide into a hip holster and gave Luke my full attention. "My…what?"

"You have your father's sense of duty, Quincy. It is one of the things I most valued in him as an employee, and most loathed in him during the time we were adversaries. Both you and he are like the proverbial dogs with a bone when you feel that someone has been wronged, and if something or someone is under your protection, you will move heaven and earth to help them, protect them, or if necessary, avenge them."

"And who exactly was I avenging by getting into a pit fight with a bunch of monsters?" I asked.

"The city, of course." Luke's expression was unreadable, but it seemed like there might have actually been a hint of pride on his face. "For some reason, you have appointed yourself the protector of this city, and of all the denizens herein, be they human or supernatural. You discovered something that you considered a threat to those citizens, and you were obligated to neutralize said threat. Not from any onus put upon you by an official, or even unofficial source, but from your own sense of duty. You are an honorable man, Quincy Harker, no matter what you may think about yourself. And when someone threatens those under your protection, you do what honorable men must do—you fight."

I turned back to my gear, holstering my pistol and double-checking that I had a couple spare magazines in my back pockets for the Glock. "You're right," I said without looking at my uncle, perhaps the most famous monster in history to have never been elected to public office. "I do feel like the people of this city are my responsibility, and I do feel like they need to be protected from things like the Colosseum. If it was a straight fight, that would be one thing. People who chose to fight and could choose to leave—I got no problem with that. But Mort put his thumb on the scale. Nobody was getting paid but the house, and that's not fair. So yeah, he was taking advantage of people I promised to protect. And now I gotta go kick his ass."

"No, babe," Becks said, coming out of our bedroom in all black tactical gear, complete with a custom chainmail shirt made of ceramic links for lighter weight, woven tight enough to stop all but the tiniest of fangs or claws. She fastened a choker of the same material around her neck, slipped a pair of fingerless gloves on her hands, and gave me a cockeyed grin. "This is my city, too. I might not be a cop anymore, but Charlotte's as much mine to protect as it is yours. *We're* gonna go kick his ass."

Only problem with our plan was that Mort knew we were coming. Or he'd been cowering behind a wall of monster meat ever since we'd shut down the arena, which I doubted. Way easier to have someone keep an eye on the parking garage of my building and call him when we left looking like we were ready to storm the castle, as it were. The parking lot was full when we arrived, except for one spot right up front with a sign that read "Reserved for The Reaper."

"I think he's expecting us," I said as Becks pulled the Suburban into the empty spot. I wanted to drive, but ever since one road trip where I blasted the soundtrack to *Hamilton* for six straight hours, I lost my driving and therefore my radio privileges, even on in-town trips. Mort's bar was only a few miles from my building, but she was taking no chances on me forcing her to listen to show tunes for even a moment.

"Yeah, looks like it," she replied. "You still wanna do this, or you want to wait until Glory and Faustus get back? Or maybe until Luke can come with?"

Truth be told, Luke could have accompanied us on this run. He doesn't get significantly weaker in the daytime, and although his idea of a sunburn looks more like a Roman Candle than a little pink skin, we've found workarounds before. I just wanted to do this one on my own. I would have left Becks behind if I thought there was a snow-ball's chance in hell she would have stayed home. This felt personal, and I wanted to be the one to end it. Luke had played the cavalry for me once already on this case. I didn't want to get used to him bailing me out, any more than I already was.

"Nah, let's do this. What's a bar full of demons and monsters just waiting for a chance to gnaw on our bone marrow?" I said with a bravado I didn't really feel.

"For us? Just another Tuesday," Becks said, opening the door and sliding out of the SUV. I followed, then paused as she grabbed a twelve-gauge from the back seat. She looked at me. "You okay? I know you liked Mort."

"As much as a guy with 'Demon Hunter' on his business card can like a demon, I guess. My bigger worry is what meat suit he's borrowed this time. I can't kill him if he's hijacked an innocent."

"I don't think cutting a deal with a demon to let them borrow your body qualifies you as innocent in anybody's book, Harker," she replied.

"Yeah, but there's guilty, and there's deserves to have your ticket punched guilty," I said. "But there's only one way to find out. Got my six?" I asked.

"Always."

So we crossed the crowded parking lot to the door, which was unusually untended. Mort normally had a guard of some sort floating around, but this time there was nothing. No door man, no bouncer, just an unlocked metal door. I took that as an invitation, and not feeling particularly welcome, drew my Glock and stepped inside.

41

The bar was packed, something I'd never seen during daylight hours, and every head swung around as I stepped inside. None of them were smiling, unless you count the few that had bloodthirsty grins plastered across their faces.

Maybe you should wait outside, babe, I sent to Becks.

Maybe you should go fuck yourself. My vocabulary was obviously rubbing off on her.

I'm just saying that you're completely human, and these monsters aren't going to be very discriminating about who they kill in order to get to me.

Then I guess it's a good thing I brought the big gun, isn't it? And she had. Becks carried a modified GForce GFY-1 semiautomatic bullpup shotgun with a ten-round magazine. The DHS armorers had reinforced the barrel to handle the exotic loads we used, including the Dragon's Breath rounds we both preferred for vampires. I noted a couple extra ten-round mags on her tactical vest, along with her Glock and three or four spare magazines for that. My girl came loaded for bear.

I did, too, just less in the conventional weaponry department. I had my pistol, and a few extra magazines, all loaded with alternating silver and cold iron rounds. And I had a pair of silver-edged daggers strapped to my belt, plus a backup gun on one ankle. But most of my power wasn't going to be in bullets and blades; it was going to be in fists and fireballs. So I had a new pendant hanging around my neck, with a big chunk of labradorite hanging from it. The iridescent colors of the stone swirled around like a wild mosaic, spinning from one end of the spectrum to another.

I'd spent a week when we got back from our "vacation" to Manteo pouring magical energy into the stone, figuring out how to use the rock as a focus for power that I could draw upon when my own reserves ran out. I'd also gotten my tattoos redone, but I had to empty those out in the Colosseum, so that backup power source was done until my next trip to see James, my tattoo artist in Atlanta. Hopefully the labradorite was as mystically powerful as the books said it was, because I figured I was going to need all the juice I could draw on for this one.

"Hello, Mort," I said. "Looks like you've been expecting my visit."

Mort stood behind the bar, no longer wearing the Indian woman's body he'd been inhabiting the last time I saw him. Now he was in a completely unexpected vehicle—a vampire. I'd never seen Mort hitch-hike a para before, and kinda assumed he couldn't do it, although I guess there was no reason he couldn't. But a vampire? A demon inhabiting a monster that already had a sliver of the demon Skyffrax inside it? This was new to me.

Mort was about six feet tall in this incarnation, with long blond hair pulled back in a ponytail, a chiseled jaw, and blue eyes that would make any reasonable person think he was the model for Keifer Sutherland's character in *The Lost Boys*. He even had on the long jacket, but he didn't have the trademark grin that featured in so many of the younger Sutherland's roles. "Yeah, Pete called as soon as you let him go. That was sweet of you, ya know? Not killing him. Didn't matter, of course. He knew too much, and he blabbed about my business to the enemy, so I handled him."

Mort reached down behind the bar and hauled up Pete's corpse, obviously drained. Mort held him by the hair and waggled the body at me. "This is what happens to people that help you, Harker. They end up dead. Just like Christy. Just like my baby girl, you sorry fuck."

"Is that what this is about?" I asked. "After all this time, *now* you're coming after me for getting Christy killed? Come the fuck on, Mort! You know I didn't kill her. You know I felt terrible about her dying, and you know I killed the motherfucker that murdered her! What the fuck more do I need to do?"

"You can't do anything, Harker. You can't do anything but kill. I thought I'd forgiven you, but then I found out it wasn't Smith that killed my daughter, and it wasn't Orobas. It was you, Harker. You cut off my daughter's head so that fucker could help bring Orobas into this world, all so you could be the big hero and send him back to Hell!"

"What the fuck are you talking about?" I was honestly confused. Mort's daughter, the cambion named Christy that I thought was just his badass bartender, had been murdered by an asshole using the original pseudonym "John Smith" in order to bring the demon Orobas to our world and give him permanent residence here. Mort had been with me when we confronted Smith and Orobas, and he knew exactly what went down.

"You did this, Harker! You cut off my daughter's head, and now I'm going to cut off your girlfriend's. You're gonna know what pain feels like, Quincy Harker, I swear it by every demon in every Circle of Hell!" Then Mort leapt over the bar at us, clearing twenty feet in a single bound, and all my thoughts of figuring out what sent Mort off into Psycho-land vanished as every monster in the place came at us, and the shit well and truly hit the fan.

There were easily fifty shifters, vampires, faeries, and monsters from all corners of the magical world in the room, and I had one human standing with me. But it was the one human I loved more than anyone in the world, so I knew there was no better backup anywhere. Becks opened up with her shotgun, filling the bar with gun smoke and thunder, while I spun up a one-sided shield a couple feet in front of us. It wouldn't hold anyone back for long, but a few seconds can be the difference in a fight for your life.

The shield stopped the first wave of attackers, and Becks' torrent of silver and iron buckshot took down half a dozen in the first few seconds. I drew my Glock and put six rounds in faces from less than a yard away, dropping more bodies. Then the shield failed under the pressure of three dozen angry monsters, and I dropped my pistol, holding both hands forward, palms out, and calling power.

"Forzare!" I bellowed, channeling kinetic energy through my hands to push the pile back. If they swarmed us, we were done. The power coursing through my hands shoved me back a foot, but it flung ten or so of my opponents ass over teakettle backward throughout the bar. I summoned my soulblade and stepped forward, slashing through limbs and necks with every step. I didn't even look at where I was swinging, just moved forward like my sword was a scythe and it was harvest time. They wanted the Reaper, well it was my fucking time.

Becks's shotgun boomed again and again, and every time she fired, monsters fell and the screams of the wounded grew louder. I hacked through arms, legs, chests, and necks for what felt like forever, until my arms felt like they had anchors tied to them and my shoulders felt like knots of rusty steel cable. The fight was short, loud, and bloody, as Mort's hired (or more likely volunteered, given my popularity with the local monster populace) goons fell like toy soldiers. It was barely two minutes after they charged that the only ones left standing were Becks, me, and the vampire Mort was riding in.

Mort stood at the back of the pack, just watching us and grinning. When the last of his henchmonsters fell, I banished my blade just as I heard Becks click empty on her shotgun. She dropped it to a nearby table with a loud *thunk*, and I saw her lean against the back of a nearby chair for support.

You okay? I asked.

My shoulder feels like hamburger, but I'm not injured. Just a little sore. You?

None of them even got a scratch on me. They didn't stand a chance. Not sure what was up with this. If they had no shot at taking me down, why throw their lives away?

I looked at Mort, who just stood there grinning. "What the fuck are you smiling about, jackass? We just killed your whole crew."

"But now you're tired, and I'm still here. And this body I borrowed is almost as old as your dear uncle, so he's one of the most powerful vampires in the world. Time to reap what you've sown, Harker."

Then he sprang at us, and all the bullets in the world wouldn't have done me a bit of good. He slammed into Becks, shoving her roughly against the front wall of the bar, and jammed his mouth down over her throat. In half a second, he had her head turned to the side and his fangs buried in her carotid. Except instead of a scream and a gout of blood, we got the *crunch* of breaking teeth as he bit down into her chainmail choker instead. Mort jerked his head back, spitting teeth onto the floor and glaring at my fiancée.

"Won't save you from a broken neck, bitch," he snarled, broken teeth making him lisp a little.

"This will, asshole," Becks growled back, then pulled the trigger on the pistol she had wedged up against his ribs. She slammed all fifteen rounds into his midsection in the span of a couple seconds, and Mort staggered back, shock spreading across his face. "You think Harker's the only one here who's taken out monsters, you stupid fuck? I faced scarier ish than you when I was a rookie walking a beat. And now I know what hurts you bastards, so I can pack all the silver and fire I need."

Becks ejected the magazine, which must have been loaded with either cold iron or regular ammunition, since Mort was still standing, and slammed a fresh one home. She took a solid stance and leveled the pistol at the vampire with a demon riding shotgun. I noticed the red paint on the bottom of the magazine and knew if she hit Mort with one of those, it was game over. "These are tipped with white phosphorous, motherfucker. You get one of these in your gut and you'll go up like a goddamned sparkler."

I called my soulblade and gripped the hilt in both hands. "You ready to call this vendetta off, Mort? Or are you ready to die for real? Because if I shove this up your ass, you don't go back to Hell. You just *go.* For once and for all. No rebirth, no waking up all comfy in a lake of fire. You're just done. Is that what you want? Is that what *Christy* would want?"

I'd hoped bringing his thoughts back around to his daughter would give him clarity, let him see exactly how fucked he was, and maybe, just maybe give me a chance to prove to him that whatever he had in his head about what happened to his daughter was wrong, and that I had nothing to do with her death.

I have seldom been more wrong in my ridiculously long life. He didn't gain any clarity, he just went further round the bend. He spun around to me and charged, hands outstretched like he wanted to rend me limb from limb. There was no plan to his attack, no strategy, just a mad rush at someone he wanted to destroy totally and finally.

Someone who was waiting for him with a very big sword. I stepped to the left, bringing my soulblade up as I did, and sliced through his neck without the least resistance. In an image mimicking Christy's death years ago, his body collapsed like a puppet with its strings cut, but his head rolled forward, sightless eyes fixed on me as every bit of light, of tortured soul, went out of them. Mort's borrowed body was turning to slurry even as it fell, but his eyes stayed locked on mine until I turned away, banishing my soulblade and walking wordlessly to Becks' SUV.

There was nothing more to say. Nothing more to do. Mort was gone, and so was one of the last vestiges of Sanctuary in my city, and my life.

EPILOGUE

EPILOGUE

W̲hat was all that really about?" I asked our assembled brain trust that night. I sat at the head of our conference table in the apartment we kept empty as a "war room," with Luke, Becks, and Xia all gathered around. Nameless had hopped up on the table itself, typically disregarding anything resembling propriety, and now lay curled up at the far end under Luke's hand. I felt oddly disgruntled about my uncle completely co-opting my cat, despite never wanting a cat in the first place.

"What do you mean, babe?" Becks asked. "It seemed pretty clear-cut. Mort still blamed you for Christy's death, and he wanted to kill you for it."

I shook my head. "Not that. I get that, misplaced as his anger was." I noticed the confused look on Xia's face and gave her the condensed version. "Mort's daughter, Christy, was a half-demon, a cambion. She was murdered a few years ago by a bad guy who wanted to open a Gate to allow his demon boss a permanent visa in this plane of existence. I had nothing to do with her death, didn't even know she was his daughter until she'd already been taken, but that didn't make her any less dead."

I shook my head again. "But Mort said some shit right before he came at me that didn't track. He talked like he'd gotten some kind of new information that implicated me in Christy's death. Like I'd given her over to Orobas for some reason. That's what made him decide I had to die—because he thought I legitimately killed his daughter."

"What would give him that idea?" Luke asked. "Our encounter with Orobas was quite a number of years ago at this point. I would expect that any information about your involvement with Christy's death would have come to light before now. Not that there is any information to come to light, of course." He added that last bit at the end in an uncharacteristic nod to my prickly feelings.

"I have no fucking idea," I said, refilling the rocks glass by my right hand. I was running low on Johnny Walker Blue, and this time I didn't even have Faustus to blame. "And Mort was standing right next to me when we confronted Orobas. I don't know how he could get the idea that

"Have you pissed anybody off lately that would be devious enough to come at you through Mort?" Becks asked, polishing off her detective skills. "You've got a lot of enemies, but they tend to come at you head on. Who wants you dead *and* is sneaky enough to use Mort to do it?"

I wracked my brain for as long as it took me to drain my glass, then set it down with a *click* on the glass. "No idea to that one, either," I said. Then something struck me. "But I had a question for you guys."

"Shoot," Becks replied.

"How did you find me?" I paused. "Let me rephrase that. The last time we talked before you showed up at the Colosseum, you were close to figuring out where the fights were taking place, but you hadn't gotten it dialed in to a specific location. Then right as I'm about to get my heart ripped out by Eleanor the Super-Vamp, you go full Ride of the Rohirrim on me and pull my ass out of the fire at the last moment. Please tell me you didn't wait until I was sure I was going to die just for dramatic effect."

Becks smirked at me. "Like you would do?" she asked.

I gave her a grin. "Okay, fair. I'd totally do that. But you're a better person than me, and Luke doesn't have the pop culture references to go full-on *Avengers: Endgame* on me. So how did you find me. Was it something you did?" I directed that last bit at Xia, our new tech genius.

She held up both hands in surrender. "Not me, boss. I could get them within a two-block radius, but there were a lot of big buildings in those two blocks where you could have been. Wish I could take credit, but it wasn't me."

"It was me, after a fashion," Luke said. "I received a phone call from a very old associate asking me why my nephew was participating in bloodfights under an assumed name. He gave us your location."

"An old associate?" I asked.

"One of the oldest of my associates," Luke replied.

"And he saw me at the fights, recognized me, and called you?"

"Precisely."

"You gonna tell me who this 'associate' is, or are we going to dance around this a little longer? Because if we're gonna keep dancing, I'm gonna need another bottle."

"I do not know what name he uses today. I first met him in Poland in the sixteenth century, and his name at the time was Jackert. Like myself, he has used many names through the centuries. Honestly, I didn't know he was in America until he reached out to me."

"How did he find you?" Becks asked.

"He reached out through social media," Luke replied. "I have a Twitter account. @therealcountdracula. Unfortunately, they refuse to give me a blue check mark."

"I think it's called X now," I said, my mouth moving as my brain continued to process the concept of Luke on social media. And that handle?

"I refuse to call it that," Luke said. "It is a stupid name. But that is how Jackert found me, and he sent me the location of the arena. Rebecca called some allies together, and we affected a rescue."

"Can I see your phone?" I asked. Luke slid it over to me, and I opened his app. He kept his phone unlocked, since biometrics are iffy when your body temp is whatever the central air is set at. I scrolled through his DMs, ignoring the staggering number of young women sending him "Turn me, Daddy" posts, and finally located a message from a user named PolishJack1564.

It read "You will find Quincy at 1234 Commercial Avenue, fighting to the death tomorrow night. I do not believe he can best Eleanor, as we both participated in her training and she was a gifted student. Best of luck. J." There was no profile photo, but his location was listed as Atlanta, Georgia.

I slid the phone down the table to Luke. "I think I met your friend Jack a few months ago. If he really is in Atlanta, that is."

Luke's eyebrows went up, and he said, "Really?"

"Yeah," I replied. "When I went down for that CDC thing where Oberon was trying to poison all of humanity? He was at the party. He said he knew you from way back, and I could feel the power rolling off him in waves. He's a badass."

"Yes," Luke said. "Jackert is one of the most powerful of my creations. The essence of Skyffrax was far less diluted when I turned him, and he was a well-trained warrior in life, so when he became immortal, he spent centuries perfecting his skills, both mundane and mystical. I have always wondered if he has surpassed even my abilities."

"Well, I hope you don't need to find out, but I think with him popping up in two of our cases in three months, we need to go to Atlanta and have a little chat with your old buddy."

Luke nodded. "I agree. It seems too great a coincidence for him to be at both Oberon's gala and this fight club. Jackert has a few questions to answer."

"Yeah, like who told *him* about the fight club," Becks said. "Okay, everybody. Go get some sleep, then tomorrow night we hit the road for Atlanta. Somebody's got some 'splaining to do."

That was the damned truth. I'd just chopped the head off another person I once thought of as an ally, and while that hurt, what really burned was the idea that there was someone behind the scenes manipulating this shit. Again. It was starting to feel like that shit with Edgar calling himself The Chancellor all over again. And this time I had a sinking suspicion that I knew who was behind it.

I went to bed with the image of a blond woman carrying my father's eyes and my mother's jaw in my mind. Because I was pretty sure that the next day, I was starting the hunt for my sister, and only one of us was going to survive our reunion.

THE END

ACKNOWLEDGMENTS

This one wasn't easy to write. Not because of any deep subject matter, although I do think I address some of Harker's inherent PTSD more in this one than in some previous books. No, this one was tough because 2025 has been a hell of a year, y'all.

I started the year with a pair of cataract surgeries, since my eye doc told me I had the cataracts of a seventy-year-old. Which would be fine, except I'm fifty-two. So I had cataracts removed from both eyes, and while I was in recovery from the second one, the docs discovered that I was in atrial fibrillation, a very common irregular heart rate that can nonetheless be very dangerous.

So instead of the two eye surgeries I knew I was starting 2025 with, I had those and followed them up with two cardiac procedures to correct my afib. The second one worked, and I'm fine now, but it took a lot more out of me than I expected. Then my wife had a hip replacement, and everything slowed down again.

We're both fine now, but all this real-life BS certainly put a damper on my fiction for the first half of the year. Hopefully I'll be able to stay healthy and productive for the rest of the year, and it won't take as long to get the next book into your hands.

But I do have some people to thank, as always. Thanks to Natania Barron for her amazing cover work and her ability to move heaven and earth to hit my deadlines even when I don't tell her about them until nearly too late. Thanks to Melissa McArthur for her help with editorial and grammar.

Thanks to K.E. Mair for helping run my YouTube and marketing. If you're seeing more of me on your computer lately, blame her.

Thanks to my sister Bonnie for her help at conventions and her advice on everything, and an extra special thanks to Theresa Glover, my right hand in managing this circus, and the person who throws sandwiches at me as I'm running between panels at DragonCon.

And as always, thanks to you. Every last one of you is why I do this, and why I'm able to do this for a living. If it weren't for you, I'd have to wear pants far too often.

ABOUT THE AUTHOR

John G. Hartness is a teller of tales, a righter of wrong, defender of ladies' virtues, and some people call him Maurice, for he speaks of the pompatus of love. He is also the award-winning author of the urban fantasy series *The Black Knight Chronicles,* the Bubba the Monster Hunter comedic horror series, the Quincy Harker, Demon Hunter dark fantasy series, and many other projects.

In 2016, John teamed up with several other publishing industry professionals to create Falstaff Books, a small press dedicated to publishing the best of genre fiction's "misfit toys." Falstaff Books has since published over 350 titles with authors ranging from first-timers to NY Times bestsellers, with no signs of slowing down any time soon. He is also the founder of the SAGA Genre Fiction Writers' Conference, where students hone their business and craft skills to write better books and make more money.

In his copious free time John enjoys long walks on the beach, rescuing kittens from trees and playing *Magic: the Gathering.* John's pronouns are he/him.

ALSO BY JOHN G. HARTNESS

THE BLACK KNIGHT CHRONICLES

The Black Knight Chronicles - Omnibus Edition

The Black Knight Chronicles Continues - Omnibus #2

All Knight Long - Black Knight Chronicles #7

Lady in Black - Black Knight Chronicles #8

BUBBA THE MONSTER HUNTER

Scattered, Smothered, & Chunked - Bubba the Monster Hunter Season One

Grits, Guns, & Glory - Bubba Season Two

Wine, Women, & Song - Bubba Season Three

Monsters, Magic, & Mayhem - Bubba Season Four

Blood, Sweat, & Tears - Bubba Season Five

Shinepunk: A Beauregard the Monster Hunter Collection

QUINCY HARKER, DEMON HUNTER

Year One: A Quincy Harker, Demon Hunter Collection

The Cambion Cycle - Quincy Harker, Year Two

Damnation - Quincy Harker Year Three

Salvation - Quincy Harker Year Four

Carl Perkins' Cadillac - A Quincy Harker, Demon Hunter Novel

Inflection Point

Conspiracy Theory

Comes a Reckoning

Lost

Histories: A Quincy Harker, Demon Hunter Collection

Histories II: A Quincy Harker, Demon Hunter Collection

SHINGLES

Zombies Ate My Homework: Shingles Book 5

Slow Ride: Shingles Book 12

Carnival of Psychos: Shingles Book 19

Jingle My Balls: Shingles Book 24

Snatched: Grandma Annie and the Cooter of Doom: Shingles Book 29

Deader than Hell: Shingles Book 40

NSFW - The Shingles Collection

OTHER WORK

The True Confessions of Fandingo the Fantastical (with EM Kaplan)

Queen of Kats

Fireheart

Amazing Grace: A Dead Old Ladies Detective Agency Mystery

From the Stone

The Chosen

Genesis

Hazard Pay and Other Tales

Have Spacecat, Will Travel

Identity Theft

Unforgiven

FRIENDS OF FALSTAFF

Thank You to All our Falstaff Books Patrons, who get extra digital content each month! To be featured here and see what other great rewards we offer, go to www.patreon.com/falstaffbooks.

PATRONS

Dino Hicks
Nick Kinney
Martin Quinonez
Rob Voss
Patti Holland
Adrienne Nichole
Josh Minchew
Jack Stubblefield
Belmura
Deanna
Bob Holland
Anja Smith
Nick Crook
Trisha Woolridge
J B
Pat Hayes
Melisa Boris
Bill Fear
Jennifer Lee Maher
Nicole Reavis

Simon Elberger
Larissa Lichty
John Kilgalion
Wolfe
Casey & Travis Schilling
Staci-Liegh Santore
Sheryl R. Hayes
Jungle
Samuel Montgomery-Blinn
Scott Norris

Thank You for Supporting Independent Publishing!

We believe that you should be able
to read your books, your way.
That's why this Falstaff Books
print edition includes a digital copy
at no additional cost!

Just scan the QR code with your device,
follow the directions on Prolific Works,
and enjoy!
You can also join our newsletter when prompted,
and never miss an awesome Falstaff Release!